THE BATTLE FOR ENGLAND

Wars of the Magna Carta
Book One

Austin Hernon

SAPERE
BOOKS

THE BATTLE FOR ENGLAND

Published by Sapere Books.

11 Bank Chambers, Hornsey, London, N8 7NN,
United Kingdom

saperebooks.com

ISBN: 978-1-912786-49-7

For Mandy, my ever patient wife — for her help in exploring the nooks and crannies of English history.

Prologue

By 1215 King John was in serious trouble. He had upset his subjects in many and various ways. He had lost the English dukedoms of Normandy and Brittany, and the counties of Aquitaine, Poitou, and Anjou, to Philip of France. He had got involved in the murder of his nephew Arthur — the heir nominated by his brother, King Richard. He had been excommunicated by Pope Innocent III and he'd had to deal with a revolt in Wales. Latterly, he had been persuaded into signing the Magna Carta by his nobles — which he reneged on, claiming that he was forced into acceptance and had only signed it under duress.

This final bad decision led to the barons inviting the French Prince Louis over the Channel to take charge of a new 'civil' war in England.

In 1216 John lost Westminster and fled to Winchester. Dover Castle was under siege, and England south of a line from the Wash to Bristol was in revolt. John was being pulled back and forth by the tides of war, travelling as far north as Berwick to quell the flames. By the autumn he was back in the south with the state of England in serious danger of becoming a French crown territory.

The eyes of England turned towards the Midlands, where, sitting proud on its ridge, stood the mighty citadel of Lincoln, a stronghold since Roman times. Lincoln must hold out if the country was to survive.

Lincoln and its nearby supporting fortress of Laxton were in the hands of two redoubtable women: Nicholaa of Lincoln, and Matilda of Laxton, both hereditary Keepers of the King's

Forest. Nicholaa and Matilda hold the lands of Lincolnshire and Nottinghamshire between the coast and the Pennines secure through the defence of their castles. They must hold firm: the central defence of England rests upon their shoulders.

Part One: The Gathering Storm, Lincolnshire 1216

1.

I had but recently escaped the permanent dust cloud of the already magnificent cathedral in Lincoln, for the relative quiet of the castle. The cathedral was consecrated in 1092 as the church of the Blessed Virgin Mary of Lincoln. I had thought it finished, in the year of our Lord 1216, but bishops were forever adding bits on. At this time Archdeacon Peter was extending the building in the absence of Bishop Hugh, away in Rome. My relief from the chaos paused when he summoned me.

'I have a new appointment for you, Father Bernard.'

Looking at him carefully I saw that great weariness which comes over men from time to time when they are struggling to see a way forward, and I wondered if he had seen me as an answer to some of his problems.

'What would that be, Archdeacon? Somewhere away from this eternal dust, I hope.'

'In the end we are all eternal dust, Father Bernard. The presence of some dust on earth might prepare you for the next life.' He grinned; it lightened his face for a moment before it returned to his naturally sad countenance. 'Would the castle suit you permanently? We need to provide a confessor to Lady Nicholaa; it is several weeks now since her beloved Father Francis died and I have been lax in not sending someone else. I believe that you are known to the lady?'

'Indeed. During the long illness of Father Francis I was pleased to be of help to her during these turbulent times.'

'Quite. However noisy and dusty the surrounds of the cathedral, Bernard, I fear there are more egregious disturbances to come ere this disagreement between King John and the great nobles of the land is settled.'

'I too fear that, and I pray for peace.'

'Surely; and if it will help the lady, 'tis well done. As Castellan of Lincoln she carries a heavy burden for a woman, and newly widowed.'

I thought to discuss that point, but held back. Not everyone would have placed Nicholaa de la Haye in such a position, and some would have had her out of it. But she had inherited the office and with her it would stay. Besides, her late husband, Gerard de Camville, had been more of a hindrance than an asset in the management of Lincoln, a marriage of convenience as most folk knew — and his death aged eighty-seven might have come as a blessed relief for him after Nicholaa's staunch defence of her rights. I knew her well enough to understand that any attempt to oust her or indeed to place some man into a position as her mentor, or, dread thought, appoint another husband for her, would have met with a thorny response. The lady was best Damascene steel inside and brooked no nonsense.

'Indeed, a heavy burden for a woman ... as you say, and another war looming. Does the king not know what mischief he has unleashed by repudiating the charter he signed at Runnymede?'

'I fear not, Father Bernard; he has a strong head, does John Lackland.'

'And now the French prince, Louis, has landed an army to dispossess him of his realm.'

'Aye, we must pray, Father Bernard, pray like never before.'

'Does Lady Nicholaa know that I am to be sent?'

'I have written to her and she is favourable. You can tidy up here and make your way over to the castle. Keep me informed, if you can.'

Keep him informed? Spy on her more like. I wouldn't do it; and he had 'written to her' at most two hundred paces from cathedral to castle — why couldn't he walk; is the rift twixt castle and cathedral that wide? These and other thoughts kept me occupied as I crossed the wooden drawbridge leading up to the great tower gate into the castle ward.

'State your business.' Some great lumpkin of a soldier barred my way, disturbing my thoughts.

'God's business, stand aside,' I replied, as he stared down at me.

Recognising his duty, he pushed at a small postern door set into the monstrous gate and it swung open to allow me entry. I smiled at him as I passed and he bared some black stumps at me in return; a grin, I surmised.

'Bless you, my son.'

When I reached the foot of the steps leading up to the keep, I paused, straining my neck to look upwards. They were very steep, and there were lots of them. Halfway up a pair of feet confronted me and a voice from above gave me an excuse to halt and try to regain my breath.

'You are Father Bernard? The visiting priest.'

'I am,' I gasped, looking up again. He was in silhouette now.

The disembodied voice continued, 'Then you are here to see my lady, Nicholaa.'

'You are well informed,' I responded, breathing more freely.

''Tis my job. I am Oswald, captain of the garrison. I am responsible for the safekeeping of Lady Nicholaa. Are you armed?'

'I did not recognise your feet. In answer to your question, of course, I always carry a loaded censer under my robe.'

I regretted that remark. He came down onto the same step as me and I was certain that he was going to tear my robe apart to remove the offending incense burner.

'I know what a censer is; do not jest about matters which concern the lady's safety, Father Bernard. I may have to detain you in a cell until your wit cools.'

'I'm sorry, Captain Oswald, it will not happen again. I'm expected, you say.'

He glared at me for an age before replying. He smelled of efficient violence and I felt close to my maker at that point — then his face melted into a smile, I surmised, because most of his face was enveloped inside one of those mail coifs they wore.

'Welcome, Father Bernard, I am to take you straight up.'

'Thank you, Captain. Up?'

'Yes, up. You are but halfway, the lady awaits you in her privy chamber on the top floor. Follow me.'

After a further climb we reached the guard floor. He led me across it to a stairway in a corner and we began to climb again. Eventually the stairs emerged into a much better furnished chamber which stretched across the whole expanse of the tower. The atmosphere was calm with only a low buzz of conversation to be heard. There were drapes on the walls and various tables set out with food; people were sitting around talking while others were studying maps and charts laid out on tables; it seemed to be the hub of a very well-regulated organisation.

'Are you coming, Father Bernard?'

Another rebuke from the man in the metal coif. I had paused at the top of the stairs partly to take in the sights and partly to regain my puff.

'Of course. More stairs?'

'Not now; over there.'

He pointed at a very large table across the chamber behind which sat a very small woman. She was contemplating something said to her by a man, probably a merchant by his clothing, who seemed to be making an impassioned address to her.

Her eyes were studying the table top and I suspected that she had heard quite enough from him.

The mail helm stopped before her and coughed. She looked up and smiled graciously, probably with relief.

'Father Bernard, my lady,' informed the captain.

I was grabbed by a sleeve and thrust forward against the front of the table.

Lady Nicholaa smiled at me. She was an impressive woman, in her sixties and very much in control of herself and her surroundings. She was wearing a fine burgundy chainse with a matching ganache around her shoulders, while her hair was covered in a simple white amuse held in place by a fine silver filet.

'Father Bernard, we meet again.' Her voice was rich in tone, deeper than her size indicated, and well-modulated.

'Indeed, my lady, I am privileged.'

'And I. Perhaps we can enjoy some more quiet conversation, when I have time.'

'I am looking forward to that, my lady.'

'Good. But for now I have business, you understand. Perhaps you would care to sit near and listen; it may help you to understand the world outside of the cathedral a little better.'

'I am always curious, my lady; thank you.'

I felt a tug at my sleeve. The face in the metal coif was a little gentler this time as he found me a chair at the end of the table and plonked me down in it. I wondered if I should ever move again without his assistance.

As it happened my escort left once I was settled and I watched with interest as Lady Nicholaa dealt with a few more plaintiffs. There was clearly a high degree of respect for the lady in the town, regardless of their view of the king — if they were confident enough to bring their grievances to her rather than settling them through violence or other means, it would better preserve the peace.

By late morning she was done, and rising came over to me.

'I think that your duties can begin with you leading midday prayers in my private chapel, Father Bernard. What say you?'

'I say, my lady, that I am delighted.'

'Then let us go. As you know, I usually go down into the ward to attend the garrison chapel with my household, but for today it is convenient just here.'

A young woman, a handmaiden no doubt, drew back a curtain to reveal a small wooden door which she opened and stood aside from.

'Thank you, Basilea. Father Bernard is appointed as my confessor and he will guide our spiritual needs from now on.'

Basilea smiled and bobbed. A very pretty girl, I thought, she will cause some heartache among the men.

'Thank you, my child,' I said, following Lady Nicholaa into the chamber. It had a small altar at the end and four Prie-Dieu kneeling chairs, two on either side. One window slit gave a little light, as did two candles burning either side of the crucifix in the centre of the altar.

The two ladies knelt as I genuflected in front of the crucifix before saying a small prayer.

Turning, I gave out my blessing and thought that I should say a little more.

'I would like to thank you, Lady Nicholaa, for the privilege of prayers with you, and of course with your companion, Lady Basilea. No doubt we shall have many conversations, by your good grace, in the future. But is there anything of special note to which we should pay attention this day?'

She thought for a moment before answering. 'I think that we should pray for the guidance of the king. He has upset many by seeking to set aside the great charter he signed last year — that was unwise.'

I agreed. 'It has given some the excuse they were looking for to bring French Prince Louis over the sea to challenge him.'

Lady Nicholaa gazed at me with sad eyes and, taking Basilea by the hand, stood facing the crucifix. I thought to ease her discomfort and intoned a short prayer.

'Lord, if it is to be war between our countrymen, let it be short, and let it be justly won by our king.'

Genuflecting first she turned away from the altar and went towards the door.

'I will take a little nap now, Father Bernard, as is my custom. We will speak later. We must prepare the castle for the king's impending visit. I have word that he has recaptured the donjon at Rochester and is now seeking out his other enemies who are laying waste to the land. I believe him to be close to Worcester at present but we must wait to see the direction of his travel.'

I was assailed by sudden dark thoughts; oh what hounds of war hath this impetuous king unleashed now! May God have mercy upon our souls. Then I wondered where I was expected to live and sleep, so after blowing out the candles I went off to find the chamberlain.

Eventually I was installed in a little chamber at the back of the garrison chapel in a little wooden hut in the bailey, and very cosy it was. Having my own space was a luxury and I would have been very comfortable except — except that the town was with the cathedral, and they and the castle were drifting apart, according to rumour, and a conflict of interests between them might not be very far off.

I had only attended Lady Nicholaa for a week when the first of King John's advance riders appeared. I was on my way back from the cathedral after another of Archdeacon Peter's inquisitions. Passing through the graveyard outside the cathedral I had already crossed by the top of the steep hill and was nearing the castle when I heard a horse coming up behind me. It clattered by, breathing heavily after ascending the hill, and was no doubt pleased to be brought to a halt at the gate. There the rider was stopped briefly by the guard before being let into the bailey. The main gates were closing behind him as I scuttled through after him.

I was well known now and had no difficulty in obtaining access to Lady Nicholaa's impregnable last refuge, the Lucy Tower, rumoured to be named after some long dead female castellan — and designer of the infernally familiar multitude of steps leading up to the guard floor.

Lady Nicholaa was standing proud by the fireplace issuing instructions to her various captains. I made such a fuss, almost running, that she looked up from her plans to call out to me, 'Are they here, Father Bernard?'

'Indeed, my lady, the king's first herald is within the east gate.'

'Then we must go and make him welcome, his master will not be far behind.'

'Very well, my lady.'

Quickly, she sped off to the top of the tower steps to descend into the bailey. She was sprightly for a woman in her sixties, apart from a little hesitancy descending the steps.

I made so bold as to give out an opinion. 'I trust that the king is coming here to give proper thanks for your loyalty in holding this place secure against all his enemies.'

She stopped halfway down the steps and tutted at me for my words.

'Father Bernard, hold back such remarks, King John would be offended to hear suggestions like that. He is, after Richard's death, our undoubted king by right of accession. Let's hear no more of it.'

'I am sorry, my lady, they were wild thoughts and unworthy. I'll do some penance.'

'See that you do. Now quickly, I'll not be found wanting in my greeting, creaking bones or not.'

We were followed by courtiers, anxious to be at the front when Lady Nicholaa first greeted the king and at the same time trying not to crowd the lady. They were a nuisance and I found it difficult to keep my place next to her without tripping on my robes.

At the bottom she halted suddenly, causing more chaos behind as she demanded, 'Where's the key, I must have the key to the castle.'

'I have it.' Basilea came pushing her way down the crowded steps holding the key up high.

Lady Nicholaa was less than pleased and snapped, 'The cushion, girl, where is the cushion, we cannot hand it to the king without a cushion.'

Basilea turned, calling to someone unseen above the heads of the crowd on the steps, 'The cushion, Lucette, the cushion.'

A hand-held cushion appeared above the heads of the crush and it flew down over their heads. Being too slow to catch, I was hit in the face by it but snatched it to my chest.

'Ah! Father Bernard, you have it. Let me place the key on it, then keep hold of it, you shall be by my side when I speak to the king.'

That caused a few grins to fade; a mere priest next to the king? Some knights, and especially the ladies of some knights, were well put out.

It was a dank end to September, this year of our Lord, 1216. The harvest was hardly in before a leaden gloom descended on the land. It matched the mood of the people still astounded by the loss of lands in France, a result, many whispered, brought about by the incompetence of the king, although none spoke these words outside a circle of their friends.

I watched with admiration as Lady Nicholaa stood calmly in the bailey, directing the comings and goings of a seeming myriad of functionaries, all intent on making their best efforts count for the reception of their rightful monarch.

Being nearly done she turned to me and asked with a calm smile, 'Father Bernard, think you that the king will be satisfied with my arrangements?'

'I'm certain that he will, it will be the friendliest welcome that he has experienced for a while.'

'Oh, you are wicked. I still wonder if he will be satisfied sleeping in yonder pavilion.' She waved an arm in the direction of the flag-bedecked marquee she had set out for the monarch near the great hall.

I looked past the lady towards the steps leading up to her stone-built eyrie sitting dizzyingly atop its motte.

'It will be preferable to mounting yonder steps, my lady.'

'Think you that he is incapable of climbing such an obstacle? He is, after all, a warrior king.'

Aye, and one who has recently lost the counties of Maine and Anjou and the duchy of Normandy to the French king Philip. But I kept those thoughts to myself.

'Do you think that he might prefer your bed, my lady?'

That came out a little wrong, but she giggled nonetheless.

'It is a while since anyone sought out my bed, Bernard. It is true that the king has a certain reputation for ladies' beds, but I believe that I am safe in that regard, don't you think?'

She had turned that remark neatly back upon me, the king's salacious appetite for bed companions being yet another of his traits which many found unappetising.

'I'm sorry, my lady, I had not intended to include you in that suggestion.'

She laughed out loud, attracting the attention of all around her. 'I'm teasing you, Bernard, I'm the wrong side of sixty to worry about that kind of thing, but still I'll have my privy chamber prepared for his use.' She called out, 'Where is that chamberlain? Have him prepare my chambers for the king.'

There was a commotion to the right as the great gates swung open and admitted a Serjeant of the guard and his patrol.

They had been out in the town, which lay just beyond the gates, on an inspection. There were many out there who would have gladly seen King John despatched to an early grave, such was his unpopularity among diverse lords, knights, merchants, and others, whom he had been squeezing for cash these many years since he had been crowned — or even before that, when he had been forced to scrabble around for money to support the deceased King Richard's adventures in the Holy Land, *and* pay his ransom when the reckless king had been apprehended on his way home by some unscrupulous Austrian lord — the ransom had almost ruined England, a habit which John seemed to find difficult to relinquish.

Whatever their grievances, John was the ordained and anointed king, and today was not one to argue the point.

Another great shout to open the gate came echoing across the crowded sward of the bailey.

'Are you expecting any other visitors, my lady?'

'Indeed I am,' she replied, at the same time giving out more instructions to the chamberlain, now appearing especially harassed. 'My friend, Matilda of Laxton, is coming. She does not intend to miss this opportunity to petition further the king regarding her domains.'

'I see. Is the High Sheriff of Nottingham still interfering in the running of her forest?'

'He is. Philip Marc sits far too heavily upon her shoulders regarding the forests of Sherwood and Derbyshire, it is time that the king told him to restrict his interest to the town of Nottingham.'

'I thought him precluded from that office in the great charter?'

'He was, but he continues to petition his case with the king.'

'A persistent rogue,' I answered to a disappearing back, which I followed as Lady Nicholaa moved closer to the gate.

It was not long before a cavalcade made an entrance. There was a hush as the first rider trotted through the gate. He was a well-built Saxon dwarfing the pony he was perched upon. Carrying one of those dreadful warbows, and wearing a mail hauberk with a short sword in his belt, he seemed supremely confident in his potentially perilous position at the head of the column. With his long blond hair flowing freely around his head, he was a terrifying sight to all who might wish him harm, but he smiled as he made his stately entrance.

He reined his horse to one side and his accompanying men, all Saxon archers by their appearance, formed an alley of twelve, six on either side as a welcoming party for their mistress, who closely followed them in.

It was Lady de Caux, named Matilda, who they escorted, and I imagined that it could not be grander than the one we were expecting for the king — for behind her rode a priest and twelve Norman knights to complete the rear of her cavalcade.

'Times must be dangerous in the forest, my lady,' I ventured to say to Lady Nicholaa.

'Indeed, it would be dangerous to run into this lot, methinks.' She laughed and called out, 'Maud! Maud, my dear, how nice to see you once more.'

Lady Matilda guided her horse towards us and, to my surprise, cast a leg over the beast's neck and sprang down to grasp Lady Nicholaa tight around the shoulders. She was very manly in her dress, apart from her hair, which was wild and dark, and scarcely covered by a scanty gauze nebulae. Her nether region was clad in what appeared to be a fine doe-skin kirtle, but it split in the middle to reveal that it was designed like a man's breeches to allow her to sit to horse as a man, and a blouson top which had unseemly buttons down the front. She stepped back from the embrace and fixed the gaze of her hazel eyes on my lady.

'Nicholaa! Have we arrived before the king?' she demanded in a voice which probably reached over the castle wall into the town.

'You have, my dear.'

Matilda called to a young woman who had been riding behind her. 'Orva, see to my horse if you will.'

Orva, a very pretty woman with wild blond hair flying about her head, also in breeches, and to my alarm with a wicked seax strapped to her waist, collected the reins of Matilda's horse and took it over to the Saxon leader. They leant towards each other and exchanged kisses on horseback.

'Who's that man?' asked Lady Nicholaa. 'And the maid?'

'That's Ælfgar … and,' she answered, looking at the amorous pair, 'Orva. They are very good friends.'

'So it would seem. How can you afford so many Saxon archers? I have only crossbowmen.'

'Ælfgar's family have lived on my lands since time began. He attends me for little reward and mostly because of the many Saxon families who still live within my curtilage.'

'The king is not far behind you, he should be puffing his way up the Dane's Gate Hill, or even have reached Castle Hill as we speak.'

'Where can we stand?'

'You stand with me; there are questions about the forests that we want answers to … which reminds me: Chamberlain! Are my privy chambers prepared for the king if he wants to make use of them?'

'Indeed they are, my lady, as requested. And where will your visitor sleep tonight, my lady?' he asked, looking at the lady Matilda.

'With me, of course, wherever that may be.'

'Father Albric will need a privy chamber.' Matilda beckoned over the priest, also a Saxon by his appearance. He dismounted and approached. 'This is Father Albric, my confessor.'

'And this is Father Bernard, *my* confessor.'

'We are well shriven, Nicholaa,' laughed Lady Matilda.

A great shout went up from the battlement above the gate. 'The king! The king's fore riders are here.'

23

I grasped Albric's hands and welcomed him. 'Welcome to Lincoln, Father Albric. Have you seen our cathedral?'

He was a pair of heads shorter than I but as I looked down on to his pleasant face I thought that we might get on together.

'It is difficult to miss, Bernard. When the sky is clear we can see this ridge from the top of Lady Matilda's donjon, fully sixteen miles away, so I'm told.'

'Really, so far?'

'Come, Maud,' Nicholaa called, 'tell your Saxon to line up his men inside the gate with mine and we will go to stand outside the barbican. King John is almost here.'

So we went through the east gate, beneath the walls of the barbican, and lined up to await the appearance of King John.

Taller than Albric I might have been, but I felt very small standing, as ordered, by Lady Nicholaa. She was clearly concerned that her arrangements were sufficient to please the king. Here in the open square in front of the looming castle gate, the battlement of which was prickly with protruding weaponry, we were hemmed in by men-at-arms keeping the crowd back and warriors on horseback fully armed to impress — who would dare to threaten the king with such a show of strength to guard him?

Across the square facing us was the great west front of the cathedral, still impressive despite the gloomy day, while from the direction of the Castle Hill to our right cheers and jeers rang out in equal measure, louder and louder, reporting the steady progress of King John as he neared.

'Is it in regard to Richard de Lexington that you wish to speak to the king, Maud?' asked Lady Nicholaa, shouting to make herself heard.

'Aye, that poxy relative of mine did usurp my domain when last I was widowed, and now that he hath offended the king I will chance to get it back.'

'He was fined for rebellion at Berwick, I have heard.'

'Serve him right. Lords wanting to get their hands on my domains are as numerous as flies around that horse's backside.'

'Maud, have a care, you are embarrassing our priests,' said Lady Nicholaa, grinning at me.

'Nay, my lady,' I responded, 'I have not been cloistered all my life, once I was a carpenter before I received the calling.'

'Were you indeed,' retorted Lady Matilda, 'and is your name Joseph?'

'Nay, 'tis not,' answered Lady Nicholaa on my behalf, 'but I knew not that you were once an artisan, Father Bernard,' said she, looking at me.

''Tis in the past, my lady. But look, here is the king,' I cried as the royal cavalcade turned the corner; only fifty paces away and the excitement swelled the noise.

There was a splendid white palfrey standing at the corner of Castle Hill, all caparisoned in finery, and we watched as King John dismounted from the very large farming beast which had carried him up the hill, then after donning a finely embroidered cloak he clambered on to his new steed and sat still while his attendants fussed around him, adjusting his clothing to make him regal in appearance.

'A man of some style,' I remarked to Father Albric.

'But little substance, I fear,' whispered he into my ear.

'He intends to make a grand entry into the castle, Nicholaa,' said Matilda.

'Indeed, his ornaments brighten up the dull day.' Lady Nicholaa stepped forward to greet the bejewelled monarch now upon us.

He was tall atop his horse, but when he slid off awkwardly he was no higher than me, or anyone else for that matter — not the mighty warrior which his deceased brother Richard had been, that's for sure. Close to, his face bore the ravages of his worrisome and dissolute life, he wore a kingly gold filet on his head, a little askew I noted, but the rest of him dripped finery and jewellery enough to pay the ransom of several kings — or feed the whole congregation of the cathedral for a month, which building sitting behind him he ignored.

'Lady Nicholaa.' He had no difficulty in identifying the keeper of his forests and castle in Lincolnshire, for everyone had stepped back and ensured that she stood to the fore.

'My lord, your keys.'

Nicholaa, not to be outdone with regard to finery, nevertheless made herself small as she greeted her monarch.

'My beloved Nicholaa, why do you offer me the keys? For you are surely better at guarding my possessions than I am.'

'At least that's honest,' whispered Albric.

Nicholaa bowed a little and proffered once more the cushion upon which the castle keys reposed.

'I fear that I have left too many summers behind me, my liege, and my body fades by the day; perhaps 'tis time that I handed these things over.'

'My beloved Nicholaa, I will that you keep the castle as ordained, until I order otherwise.'

He placed a hand upon the keys then withdrew it, although his eye had alighted on Basilea and he had difficulty in returning Nicholaa's fervent gaze.

'Come, Nicholaa, escort me beyond this forbidding gate, for I wish to see what delights await me within.'

His speech was to my lady but I saw that his eye had returned to the maiden, who began to blush at his obvious attention.

Nicholaa was not without a sharp eye and stood firmly betwixt the leery king and Basilea, seeking to distract him with prattle.

'Will your majesty meet with my friend, Matilda of Laxton? She holds your forests of Nottinghamshire and Derbyshire, at your pleasure.'

That did the trick and John's attention fell upon the lady Matilda.

'Is this true?' he asked, finding the much younger Matilda meat to his eye. 'That my forests hereabouts are in such beautiful hands? Come closer, Matilda of Laxton. Call Ralph Neville,' he ordered an attendant, 'he has charters with him to settle the claims of these female keepers hereabouts, this is a matter overdue for settling, methinks.'

Then, to no one's surprise, he offered an arm to each of the ladies and went up through the barbican to the castle gates, closely attended by his now acknowledged female keepers.

I said urgently to Father Albric, 'His lechery shows no abatement, defeated in battle, but rather he retains his arrogance with the women. I must speak with Basilea.'

'Of course, and I have concerns for my lady Matilda, but what can I do?'

I located Basilea in the crush, and with Albric clinging on to my robes beseeched her.

'Make yourself scarce, Basilea; if you value your person stay away from the king's presence. I will fix it with Lady Nicholaa. Now go and find the oldest and most crotchety of Nicholaa's attending women to replace your good self, and do not be found as long as the king remains here. Now go.'

'Is he as bad as that?' Father Albric asked with astonishment. 'I had heard rumours, but this…'

'He cares not for other men's marriage vows as much as for the comfort of their wives. Have no doubt, Albric, the girl is safer with the villains of the forest than near to this king.'

'You don't think that Lady Matilda is in danger, do you?'

'She retains a degree of attraction, I can see that, but that other girl, Orva, might excite him.'

'He would be advised to stay clear of that creature, for she bites. Did you note the seax at her waist belt? It is rumoured that she has used it on occasion … oh dear.'

I hurried along, anxious to stay near the king. The idea of the king of England ending his reign, however tenuous, on the blade of a Saxon knife was somewhat amusing.

I missed some of the conversation but caught up with the chaotic procession by the time the king had been conducted into the pavilion, newly erected for his visit. He was seated on a throne at the far end. On either side of him were Matilda and Nicholaa. Next to Nicholaa was Ralph Neville, chancellor and half-brother of the notorious Hugh, the chief forester of England and over-exuberant exactor of taxes, and on Matilda's right was one of the king's senior advisors, Peter des Roches, the Bishop of Winchester and a former precentor of Lincoln. I knew him not well, and he seemed quite preoccupied with attempting to transfix Matilda's attentions with his charms, although with his broken English — he favoured French — he was making little headway.

Standing behind with Albric I could see that Matilda was more interested in gaining the king's ear than any attempts at a bishop's wooing and I fixed my attention on that conversation.

'We heard that you would be going to Newark, my lord. We did not expect the pleasure of your presence so soon.'

The king had been eager to sit to table. On close examination he appeared quite exhausted after only recently riding down from Berwick. He had been washing down the dust of the road quite liberally since he had taken his place. His eyes were still keen to travel, but only up and down Matilda's body, and he was leaning across the arm of his throne to engage with the lady.

'Yes, 'tis a long, long road, that great north way. But we needed to reach Newark to rest the army before proceeding further south, that French chancer has taken control of a lot of the south, we needs confront him ere long.'

He banged his hand on the arm rest causing Matilda to shy a little, but she returned to her quest.

'There is trouble with the Scottish king, I understand.'

That produced another thump of the arm and caused King John to drain another pot.

'That foreign-talking hill tribesman, Alexander. He has avoided me and goes I know not where. I'll have him on his knees before long, scurvy rogue, just you see. Wench!' he called.

A serving girl went to attend him and as she leant forward to refill his tankard his right hand went up between her legs. She smiled graciously and scooted off as quickly as she could.

Matilda turned and grimaced at me: what could I do?

A man, she mouthed. I was puzzled until it struck me. I scurried off to the buffet at the back of the hall and instructed the chief steward, Ingilf, to serve the king himself. Let's see where his hands strayed next time he called for more.

Matilda took some of the king's attention when she leant bravely towards him and asked, 'Do you see what a fine table Lady Nicholaa has prepared, my lord? There are some appetising viands prepared for your pleasure.'

'Indeed, there are.' Then with a surprising act of kindness he remembered to turn towards Lady Nicholaa and offer her a compliment, which she accepted gracefully.

'Thank you. Have you been able to address Lady Matilda's concern, lord?'

'Concern? What concern? Neville!' he called over Lady Nicholaa's head to his chancellor, 'have we a concern with this lovely lady?'

He turned back to Matilda and trapped her hand on her knee. Such public boldness.

Ralph Neville was alert to the king's behaviour and answered immediately, distracting him from Lady Matilda's limbs.

'The question of the Nottinghamshire forest, lord. The matter is quite settled now that Lexington has been removed from the position. And, if I may remind you, lord, High Sheriff Philip Marc was commanded to leave the forest in the Magna Carta last year, you agreed that Lady Matilda should resume her rights of inheritance, and that she should be appointed as the keeper of forests in the north of Nottinghamshire, including the area known as Sherwood, and retain the position of Castellan of Laxton.'

'I did, yes, yes, indeed. Now that we have both the ladies of the forest at our table together, we must celebrate. God knows, there has been little to celebrate this past summer. Girl!' he shouted and his left hand returned to Matilda's leg and his other went up between the steward's thighs but was quickly withdrawn as he felt the objects dangling there.

'Jesu, man! Art thou odd? Where's that wench gone?'

'She hath lady's problems, my lord, and I have excused her for the night. Please forgive me, my lord.'

'Forgive you? I damned near lost a finger in you. Hah! Hear that everyone? This fellow was near sticked by a kingly digit, hah!' He bellowed out great peals of laughter and those who knew him joined in with gusto.

I thought that it was going to be a very long night.

My little wooden hut kept out rain but not sounds, and the castle, thronged as it was with guests and noisy townsfolk, seemed to stay awake all night. I was up and about before dawn to make my way up to Lady Nicholaa's privy chapel. I was on my knees when I heard the door open, then the swish of skirts as my lady came to kneel beside me.

After a few moments' silence while she composed herself she indicated that she wanted to begin a conversation. I thought it best to sit and handed her up so that she might be comfortable on a chair.

'This does not auger well, Father Bernard. The king is in a sad state, and his realm fares little better. What are we to do?'

My response was interrupted by a disturbance at the door, and Basilea appeared with Lady Matilda and Father Albric.

'Forgive me, my lady,' Basilea apologised, 'your guests were wandering around the tower looking for you.'

'Oh, Maud, do come in; good morrow, Father Albric, you are welcome. We were discussing the affairs of state and the state of the king. Some news came to us during the night. It seems that King Alexander of Scotland has bypassed us here in Lincoln, travelling south, and is set on forming an alliance with the French prince, Louis, in Kent. I think that King John will not tarry here very long.'

'Jesu,' said Matilda, 'the king will be certain to take his army south. It will leave us to our own devices, Nicholaa, and we will need to serve him as best we can with what we have got. How sure are you of the townsfolk of Lincoln?'

'I'm not,' came her unhappy response.

'Both church and people still resent King John's tithes and taxes, they say that his wars in France have proved unprofitable and unbearable, and wish him naught but ill will,' I added.

'But he is the king. It is his duty to serve the nation as he thinks best,' asserted Lady Matilda.

'Alas, dear Maud,' counselled Nicholaa, 'you are well shielded from town politics deep in your woods. The people hereabouts seethe and blow like trees in the autumn winds. Even if he had not lost all of England's domains across the sea, the taxes have been too much for them to bear, they have destroyed trade and farming, such has been their impact on people's purses. The idea of a different king has been growing of late. I hold the castle secure, but the cathedral is open to all opinions, and the streets are kept quiet by my patrols.'

'Does he know this?' asked Maud.

'His advisor, Neville, knows it well enough.'

'Then you expect him to leave soon?'

'I do, and we must see to our duties. Is Laxton safe, are your forests safe, Maud?'

'Safe enough. But now that I am confirmed as mistress keeper, I shall ease the High Sheriff of Nottingham's men out of my woods, he can attend to his duties within the bounds of Nottingham town; he is not welcome in my domains.'

'Philip Marc will not bear this lightly, my lady.' Albric was quick to point out the obvious. 'He fills his purse with tithes from the forest.'

'Well, any tithes will be directed to the king's purse from now on, and they will be put to better use than Sheriff Marc is wont to use them for, let him coax his money out of the Nottingham town merchants instead.'

'Well said, Maud. Now let us see if the news has disturbed King John, he should be up and about by now.'

Lady Nicholaa led the way down through the tower and across the bailey to the great hall, arm in arm with her friend.

Sure enough a tired-looking King John was engrossed in council with his great and good and we were not invited, so we made our way back up those never-ending steps and took breakfast in Lady Nicholaa's privy chamber; a privilege which sparsely fed priests took to with gusto.

It was not long before we were interrupted as the stately Ralph Neville, a handsome man, and who I suspect was as near to the king as any, he was escorted in and invited to join us, which courtesy he refused, saying, 'We have not had enough time to enjoy your hospitality, Lady Nicholaa, for which I apologise and hope to repair that omission at some time in the future. However, things are pressing and the king must hence from here. We have also decided to confirm your appointment as the Sheriff of Lincoln; it sits well with your other duties. We must leave for Newark within the hour.'

With that he went, leaving Nicholaa and Matilda gazing at each other.

Matilda broke the silence first. 'Sheriff?'

'Sheriff, castellan, and keeper, all at once. We might need longer days to go about our business.'

The pair grasped each other and there was a certain moment of merriment as they held each other up, laughing.

'This is Neville's doing,' said Matilda, 'he guides the king's thoughts, surely.'

'Probably,' responded Nicholaa. 'Come on, everyone, be about your business,' she exclaimed when the mirth subsided.

There was an immediate scatteration of people as Nicholaa and Matilda went off to gather their followers and make them ready to give the king a proper royal send-off.

King John did not seem a well man as he mounted, or rather was assisted to mount his horse, a fine grey which was deemed sufficient to see him safely to the bottom of Castle Hill and on his way to Newark. But he departed with kind words.

'Lady Nicholaa, thank you for your hospitality; my visit was much too short. But I pray that you continue to hold secure this loyal castle against my enemies, and see that you find help sufficient to enable you to discharge your duties in regard to our royal forests of Lincolnshire. Although I am certain that you are capable of keeping them safe I have instructed Chancellor Neville to make funds available sufficient to assist you in this matter.'

He leant down to offer his hand, which Lady Nicholaa took in both hands, kissed, and pressed against her heart, saying. 'God speed you, my king; God give you strength to safeguard the realm and scatter thine enemies.'

He was moved by this entreaty and I spied a glisten in the corner of his eye before he turned to Lady Matilda.

'Maud, my dear: another who many men should find their actions shameful in the face of thine. I am privileged to have such brave women on my side — would that God had given your hearts the strength to bear arms at my side! Instead I will rely upon your steadfastness of spirit to succeed in your duties. Now, Maud, if you have any trouble with Sheriff Philip Marc, and his propensity to stray from his proper territory, feel free to persuade him back inside his recognised borders. Do you understand?'

Lady Matilda, looking to speak, tried also to catch hold of the king's hand, but there was a shout as Chancellor Neville evidently thought that the goodbyes had lasted long enough, and upon which King John kicked at the sides of his mount and set off towards the top of the Castle Hill and out of our domains.

As he made to follow his king, Neville also shouted across to the ladies. 'Act wisely, Mesdames, and without favour; the king hath faith in you.'

An open invitation, I thought, and I wondered how these two grand ladies would discharge their duties, having been confirmed in their authority to act upon the king's behalf.

Departures such as these after visits by great persons oft-times left a sudden gap in activities and led to a silence. Not so today. Lady Nicholaa called for her castle chamberlain, Turstan, and set about attending to the duties of the Constable of Lincoln Castle, Sheriff of Lincoln, *and* those of the keeper of the king's forest in Lincolnshire.

Taking Lady Matilda by the hand she led off towards the Lucy Tower saying, 'We need to consider how to keep the peace hereabouts. These are dangerous times and without the king's army we must keep control of forest, town and castle using our few brave soldiers and our wits. How do you see it, Maud ... Keeper of the King's Forests of Nottinghamshire and Derbyshire?'

The lady concerned stopped and brought the procession behind them to a sudden halt.

'Frightening ... and exciting all at once.' She looked around her, and not seeing her guardian, for he was hemmed in by the throng, called out, 'Ælfgar!'

There was a disturbance in the crowd as people were swept aside by the imposing warrior.

'Here, my lady,' came the reply as Ælfgar appeared by her side, and not a few picked themselves up from the ground where he had left them.

'If you and Orva can disentangle for a few moments, there are matters of importance to discuss. Stay near me now, d'ye hear?'

'Aye, my lady,' answered the giant.

I was set to follow but a tug on my sleeve halted me. It was a young lad from the cathedral.

'Please Father Bernard, Archdeacon Peter would like to see you in the cathedral.'

I looked down as he panted, all flustered and out of breath.

'Very well. Tell him I will attend him shortly. Go now … and don't trip up,' I called after him as his little legs sped him across the crowded bailey.

'What now?' asked Albric.

'I'll ask permission from my lady, then see what the mighty archdeacon wants. He is bound to press me on matters, to see what is being conspired within these walls. I'll needs think of something to tell him, but I'll not betray any confidences. Now where is Lady Nicholaa seated? Ah! There they are.'

Lady Nicholaa was almost ready to commence a briefing. She was sitting in the erstwhile king's throne, now reverted to its normal use as her chair — which had been brought down from the tower especially for the king. Seated beside her were Matilda on her left and Geoffrey of Serland, one of her foremost knights, on her right. Attending were other important men necessary to her needs to keep safe the castle: Chamberlain Turstan, Steward Ingilf, Captain of the Guard, Oswald, the captain of crossbowmen, Serjeants of the infantry, and the captain of cavalry, such as she had at her disposal, which was not a lot; horsemen were not especially useful in defending a castle — and expensive to maintain.

I quickly sought her ear before she could begin. 'The archdeacon has sent for me, my Lady, may I have your permission to attend him?'

'Oh dear me no, Bernard, you have a vital part to play in the defence of the castle, the archdeacon must wait. Now, what I require is a scribe, someone to accurately record events. We may well come under siege if things go badly elsewhere. So get yourself a seat and some writing instruments as quick as you can and join us here, if you please.'

Dashing up to the lady's chapel where I knew that I could find vellum, ink, and quills, I found myself rejoicing — Lady Nicholaa had made herself quite clear, the castle came first and the archdeacon was next.

By the time I returned, panting, to the table, a space had been cleared for me and that bulky Saxon warrior of Lady Matilda's had also been found a chair.

'Thank you, father Bernard, now record a diary, and when we want lists, you can set them down for us.'

Lady Nicholaa then swept her gaze around the gathering, taking everyone into her confidence, before commencing her briefing.

It was difficult at first, ideas and exchanges swept back and forth across the table, and methods of defence and war not being within my expertise, I struggled, although dealing with the aftermath had been my lot on too many occasions. So I reverted to scribbling quick notes meaning to write them down with care later — and that was much easier.

Eventually I had recorded lists of duties and methods of defence all agreed on, so when Lady Nicholaa released me I went straight up to my priest's chamber to write my notes properly. The archdeacon would have to wait until morning.

It was chilly and damp in the morning, a heavy mist hung in the air on top of the castle ridge, and it seemed just as chilly when I entered Archdeacon Peter's office. He was in a solemn mood as I knelt before him for a blessing.

'Sit, Bernard,' he commanded when the formalities were done, and I took the chair provided opposite him. 'Messages seem to have taken a roundabout route before they reached your ears.'

'Indeed, Archdeacon, I was in a privy meeting with Lady Nicholaa.'

'Indeed?'

He waited for me to elaborate, but I merely returned his gaze — becoming impatient he decided to come to the reason he sent for me.

'The king has left, I hear, whither is he bound?'

'Newark, as far as I know, Archdeacon.'

'Mmm. What mission has he in mind?'

'I am not privy to that, Archdeacon. But it is reported that the Scottish king is on his way to join with the French prince in Dover. What would it matter, Archdeacon Peter?'

'I know about King Alexander. How close are you to the lady?'

'She shares her confession.'

'I mean in temporal matters.'

'I am appointed as her scribe, all she tells me is in the strictest confidence, and I have given my oath on it.'

That was nearly true, I had accepted that what I heard in her presence was in confidence, without being asked to take an oath, military privacy was necessary, and I knew it. A fine point, but one which did not damage my soul, I feel.

'You know that feelings are running at fever pitch in this town?'

'I listened to the reaction when the king ascended the steep hill.'

'He has extracted too much money from the merchants and lords hereabouts to waste on unsuccessful wars, and the church has not been exempt either. We have sent off too many barrels of silver coin for him to waste on his futile adventuring. His tax collectors will receive little more from Lincolnshire, I believe.'

I paused for a moment to try and work out where the message was in that last statement. 'Is that a rumour, or something more certain, Archdeacon Peter?'

He looked at me strangely, perhaps considering where my loyalties lay.

''Tis but gossip, but gossip oft-times hath legs … you understand?'

'I understand that the king pushes some things to the limits, Archdeacon.'

'Then understand that in this regard he has met his limit, and that there are those minded to prevent his further straying beyond that. Have a care, Father Bernard; have a care when it comes to choosing sides, for that day may not be far off.'

I stood, not knowing what to say, and thought for a moment. 'And when I return to the castle, to the lady Nicholaa?'

A shadow passed over the archdeacon's face and he stared at the floor before responding.

'I will not ask you to choose between your duty to the lady and your duty to the church, which will lie within your conscience, Father Bernard. But take time to think on it, and choose wisely. You have my blessing.'

He gestured for me to kneel and placing his hands upon my head muttered a few words of prayer before dismissing me.

As I reached the door of his office he called out gently, 'If I do not see you again on this earth I pray that we will meet in heaven.'

That bad? I turned to face him. 'Thank you, Archdeacon Peter, I will pray for you too. God be with you.'

Deep in thought I made my way along the gloomy cavern of the empty cathedral, but found a spot to kneel and pray in front of the altar screen before I left through the postern door and into the chill of the graveyard. The door was slammed shut behind me as I headed towards the castle. Mist swirled around the half-hidden gravestones, and I thought that I heard voices: approving or condemning? Who's to say? I had made a choice but left the cathedral's great door behind with a heavy heart.

In the gloom I thought that I heard another noise and turned. The cathedral was now lost in the mist, no longer visible. Perhaps I had left that life. Stuck in the mists of in between with neither castle nor cathedral to guide me. Dear Lord, where are you taking me? It was only two hundred paces door to gate — the longest journey of my life. I had made my choice, to live or perish within those mighty walls. But had an unseen hand hidden both gates from my view for a reason? I shuddered as I approached the barbican but the grumpy guard recognised me and gave me a cheery greeting, spitting on the ground as he did so.

'Evening, Father Priest, uncommon misty today.'

He cleared his throat and I swished on past not wanting to be engulfed by his expectorants.

'God bless you, my son,' I uttered swiftly — then paused as the vista of the inner bailey, now cleared of mist, revealed that all of the pavilions had been spirited away. Were they already clearing the ground for war?

Jesu! Those donjon steps again.

The morning was well gone by the time I swept into the guard floor of the donjon, bringing a waft of the damp air with me. The ladies were there, saving me the climb up to the top, and deep in conversation. Ælfgar looked up, a frightening sight, as if I had disturbed their thoughts but I was hailed by Father Albric and went to stand and steam near the fire place while he inspected me.

'Something disturbing you, Father Bernard. Can I help?'

His question startled me, how had I managed to find my way here so distracted.

'Father Albric, is all well with you?' An odd question, perhaps, but all I could think of.

'Indeed, I am fine. Would that the world was as ordered.'

'Yes, yes, there are dark clouds looming.'

'You brought some in with you.'

I stared at him, not understanding.

'You are damp, Father Bernard.'

''Tis but the morning mist, Father Albric, the dark clouds are yet to come; there is much unrest outside these walls.'

'This I have been hearing. The ladies are preparing for a state of siege.'

'Oh my God, 'tis true; the archdeacon also hath prophesied it.'

Albric put a hand on my shoulder, which was difficult as he had short arms and I was tall. 'Come, we shall listen to the ladies.' And he led me over to where they were congregated.

Gathered around the great table at the head of the hall, the ladies Nicholaa and Matilda were together, flanked by Basilea and Orva respectively. I looked around for our Saxon warrior, Ælfgar, he was now at a window blocking out the light and talking to one of our Serjeants. Lady Nicholaa's chamberlain, Turstan, was also present together with Geoffrey of Serland,

and Captain Oswald. We sidled over to catch the conversation, but Lady Nicholaa spotted me and beckoned me to sit opposite her. There were blank parchments and writing materials laid out awaiting me.

Lady Nicholaa fixed a gaze me, drumming the table with her fingers.

'What news from the cathedral, Bernard?'

''Tis not good, my lady, there is more unrest in the town.'

'This matches our intelligences, my lady,' added Geoffrey, 'what my spies and agents have gathered in from around the county, there are murmurings of discontent, rebellion even.'

'It does,' she agreed, 'but there is more, is there not, Father Bernard?'

Fixed by that stern visage I thought that nothing but the stark truth was required.

'They are having difficulties, my lady, the archdeacon…'

Nicholaa finished the sentence for me. 'The archdeacon cannot lend his support to the king. Is that what you are going to say? *Ut representativum episcopus.* On behalf of Bishop Hugh, the archdeacon is minded to side with the people?'

It caused me some distress, but what her spies in the town had learned matched too sadly with that I surmised from my meeting with Peter, so I merely confirmed Nicholaa's assessment.

'Just so, my lady.'

'And you, Bernard, whither are you on the issue? Are you merely a messenger, has the archdeacon withdrawn you?'

'I am here … my lady, because it is my choice, should it be that you wish it so.'

She smiled at me gently. 'Ah, good priest, that is indeed what I would prefer. Know you what God's will is in this matter?'

I relaxed, accepted by her, and almost broke into a smile.

'Thank you, my lady, thank you. And I am certain that God is indeed with me today. Archdeacon Peter also referred me to the wisdom of the Almighty and left me to follow my conscience: it brought me here. There is too much attachment to silver out there … and too little to duty, I fear. However, there is hope. Although Bishop Hugh remains in London for his duties as a royal judge, we may expect some guidance from him, if a suitable letter was to reach him…'

I watched her reaction closely, a priest proposing a letter to his bishop suggesting that he guides his archdeacon differently; this runs close to disloyalty.

The lady took the decision away from me with haste. She read men well.

'I see, Father Bernard, well said. Prepare some notes and construct a missive for the bishop. Now you shall see how we prepare for war in this king's castle. And I shall consider your words for the bishop.' Nicholaa then turned to Lady Matilda. 'You have had time to reflect overnight, Maud, how much help can we expect from you in the defence of Lincoln. Can you stay?'

'I fear not, Nicholaa, I must see to the defence of Laxton; who's to say that this unrest in Lincoln will not spill over into the wider forest. Besides, we are now in October, winter will be upon us soon and we must make preparations for it, Laxton and Sherwood are my first duties.'

'I can't fault you for that. I was hoping to borrow some of your archers.'

Lady Nicholaa glanced first at Orva, sitting quietly with a satisfied smirk on her strong face, and then at Ælfgar, who was behind Orva, kneading her shoulders and grinning at her squirming neck.

43

The words, *rutting creatures*, popped into my head, but I dismissed them and paid especial heed to the negotiations going on between the two ladies, *such unworthy thoughts*.

'A nice try, Nicholaa, but they are my eyes and ears and my last resort in defence, they stay close to me at all times.'

'Ah, well, I needed to ask. I've dealt with sieges before, they are tiresome.'

'I've heard about the sieges of Lincoln castle, but not the full detail,' invited Maud.

'Oh, there's not much time, but briefly. The one in 1191 when King Richard's chancellor, William Longchamp, decided to have my inheritance off me — that lasted a month, until he got bored and departed. The next was in 1215. Gilbert de Gant turned up, and he went off with a flea in his ear; not very serious, was he.'

'The next one might not be won so easily.' Geoffrey, who had been sitting quietly, spoke up. 'We need to train more crossbowmen, my lady, every man who can lift the thing needs to be capable of firing one.'

'I agree, Geoffrey, we have men with arms as well as men-at-arms, we shall begin training immediately. Tell Bernard who we have, so that he may make a list. We do not know when unrest will turn into aggression.'

Next she inspected Captain Oswald. He was also a Saxon and dressed like one, including those monstrous moustaches and flowing blond hair — save that he wore Norman mail and oft-times carried a kite shield; not slow to pick up new ideas was Oswald.

'You know all the men who stand on the battlements, Oswald. How many are there who could bear a crossbow?'

'Quite a few, my lady. I presume that you include the likes of smiths, and cooks?'

'Everything with two legs and bollocks, Oswald,' responded Geoffrey. 'How many d'ye need to man the walls?'

'The north and east sides are the most vulnerable, we can manage with sentries on the towers of the west and south, the east gate is where I expect trouble to begin. I want one hundred on the east wall facing into the town, and another fifty along the north wall.'

'That's if we are actually under attack?' queried Geoffrey.

'Indeed,' replied Oswald, waving the garrison roster, a complete list of men of the garrison.

Lady Nicholaa spoke. 'Add Oswald's list, if you will, Bernard. Also ensure that the west gateway is sufficiently manned at all times, it may become critical to hold it if the east gate comes under pressure.'

The western gateway, I had observed, was not quite the same as the one facing the town on the east. It consisted of a sliding drawbridge, then an outer gate and portcullis, and then the barbican, an alleyway overlooked by the battlement, the killing ground for anyone trapped in there, and then another huge gate, that the final defendable entry into the bailey. Since it was not as busy as the eastern gate there was only a pair of sentries on the wall above, at most times, but they could only provide a warning of mischief.

Geoffrey let out a laugh. 'You are ahead of us, my lady, have you any other thoughts to share with us?'

Nicholaa grinned back at the grizzled knight; he had more than one scar to bear witness to his battlefield adventures, then she replied, 'There is a small gateway set in the town wall, just to the north of the castle wall, a portal, almost invisible with rubble scattered near it. It is used, I hear, by fellows of low repute, and others who do not wish to be questioned by the town porter at the Roman arch before entering the town. Is that so?'

'Indeed, my lady,' replied Oswald, 'it is watched from the battlement of the castle west gate, but as it only allows entry into the upper town it is not of much interest to us.'

I wondered what improper purposes a gate which provided access in and out of the upper town would allow, especially if the garrison sentries could observe its comings and goings, and I resolved to find out more later.

'Well, it is now of interest,' declared Lady Nicholaa. 'Send a carpenter and a mason to fashion a proper door in the hole in the wall, one which opens outwards, and make it secure. Then keep it under observation. Shoot at anybody who approaches it to warn them off.'

'As you wish, my lady. And the purpose?'

'A postern gate in the western town wall will be nowhere near big enough to admit cavalry, but if we become besieged we could bring any relieving force in though the castle west gate. The south is too difficult with swamps, rivers, and that final steep hill through the lower town. You see, Geoffrey, I am expecting any relief to approach from the north, but if they tried to access the upper town they would need to attack the old Roman gate and I expect that to be heavily defended by the rebels. If, by using this newly fashioned town wall postern gate we can get men in *behind* the Roman gate, it could scatter the rebels from that position and open up the entry to the upper town.'

'I'll need more men to man the castle west gate,' said Oswald, to no one in particular, extra guards being his problem.

'More lists, Bernard, I want to know about all our assets,' Lady Nicholaa advised me, but I was already scribbling.

'And, if it comes to it, we'll need to make, and keep good contact with any relieving force, someone will have to guide them in.'

'Indeed, Geoffrey,' responded Lady Nicholaa, as the craggy knight added some sage advice.

'I know just the man,' said Oswald with a twinkle in his eye.

Geoffrey returned their gaze. 'Me?'

'You,' confirmed Lady Nicholaa, leaving the good knight Geoffrey to consider silently his new position, that of an emissary to an as yet unknown army, during a non-existent siege in an as yet undeclared war.

Lady Nicholaa continued her preparations apace, her mind working as if she were twenty years old, not gone sixty. She had reached another decision.

'Captain Oswald, scour the stables, kitchens, smithies, cellars, and dig out any layabouts that you can find and get those organised into companies of crossbowmen. Chamberlain Turstan, see how much more we have to spend on supplies, we will need to get through this winter with what we have in store in the castle. Steward Ingilf, I want the wells protected by stone-built walls, and all the roofs within the bailey covered in grass turves, we must preserve the water and prevent fires; who knows what projectiles will be ranged against us. In addition, get as many trees cut and brought in and as many willows and thin branches as can be found, to make wattle shields. This castle *will* be defended, in the king's name, until the last man dies.'

She cast her eyes around the room as if seeking defiance, but she found none. I believe that if it was her wish, then whatever anyone thought about the king, it would become everyone's mission to satisfy the lady's demands — and so it proved. There was a murmur of consent and she stood up.

'So be it, my friends, whatever transpires we shall be ready for it. Thank you for your loyalty. Now, be about your tasks: work until sleep claims you, and then work again. And Ingilf, while I think on't, set the kitchens to work. I want a permanent cauldron of pottage to be kept hot at all times, the workers must be fed whenever they need it.'

I stirred myself, this part of the church will give her support. 'May I lead us in prayer, my lady, the pottage to stiffen the body and prayer to stiffen the soul?'

2.

Lady Matilda

It was late, the day having flown by as information was dissected, ideas were exchanged and plans were plotted. I watched as those who had been at the table split into little huddles, each no doubt discussing their own special parts in Nicholaa's plan.

After a while the lady Nicholaa spoke up. 'Maud,' she said, 'do you think that you could help in any way, my dear?'

'I've been thinking about that, Nicholaa, I may be able to give you some indirect help, whilst at the same time safeguarding my interests.'

Nicholaa sent everyone away from the table, and called for drinks to be served as I explained further.

'I must leave either on the morrow, or the day after, Nicholaa, you know that, as much as I would like to stay, but if we lose Laxton it will be as another brick out of the wall here in the middle of England, and another success for the Frenchies and those traitors.'

'You are right, dear friend, but I grow weary of it all, 'tis not as if I have not been fighting all my life to preserve my family's inheritance, but a war at my time of life may be too much, Maud, too much.'

'I know, Nicholaa, and you should have no need to defend your rights and defend the king's in this manner, but the way the world is ordered makes it necessary.'

'There are too many idle men in high places, they envy me my domains, my appointments, but quite the worst thing about

49

their regard is that they believe me to be incapable of ordering my life and the lives of those who depend on me.'

'They see you as an opportunity for advancement, get you removed and it's an easy gain for not a lot. Same as me, except that I can name my protagonist. That twerp Marc, High Sheriff my backside, the only thing high about that common varlet is his stink.'

Nicholaa snorted at that. 'I remain astonished that, having been removed from office in the Magna Carta two years ago, he is still clinging to his appointment. But things have been … chaotic. Chaotic, since John repudiated the document and nobody has had the time nor the wit to get rid of him.'

'Quite, and that is one thing which I intend to do as soon as possible. If Sheriff Marc wants to visit my forest then he can ask, other than that he can rot in his castle in Nottingham. But I will consult with my commanders to see what aid we can send you. Meantime, Ælfgar, take a look at the garrison staff and see if you can help Captain Oswald in their training.'

The following day, after prayers and breakfast, I went over to the gatehouse which faced the great cathedral and found Nicholaa and Captain Oswald waiting for me at the top, he had gathered together such artisans and assorted castle staff as were available and Ælfgar was eyeing them up looking for talent, he did not seem hopeful.

'Good morrow, Ælfgar, they've found you some fine fellows?'

He looked at me as if I was mad, and grunted. 'Morning, my lady.'

Obviously not, I thought.

'Oswald,' Ælfgar said, 'gather your Serjeants together and I'll see how much they know.'

Oswald stood patiently as the Saxon explained to the Serjeants how they would need to play a part in the training of our tyro crossbowmen.

'What's wrong wivvem?' complained one young fellow, who had probably not yet witnessed the devastating power of a full warbow.

'I'll show you later. Lady Nicholaa? Will you stay.'

'Yes, we can watch you for a little while, I have much to do elsewhere besides watch this, important as it is.'

'My lady.'

It was a bit crowded up here on the gate house battlement, but it was a good place to start and Ælfgar addressed the assortment placed before him.

'Attend me now, men ... and boys. I see a couple of youngsters, well done, and I will explain my views on this device. The crossbow is not my weapon of choice, it is clumsy to load and can't match the rate at which we archers can nock and loose arrows from our warbows. However it will be easier to train you, the unskilled, into a defensive force for Captain Oswald, than find some ten-year-olds to turn into archers, for that is when we begin to train them.'

That raised a few eyebrows but no questions. I nudged Nicholaa, and she grimaced, 'Ten years old? We've left that a bit late, Maud.'

Ælfgar hushed us with a glance.

'In the field a crossbow team might have up to three men; the bowman, otherwise known as the arbalestier; someone to assist in loading and carrying lots of bolts, and sometimes a man carrying a shield known as a pavise to guard the pair against enemy bolts, then again they might work in pairs one firing whilst the other is loading his weapon.

'Here in Lincoln Castle you are going to hide behind the battlement crenellations while you load, so all you need to learn is how to wind back the string, load the thing with a bolt and try and hit something while hiding behind the wall. Any questions?'

'Are you going to show us your war bow, lord?' one eager youngster asked, keen to learn.

'Aye, later, let's get you going first. This is what we'll do. Look over into the castle bailey being us, we've set up some targets over there.' He pointed out some empty greensward, or bare earth as it was, all the grass having been cut into turves and laid upon the roofs. 'Those sacks of straw are your targets, and we'll have you practise hitting them from up here on the battlement.'

Ælfgar and Oswald split them into small groups to practise the handling of the weapon and when they were capable of loading it, let them shoot at the targets. There were a few of the garrison soldiers who were versed in the art and, with the guidance of the Serjeants, and some of my men, to my great surprise, the assortment of volunteers were soon achieving passable results, hitting the sacks at a range of almost one and fifty hundred paces, hopeless really, but good enough to cover the open area in front of the gate.

Oswald questioned this public demonstration of our firepower. 'Everyone will know what we have.'

'Quite!' replied Ælfgar, 'they should know, better to discourage them than get into a real battle, you have not enough men as it is.'

'Ælfgar,' exclaimed Nicholaa, 'I see that most of the bolts are now striking the sacks, we are improving?'

'Yes, my lady, they are becoming useful now, if they stand and fight.'

'They will. How many have we now, Oswald? Including these parvenus?' she asked.

Ælfgar answered for him. 'That's the thing that you should keep secret. When we leave to go back to Laxton with my lady, Captain Oswald will continue to practise them every day, at least twenty bolts each, within the walls. That way those outside will be kept guessing at your strength, and it may help to stay their hands a bit more if the time comes.'

'How can they see into the bailey, Ælf?' asked Orva.

'Up there,' I pointed at the top of the cathedral, 'you might see a bit of the bailey yard from up there, and there are spies in here I suppose.'

'Very wise,' spoke Oswald, 'I wish that you could stay, but I suppose that you must see to your own defences. God willing it will not come to a war, but the portents are not good.'

'No, Oswald, this king has not been good for this realm; would that he had stayed in France.'

'Many think that, but it would be unwise to repeat it,' added Nicholaa, crossly.

I said naught, the Saxon Oswald and I thought alike on the subject. Then he asked Ælfgar a question.

'These new crossbowmen have worked it out that you think little of their weapons and are boastful regarding your own. Perhaps a demonstration?'

He laughed. 'Line them up on the battlement.'

Ælfgar collected his bow staff and I looked at Orva, she had a little smirk playing around her lips, she knew, and I knew what would happen. Ælfgar stringed his bow and the new crossbowmen lined up along the wall, waiting and watching, as were the normal sentries.

'Captain Oswald,' shouted Ælfgar, so that all could hear, 'how far is that cathedral great door?'

Oswald squinted through the afternoon gloom and replied, 'Near one hundred and eighty paces I reckon.'

Then Ælfgar called out, 'Can I hit it?'

A chorus of, 'yea's and nay's and never's,' rang out as Ælfgar picked up his sleek piece of wood, hardwood on the outer front and soft inside, fashioned from one piece of carefully chosen yew. He picked an arrow up, nocked it and feeling it against his cheek loosed it, then there were three in the air all at once before the onlookers could draw a breath. They struck the great door one after the other and the sound came back to us, thud, thud, thud.

There was a silence as the crossbowmen began to realise their shortcomings, then the small postern door next to the great door of the cathedral opened and a shiny head popped out, failed to observe the quivering arrows above then withdrew, closing the door.

'Ooh, Ælf,' chuckled Orva appreciatively.

'He is good, Maud,' added Nicholaa.

There was a great cheer from the battlement in praise of Ælfgar's bowmanship, but then he called for attention.

'Listen to me. That was normal for an archer, masters of the bow, but, as I remind you, we are trained from the age of ten. Do not think that you will achieve such results with that crossbow. Remember that you are training to repulse an attack on this castle, and you do not need to hit the cathedral door, not that anyone will notice.' That raised a laugh and he continued. 'Remember your training, Oswald, twenty bolts per day … to keep the bailey safe. Lady Matilda, are we done here?'

'Indeed, Æflgar, we have done all we can in the time. We must get back into our forest.'

'May I assist you down the steps, my lady?' Ælfgar asked Nicholaa.

'Ælfgar, I could take that offer as good manners or an insult, I can manage going down the steps, thank you, but I would appreciate your hand. If you don't mind, Maud?'

'Don't ask me,' I answered, 'ask Orva, she's the one with the seax.'

As dark fell we gathered in the guard hall for food, Nicholaa picked a little but was clearly tired and rose to leave. 'Thank you Maud, that's my day done, goodnight all. See you at Prime.'

A chorus of, 'goodnight my lady,' followed her out as Basilea helped her up the steps to her privy quarters.

Geoffrey of Serland placed some morsels onto a platter and came to stand next to me and father Albric.

'It has been a hectic few days, Father Albric, is it how you expected it?'

'Hah! Not quite, I expected that the king's visit would provoke some interest, but I much prefer it in among the trees.'

'Have you always lived there?' Geoffrey asked him.

'Mostly. I was born in Mansfield so I jumped at the chance to become confessor to my lady, Matilda de Caux, or as her friends know her, Maud of the Forest. As confirmed by the king yesterday.'

'Ah, that doubt is well removed. You are safe, my lady, I am sure,' grinned Geoffrey.

'With God's blessing, and if we all survive this unrest.'

'Father Albric has always lived in the forest. Have you?' Geoffrey asked me. His eyes were following a path down my loose-buttoned shirt front.

'For a long time now my family have been the keepers of the forest in Sherwood, all through the turbulent years after the first William was succeeded, first by his son William Rufus, and then in dubious circumstances by his youngest son Henry, even though the natural successor was Robert the elder. In time, through marriage, the domain of Brampton was added and when my parents died I inherited the lot.' I decided to make an announcement regarding giving support to Nicholaa. 'Ælfgar, I wish you to have a couple of bowmen stay on for two more days. They can help to train lady Nicholaa's new crossbowmen. Father Bernard and Captain Oswald have their list of candidates.' I caught Bernard's attention and beckoned him over, in time to hear the end of my statement. ''Tis beneath Ælfgar's skill level, but we are willing to put that to one side for the sake of unity, are we not my blond warrior?'

'Beneath them?' asked Bernard.

'Aye, priest,' answered Ælfgar, 'anybody can pick up a crossbow and, provided he hath the strength to wind it, lift it, aim it, and press the release. 'Tis no great skill.'

'Thank you, my lady, we need all the help we can get.' Bernard smiled and put a hand on Ælfgar's shoulder as a gesture of appreciation.

'I might be able to do more,' I continued. 'Between here and the river Trent is about nine miles, and beyond that the great north way, leading onwards to Scotland, then about six miles west of that is Laxton. I propose a regular patrol, to set out from here and Laxton each day, and meet on opposite banks of the river to relay any news which we may want to exchange.'

'Good idea,' said Bernard, 'that way we will gather knowledge of movements in the area between here and you, and feel safer for it, no doubt.'

'Certainly better informed,' I concluded. 'Record that Father Bernard, if you please, there will be no accusations that two women cannot defend the king's realm as well as anyone.'

Nicholaa was right, when she had insisted upon proper records, this needed to be presented as a record of truth when this was all over.

The sun had raised its torpid head high by the time we had eaten, mounted and waited while Father Albric heaved himself onto his horse, or rather the pony that he had been allocated. No great destrier for him, this little mare was quite enough for a priest in robes and he still struggled to lurch himself on to its compliant back.

Ælfgar wanted me in the middle of the cavalcade.

'We know not what the sheriff has been up to while we have been in Lincoln, Lady Matilda, if it please you to travel in the centre you will be as safe as can be.'

Seeing as I appointed the man as my personal protector I could hardly refuse. He would send out his pony mounted archers ahead and around us to scout once we left the safety of Lincoln, and I hardly expected to see them again such were their secret ways of concealment. Then there would be six knights riding before me and six more behind, the king himself could hardly expect more.

I spent a few moments talking to my mount, asking the beast nicely if it could give me an easier return ride, my backside still sore from the ride over here. Then I went amongst the men, chivvying them up and speaking my mind.

'We are returning to Laxton, as you know, but along the way we have some business to conduct with the High Sheriff of Nottingham. Philip Marc has been taking too much for granted and has been increasing his influence in our forests of Nottinghamshire and Derbyshire, especially the area known as Sherwood. King John has rejected the sheriff's claim to governance of these places and confirmed mine own. We are therefore going to visit the forests and return them into my control, we will also carry out some much needed repairs and improvements, and this is why the good Lady Nicholaa has supplied some extra wagons, so that we can stay in the woods until I judge it time to return to Laxton. In return we will support Lady Nicholaa, if, or when she finds herself in need of assistance.' Then I walked up and down the line of horses and men and smiling, hoping to instil confidence in them before asking, 'Do you like the idea of bringing discomfort to the high sheriff?'

'Aye!' came the shout.

'Should we take the long road back to Laxton?'

'Aye!' Louder again.

'Will you do without the comfort of your wives for a few more days?'

The aye for that was a little more muted until they saw the humour in it and then the greatest shout of all saw the cavalcade prancing and laughing. 'Aye! Lady, aye.'

In my riding gear, clothing quite unsuitable for a lady — my head hardly level with the saddle of the steed, I waited while Nicholaa came to me.

'You appear very fierce, my dear, can you use that thing?' she asked, eyeing my short sword.

'If I need to. I prefer to rely on Ælfgar, though.'

Ælfgar's sculptured face lit up as he approached and bent his back in a slight obeisance.

'My lady,' he said.

'Ælfgar,' I held his gaze, 'are the men all ready?'

'Indeed, my lady, ready for two weeks in the field as you ordered, our twelve archers and twelve cavalrymen, with three borrowed baggage wagons and several artisans. We shall fare well, even without any hospitality along the way.'

'Nevertheless, I shall expect a welcome from my various lords. But 'tis better to be prepared, we shall send back to neither Lincoln nor Laxton if we have planned all properly.'

'Indeed, my lady, we will be somewhere in the trees. Now shall we be off and disturb the Sheriff of Nottingham's composure?'

'Indeed, Ælfgar. Your knee, if you please.'

The blond warrior knelt and I stepped upon his proffered knee, using it to spring upon the back of my horse. As my right leg passed over his head I suddenly wondered what the audience might make of this unseemly event, I couldn't stop myself from looking at Orva to see her reaction, but she was busy flirting with one of Ælfgar's archers.

'Jesu, Ælfgar, this mail cote is heavy,' I said as I settled into the saddle.

'Yes, my lady, but I'll rest easier it you can persist with it.'

I waved at the troops and another great cheer went up, this time the whole garrison, on top of the gate house and gathered around inside it joined in and Ælfgar was beaming anew.

Hearing the cheer I set off, and as I did Ælfgar, who pulled his horse alongside mine.

'What will Sheriff Marc do when he finds out that you are taking back control of the forest?'

'What he normally does, Ælfgar, when he cannot get his own way. Spit and rage, I expect.'

'He might complain to the king.'

'He'll have to get past Neville before he gets to the king, and if he does he will not enjoy the result.'

'You are secure with the king?'

'I am.'

As the track widened Ælfgar moved forward to meet two of his scouts waiting on the track ahead and Father Albric moved alongside of me.

'I'm not certain that I understand all this, my lady, why are we not going directly to Laxton?'

I looked down on him, his pate shone a little in the weak sun, and he jiggled a lot on his little pony.

'We have a line of small motte and bailey donjons spread across the northern edge of the forest, for security, you understand?'

'I do.'

'The one at Egmanton has been chosen for improvement, even though it is not far from Laxton, simply because it is garrisoned by my troops and in need of repair. The commander will not be expecting us.'

'A surprise visit. Keep them alert, eh?'

'Indeed.'

'Who are those riders ahead?'

'Ælfgar has scouts out and about to sniff out any trouble, seeing but not being seen is their motto, the forest has ruffians within it and perhaps some of the sheriff's men would be lurking.'

'It is a pleasant afternoon.'

'Aye, a late boon, we missed the rain and the forest is doing its best to hold back the approaching winter sleep.'

'God's seasons, as he intended.'

The track narrowed and Albric was forced to slow and fall in line behind me. The birds were about their late business among the near leafless trees, the branches still dripping from a brief shower which I saw pass ahead, and the weak sun picked out the drops and made them into jewels.

I moved forward to join Orva, she silently keeping station with her lover Ælfgar about one hundred paces ahead.

'Not far to the Dun Ham ferry,' I ventured.

'No my lady. I trust that there is a sound roof at Egmanton, it'll be chilly tonight.'

'Mm, I have no reports that it isn't. Ælfgar is waving us on, we'll soon find out.'

The ferryman was alert and soon I was on the river. Ælfgar split the party into three, sending me and the archers over first, followed by six knights, leaving six to safeguard the baggage train and come over last, by which time we were ahead and on our way to Egmanton, about seven miles away.

It was in the late afternoon that we arrived. We smelt cooking before we saw the place, the sun was on the horizon and the castle was lit by the last of the light coming through the trees, it being naught more than a wooden donjon atop an earthen motte. The small garrison of ten men were standing alert at the bottom of the motte, warned by the appearance of our scouts, and their commander came over to greet me.

'My lady, we are pleased to see you. Do you intend to stay with us? The quarters are simple, but dry.'

'Thank you, Serjeant Luc. We are here to carry out the repairs that you have long complained about. We will stay one night, possibly two, depending on how long the work takes. Have you a list?'

'Indeed, my lady. We need more planks to finish the paling, and…'

'Not me, please.' I waved in the direction of Cedric the builder. 'Give it to that unhappy horseman over there, he will be glad to get the weight off his backside.'

'There's not much here is there, my lady?' Ælfgar murmured, as we looked at the small castle standing bare atop its mound, the palisade encircling the bailey unfinished.

'No, it has long needed the completion of the protecting outer bailey, we cannot risk our men falling prey to a night-time raid. However they do have a nice cooking fire on the go.'

We inspected the site of our evening meal, I prayed it was so, a fire surrounded by logs to sit on and a haunch of venison on a spit, there was also a cauldron set on the side of the fire, a pottage I presumed.

I dismounted and strode past a fire blazing away near the steps and up to the donjon door. It was gloomy inside on the ground level, the guard chamber, although some sunlight was finding its way in through the seams of the wall. The men's equipment was placed neatly around the walls next to their truckle beds.

'A tidy chamber, my lady. Your guard searjent, Luc, seems a competent man.'

'Thank you, Lord Ælfgar, we try.'

I focused on the man now standing behind us in the doorway, his features hidden by the light.

Ælfgar responded, 'You know my name, Luc?'

'Yes, my lord, everyone knows of Ælfgar, Lady Matilda's greatest warrior.'

'Let us climb those steps over there, ere Ælfgar's head gets too big to fit the stairway,' I suggested, feeling side-lined.

It became a bit lighter when we reached the next level. This was set out for the comfort of the Serjeant, with a table and some chairs. There were plates and cooking pots on another table in one corner and I had seen the cooking iron set over the outside fire at the foot of the motte steps. The next level, I could see, was reached by a ladder and I wondered about going any further.

'Is this where I am to sleep, Serjeant Luc?'

'If you wish, my lady. I will clear out my stuff to stay with the guard and have some new straw palliasses sent up for your comfort.'

'Thank you. We might as well climb further,' I said, looking at the final ladder up to the roof, and set off up. I soon emerged onto the roof and looked back down the ladder.

'Oh look, my lady, there's a goodly view from up here,' Orva said as she joined me.

With the last of the direct sunlight gone, the ground immediately in front was lit by firelight and I still had a full view of the glade below and the treetops of the surrounding forest. I thought that the light in the distance to the east might be on the top of Laxton donjon.

When Albric asked why not go back to Laxton, here was the answer. From Lincoln, but not at Laxton, lost in the trees, who would know where we were. Fully provisioned for a week in the field so that I could demonstrate the length of my reach, and who could know where we might turn up next, unexpected — this could turn into a very long journey of inspection and one full of surprises.

Appearing very small below, Gavin, our Captain of Horse was organising his cavalry and the Saxon, Serjeant Brant, was doing the same for Ælfgar's archers. Whether the palisade was finished or not, tonight we would be safely inside a cordon of metal.

We wandered right around the rooftop, it didn't take long, and when we were back where we began, I set out my requirements.

'There would normally be sentries up here all night, Ælfgar?'

'Indeed, my lady, in spells, and as long as the outer defences are not complete it is sensible to keep sentries up here.'

'But tonight we will be guarded by a circle of your men, will we not?'

'Of course.'

'Then we will occupy the floor beneath us. Serjeant Luc can share the guard floor below that.'

'Very well, my lady, and me?'

'Arrange a curtain for us, and you can sleep at the top of the stairs. Can we get some food organised?' I asked as Father Albric appeared from below, huffing and puffing. 'And help me out of this damned mail cote, Orva, then you and Ælfgar can stand down for a while.'

They were clearly twitching to grapple with one another.

Now relieved of that heavy metal cote — Ælfgar would not let me stray far without it — and with the lovers having disappeared down the stairs to find a leafy glade to frolic in, I was left to pass the time with Father Albric.

Sitting, as I was, on the side of Serjeant Luc's truckle bed, I wondered if a little time to contemplate life, with my confessor, might be appropriate.

'Father Albric, we have some time for a privy conversation, I believe.'

'Indeed, my lady, and nearer to heaven it would seem,' he said, looking up at the hatch in the roof.

'The light has left, but the view is still grand, let's go up, if you can manage it?'

'I'll make it,' he wheezed, and I let him set off upwards.

I gazed in peace at the treetops, the forest had gone quiet and I supposed that the birds had found their nests, or wherever they go at the end of year, and the creatures of the night were stirring — ever a place of change, I had always observed; nothing in these delightful woods stands still for very long.

'Are you content, my lady?' asked Albric kindly, leaning over the battlement and recovering his breath.

'Not entirely, but life is not a level path, do you not find?'

He coughed and wheezed a little before replying. 'Are we close to home, my lady?' he asked.

'Indeed. Yonder beacon on the horizon, I believe is home. I want to be capable of operating without the direct support of the castle, this is in the way of a training mission with a purpose.'

'Your thinking is very complex, my lady, I could not have dreamt of this one.'

'Perhaps, but I needs think like a man, like a general. I am in a man's position, you see.'

'I do. Is this what you want?'

''Tis my duty, to my people and my family. Why do you think those such as Ælfgar support me? My position as the keeper of the forest has been confirmed by the king, but Philip Marc, sitting safe in Nottingham, will be reluctant to relinquish his hold on the forest.'

'Yes, my lady, and you seem aware that with a man's position comes the problems of a man.'

We paused as the sky had no light, not even a moon, and we were left in the near stygian blackness, save for the stars and the fire casting light on the trees around the glade below. A rainless night though — perhaps a better place to air one's worries.

'Perhaps that is not the thing lying deep within me which is the real problem. Two husbands gone by and not a wain to show for all that striving with either of them.'

Albric coughed his alarm at this mention of earthly things, but he was there to listen and I was in the mood.

'This saddens me, Albric, and it leaves me viewing the forest as some kind of compensation. Is this to be my only lifetime reward for all the struggling I have experienced? It has been hard winning back my inheritance. "Just a widow." I heard the comments whispered in King John's court; well I'm a bit more than that. "Not a proper person" hurt the worst, and this quest to clear the forest of scallywags, thieves, and sheriff's men, it might be a man's work, but a way of avoiding the truth of my life.'

I left those words hanging in the dark. I had discussed before, in the gentlest terms, my situation with Albric, but he always demurred from discussing such things, and his response was the same tonight.

'My lady,' he spoke, clucking like a mother hen, 'do not let such thoughts enter your head. You have always been the sweetest and most devout lady, and I have known you since these many years have passed. Now be at peace with yourself, for God has surely chosen your path.'

My sad thoughts were interrupted when I heard scuffles on the ladder; it was Serjeant Luc, who stuck his head up over the top.

'The food will be ready soon, my lady, will you take it up here?'

'No, Serjeant, I'll join you if I may.'

'We tend to eat outside, sitting round the fire, my lady.'

'Fine, I'd like that. Are Ælfgar and Orva back?'

He coughed in the candlelight. 'Err, well, they may be soon. I heard them on their *walk*, or perhaps it was a screech owl going off in the trees, or possibly a dog fox barking.'

I held my hand over my face to suppress a giggle. 'Say naught when they turn up, Luc, and join us, we do not want to discourage them from their duty, do we?'

'No, my lady, a fine breeding pair like that. A haunch of roasting venison and a cauldron of pottage is waiting outside. A local goodwife provides fresh bread every day and your waggoners have brought a cask of fine ale, so we shall eat well tonight, my lady.'

'Then I shall be down directly.'

It was very noisy below, the carpenters and others were hurling things off the wagons — tools, and timbers, and suchlike. They seemed to delight in making as much noise as possible with as much strength as they could muster and when I emerged it seemed to me that there was enough timber lying on the ground to build several palisades.

There were not many gathered around the cooking fire when I got there. One man was doing the cooking and a couple of Serjeants were chatting with Luc, Orva was sitting demurely on a very large log with Ælfgar standing behind, holding her shoulders.

'My lady,' ventured Ælfgar, 'did you take a nap?'

'Not really. I am tired though, I shall probably sleep well later. Where is everyone, Serjeant Luc?'

'They will be fed at their posts, my lady. The *equitum* stay with the horses and the *peditum* guard them, they are placed in five positions surrounding the site, and will remain there until the palisade repairs are done. The carpenters will work in the light of the braziers and rushes until their meal is ready.'

'You know your Latin, Luc.'

'Yes, my lady, I was trained for the church at my parents' insistence, but I find more worldly things interesting.'

The cook began to ladle the pottage into wooden bowls and pass them round.

There was a sudden whistle and a call. A voice came from the thick of the trees. 'Coming in.'

There was a hissing noise among the outlying troops guarding us as they slid weapons out of sheathes.

But Ælfgar knew that whistle, and the voice.

'Come in,' he called back, and two silent figures clad in dark rags came into the firelight.

'My scouts, my lady. I need to speak with them.'

'Beckon them over, Ælfgar, they can eat with us and we will hear what they have to say,' I ordered.

'Certainly, I'm looking forward to this.'

With a tankard of ale and a mouthful of venison and bread they began their briefing.

''Tis Horton-near-Walesby, my lady, about seven miles off. There's summat wrong there,' began Godric, the talkative one. Cenna never said much, but his skill with the bow was frightening. ''Tis very organised and tidy-like, the troops there are all in well-presented uniforms. If'n I was to take a guess I'd say that they was sheriff's men, begging your pardon, my lady.'

'What say you, Ælfgar? Are we facing a confrontation already?' I asked.

'I would take it as so, my lady, best to be prepared.' He stood up. 'With your permission, my lady.'

'What're you going to do?'

'Prepare for a visit.'

'May I come?'

He hummed and scuffled at that request, finally saying, 'If you will accept that I am in command, and it is my patrol…?'

I nodded.

Ælfgar looked at Luc, telling him, 'You will not be involved, Luc, remain here and keep the artisans safe while they work on your defences. Father Albric, if you would stay here?' He nodded enthusiastically. 'We will be leaving shortly and I expect to return by tomorrow afternoon.'

'You're leaving in the dark, Ælfgar?' asked Orva, pulling at his arm.

'Indeed, we will be led by Godric and Cenna, and attack the site just before dawn.'

'Will there be blood, Ælfgar?' I asked, worried.

'Only if they resist, my lady. I intend that they will not have time to resist, and then you may do what you will with my prisoners.'

'Will I be nearby when you capture these men of Nottingham?'

Ælfgar grinned. 'You *expect* to be nearby, my lady? Do I suppose correctly?'

'You do.'

A grunt and a shrug of his shoulders told me what he thought about that.

In the circle of the firelight Ælfgar began drawing a map in the ground, advised by Godric and Cenna, of the castle of Horton and its surrounds.

'From here we will travel to within a mile of the castle on horseback and the rest of the way on foot,' he explained. 'Here is a track which we can use almost up to the place but then we will move through the woods to the edge of the clearing.'

Using his sword as a pointer he guided us along the main route, which passed near here then on to Retford, showing where we'd leave it near Horton to make our final approach on foot.

'Absolute silence is needed from there on, then we will close up and wait while the scouts move forward to make the final assessment. I intend to take some of your men, Luc, and some of mine, fifteen men-at arms will suffice, and five archers. When we are ready, two sections of five infantry will move to the sides of the palisade, each with a ladder, and wait until the archers engage the main gate. I will attack that with the remaining infantry while the side groups go over the palisade; that way we will have them occupied on three sides and I do not believe that they have enough men to defend them all. Any questions?'

Brand stared at the scratches in the earth and poked at the ground a few times with his short-sword. 'Got it, Ælfgar, it hath merit. When do we leave?'

'Now. Are you ready?' He turned to me.

'Yes, Ælfgar, what do you want us to do?' I asked.

'Exactly what you are told; no noise, no conversation … you will stay behind us at all times just before the assault and I will call you forward when all is safe. Now, ladies, I want you to stand up and face away from the fire, we'll get you your night eyes. When you can see your horses in the dark we'll go over to them … and do not turn back to the light, but first,' he handed Orva and I a burnt stick each from the edge of the fire, 'blacken your faces, you are too shiny.'

When we were ready, Ælfgar guided us towards the treeline and revealed where our steeds for the night stood patiently waiting. Small Welsh hill ponies, quiet and trained to stealth; they came with two wranglers to manage them. We were safe in the middle of the convoy and in time we reached the area where Ælfgar's scouts had chosen to leave the beasts, and dismounted silently.

Ælfgar gave a final briefing as the sky began to lighten. 'We move in single file to the edge of the clearing and then split left and right; remain within the cover of the trees until you hear from us, then attack the sides of the palisade while we go for the main gate. Have a piss now, and line up in your section order, archers behind me, left section next, then the right section is to bring up the rear. Wranglers take the horses into the forest and look after them until I send back for them.'

The men moved quietly off to the left and right. Brant and his archers joined Ælfgar on the edge of the clearing and they crouched in a line, as did Orva and me staying close behind to watch.

A sentry emerged, coughed, and fumbled with his clothing and began to water the palisade wall. There was a rustle as the archers stood, followed by several twangs as they loosed, and thuds as the missiles hit their targets. The pissing man was pinned to the palisade without a cry but the watching man fell off the gate house with such a commotion as to waken the dead.

Ælfgar was on his feet instantly and hurled his body at the unsecured gate, crashing through it. His men scrambled over the palisade onto the battlement, those to the left were dropping to the ground and those to the right were on the roof of the barracks hut.

A shout came back for us to approach and Orva and I emerged from the trees. I was shocked by the speed and severity of the action, it had taken only an eyeblink to wreak death from the trees.

'Ælfgar!' I shouted. 'What in God's name? There's a man pinned to the wall, and a body obstructing the gate, and who's this naked fellow in the dust? Who's this girl? What have you done?'

'Secured your fortress, my lady, as you desired.'

'Ælfgar, I wanted to frighten them off, not carve them up. Tell that fellow to put some breeches on. Who are you?' I demanded when he was fit to look at.

'Jean. I am the captain of the guard here, my lady.'

'And her,' I demanded, looking at the semi-naked girl.

'My companion, my lady.'

'I see. You are in the service of Philip Marc of Nottingham?'

'I serve the high sheriff, my lady.'

'Then go and tell your master that there is no longer any room for him or his servants in this forest, by edict of the king, as he well knows.'

The chill between Aelfgar and I began to thaw a little as we reached the next target, the castle at Bothamsall. It was deserted. I'd time to reflect, and I was wondering if my presence was a wise thing.

Word travels fast it seems, even in the forest. We waited at Bothamsall for most of the day until the wagons were escorted in from Laxton, together with Father Albric. A bit put out he was, because nobody thought it wise to relay to him the fine details of the attack on Horton-near-Walesby. I doubted if it would receive his approval. The next place due to receive a visit was Cuckney, but as it was sixteen miles away we spent the rest of the day travelling, following the course of the River Meden, then leaguered up for the night, five miles short of Cuckney near Budby.

'Ready for the morn, Ælfgar?' I asked.

'Always ready, my lady.'

'I know that, and you always do well, and I thank you for it. Tomorrow will be the last time I accompany you on your business. I can see that it would become very dangerous for you and your men to try and do things with a gentle heart.'

'Thank you, 'tis for you that I do my duty. But be certain that my first duty is to your own well-being, and I find that the restraints of the past few days have made that all the more difficult.'

'When tomorrow's business is concluded you can return me and Orva to Laxton. You can deposit us there and get on with whatever it is that you do...'

'Thank you, my lady, a wise decision. But you take the wagons with an escort, and when you reach Laxton send out a troop of five men each to the castles we have reclaimed to garrison them.'

'Is five enough?' I asked, unsure.

'No, but they are not to defend them, merely report back to Laxton if there is an approach by the sheriff's men. You can send any spare men, as long as there is one Serjeant to control them. We have not enough trained soldiers to spread around the territory. This is my plan. We will control the forests by keeping patrols out and about. If the sheriff sends more men they will be attacked and sent back in meat wagons, he will soon tire of that game. We will behave as outlaws...'

'In my own forests?'

'Needs must, and we have not sufficient men to keep several garrisons manned.'

The next morning, after a cold breakfast and a prayer from Albric the wagons were lined up and we were ready to depart.

'Thank you, Ælfgar. We'll let you get on with your task. See you, when...?'

'The day after tomorrow. I'll leave a small garrison in Cuckney and return when I am happy.'

73

3.

Father Bernard

We paused outside Lady Nicholaa's chapel after Prime.

'Well, Father Bernard,' she commented, 'that was a terrible storm last night, fit to take the roof off. A night to remember, I had little sleep.'

'A night to remember indeed, my lady, the eighteenth of October. I expect that there will be reports of damage later. I hope that the harvests have been kept safe.'

'Indeed, it has been poor enough this year. The castle is well provided for, as usual, but we can do without further damage to the townsfolk's winter stores.'

'With your permission, my lady, I will cross over to the cathedral and see what they know about any storm damage.'

'Very well. Take your time over there, see what you can find out about the town: is there any dissent now that the king has been and gone?'

'I fear that it will be a difficult conversation, my lady, they will be anxious to find out what you are doing regarding keeping this place safe.'

She laughed at that remark before responding, 'You may inform them that we are well prepared for any eventuality, and leave the rest to their imaginings.'

'I shall leave them praying for more information. Shall I see you at the evening meal, my lady?'

'Indeed, there is much to do in between, I shall see you then.'

With that we made our way down to the great guard chamber where she gathered her most important men around her and I left for the cathedral — and a grilling by the archdeacon, no doubt.

As I walked away from the castle I decided to turn down the steep hill and wander through the town to see what gossip I could pick up. It was still early but there were plenty of merchants up and about near the river marketplace. 'A farthing's a farthing, whatever the time, Father,' replied one laying out his wares. 'What you doing down here so early, if I may ask?'

'Oh, I'm taking the air, to clear my mind.'

'Well, keep on going, the fish quay is just down there, that'll clear yer 'ead.'

I laughed, and cast an eye over his stock, all woollen items from leggings to hats, I could see.

'What's business like today?'

'Not bad, Father, they're buying winter hats this week.'

'It'll soon be Christmas. Are people content now that the king has been and gone?'

''E'll not be missed, least not his tax collectors. Half my stock belongs to them, and a man can't make an 'onest livin' fer taxes and tithes.'

He looked at me a bit curious, as if he had said too much.

'Don't worry,' I eased his worries, 'the church is paying for his wars too.'

'Not pop'lar up the 'ill, then?'

'I can't comment on that.'

He grinned and rubbed the side of his nose. 'Nuff said, but I shu'nt be surprised if'n there's bother afore too long, Gawd's name I in't.'

I wandered a little further and everywhere was the same, if the folk would engage with me in conversation it wasn't difficult to extract their disquiet about our acquisitive king.

After a while I turned and made my way back up the hill. Puffing a bit when I reached the top I stopped for a while outside the tavern on the corner — time must be rushing by, there was already the sound of boisterous conversation coming from within, before heading towards the great cathedral door. Lit now by a weak sun it still managed to impress me as I approached this great gateway into heaven, or at least as near to heaven as I'll get on earth. I removed my new hat, sweating freely, and shoved it into the purse dangling from my waist belt as I entered, not wanting to upset the archdeacon, and then I went into this enormous cavern to find him.

'Oh, it's you,' he said as I stood coughing outside his little chamber.

'Indeed, Archdeacon Peter, 'tis I.'

'Come in, Bernard, you're all of a dither.'

'True, I've been to the bottom of the hill.'

'Ah! Hear anything interesting?'

'A few roofs blown off, a wall here and there, no deaths, nothing disastrous.'

'That's not what I meant. Other things, gossip. That's what you went down there for, was it not?'

'How did you know my purpose?'

'You are an open book to me. It fits, now that you are with the castle.'

'I'm still *of* the church.'

'Indeed you are Bernard, indeed you are. Now what can you tell me?'

His demeanour did not change much, he always seemed ready to be told the worst and his melancholic face always seemed ready to hear it.

'Nothing to cheer you, Archdeacon, I fear. The merchants are restless, the king does not grow in their love.'

'He hath not much in here either, Bernard.'

'What will the church do if there is trouble?'

'Pray, Bernard, pray. And what will the castle do if there is trouble?'

'Defend itself, Archdeacon. Even as we speak the castellan is finalising her preparations.'

'The … castellan? Lady Nicholaa? You believe that she will hold the castle?'

'She will, and the garrison will die for her.'

'Hmm, let us pray that it does not come to such a pass, souls are in danger.'

He looked down at some vellums on his table and poked about with them, I could see that he wanted to say something so I waited quietly.

At last he looked up, and with little enthusiasm asked me a question.

'I don't suppose that you could persuade her to surrender the castle … if it came to that. No, I couldn't ask you that, I'm sorry. Such a waste of Christian lives, don't you think, Father Bernard?'

'I do, yet the lady is determined to hold the castle for the anointed king. She believes it to be her duty to him.'

'Ah, of course, the anointed king; the church has played its part in this matter I cannot deny. I shall not mention it again. Still it might all blow over, like last night's storm, eh, Father Bernard? Now don't let me keep you from your castle duties, come and see me next week.'

'I will, gladly, Archdeacon. God bless you.'

'And you, Father Bernard, and you.'

I made my way back to the castle but my progress was hindered by a few drunkards. It was hardly past midday and it seemed that they had been hard at work in that damned tavern on the corner already. Shouting insults at the sentries they were, though remaining ready to run if the soldiers set off after them.

'Are you the castle priest?' one mouthed at me with venom.

'Aye, a king's lackey priest,' spoke another.

'Pray for your own soul, priest,' said another, louder this time.

They were becoming more audacious as I scurried towards the gate, then a pair of soldiers burst forth and chased after the loudmouths, who scattered and ran off before they could be caught.

The guard Serjeant came over to me.

'You are safe now, Father. These ruffians are becoming bolder, last night some stones were hurled at the sentries from the cover of the dark.'

'Indeed, Serjeant, thank you. Yes, I have heard mutterings of discontent in the town below.'

'You should not go out any more without an escort. I'll report as such to my captain.'

'You think that necessary?'

'I do, we have spies out there too. This French prince invading, and now the Scottish king; things are likely to get worse before they get better, I'm sure.'

'I pray that you are wrong. Thank you for your help, I must go in now, Lady Nicholaa is expecting me.'

I found the guard hall in the Lucy Tower crowded. Evidently my lady wanted everyone to see her, and they were all seeking an audience. I detected an increased tension in the air.

'Ah, you're back, Father Bernard.' Then she spoke to Basilea who was sitting next to her, 'Basilea, my dear, would you go and sit in Father Bernard's place at the end, I wish to hear what news he has brought back.'

That might have pleased Geoffrey of Serland, who Basilea was now going to sit next to, but it pleased not sweet Basilea, who didn't like the man, which showed in her expression.

'Now Bernard, tell us about your day, what news from the cathedral?'

'I can give you news from further afield than that great pile, my lady.'

'What! Like you not that magnificent edifice?'

'It is fine, except that I would have spent the money wiser, there is plenty of poverty during the winter.'

'Indeed, a point worthy of consideration. Think you that cathedrals are more for the glory of bishops than God?'

'I couldn't possibly say, my lady.'

'Quite. So where is this *further afield*, which you mentioned?'

'Oh, from within the town. Things are not tranquil, I must say, the king is not popular and I suspect there are those who would ferment the ill-feeling into something more terrible.'

'A revolt, you mean.'

'Perhaps even that. The French are now combining with the Scots, it is not good. This country has not suffered such a humiliation for one hundred and fifty years, since the Conqueror landed and made his appearance.'

'Geoffrey!' she snapped. 'Pay attention, move closer and leave poor Basilea to eat in peace.'

That pithy remark drew the attentions of Captain Oswald, who had also been feasting his eyes upon the delectable Basilea.

'Listen to me. Bernard has been into the lower town and things are already much more delicate than we had imagined —'

Lady Nicholaa was interrupted by a commotion at the doorway. A Serjeant was waving at Oswald, trying to attract his attention.

'What does he want?' demanded Lady Nicholaa.

'Serjeant, draw near. This had better be urgent,' called Oswald.

'There is a messenger, my lord.' He turned and beckoned forward a knight, all bedraggled and sweating profusely, showing that he had been riding hard for some time.

Oswald glanced at Lady Nicholaa, and receiving a nod waved him forward.

'Speak, what is it?'

The knight drew back his hauberk to reveal his dripping head and, with a little bow, he told her, 'The king, Lady Nicholaa, the king is dead.'

There was silence, which lasted only a little while before the hall erupted into pandemonium.

Lady Nicholaa stood and beckoned the unfortunate messenger closer. Shouting to make herself heard over the tumult, she demanded, 'When, where, how, tell me more.'

'Yesterday, at Newark, of a fever.'

Taking it all in Nicholaa slumped into her high-back chair — at that moment she seemed to be very, very small, in a very big world.

'Oh my God, have mercy. We must speed the preparations. Send a messenger to Lady Matilda. She needs to know about this as soon as possible.'

4.

Lady Matilda

We were almost at the gates of Laxton when one of Ælfgar's scouts came galloping towards us, closely followed by another rider.

'My lady,' he cried, pulling up his pony and covering us both with clods of earth, 'this fellow brings news.'

The following rider came to a standstill with more dignity and fewer flying clods than our scout, but had evidently been riding hard and was breathing deeply.

'What is it?' I asked.

'Lady Nicholaa, my lady, she sent me to find you. I have bad news.'

'Bad!' I repeated. 'Tell, fellow, spit it out.'

'The king, King John is dead.'

A gripe seized my stomach and the hairs on my head prickled.

'Dismount,' I commanded, 'tell us more. From whence came this news?'

'From Newark. The king died and his remains are at Newark, of a fever, 'tis told. Lady Nicholaa sent me to warn you. Things are likely to change, if this emboldens the king's enemies…'

'Dear God, this is dreadful. What should we do next?'

'Lady Nicholaa asks if you can come back to Lincoln, to support her.'

'What! Leave Laxton?' I stared at the messenger. 'I cannot, will not, desert Laxton, it is vital to hold this side of the river, 'tis part of Nicholaa's defence. We agreed.'

'Lady Nicholaa would like to see you, she asks that you return to discuss this new turn of events.'

'Ah, very well. Come into Laxton, fellow, and wait until we have decided our next play, it can wait overnight, surely.'

'As you wish, my lady.'

'The game hath changed,' Father Albric murmured.

'You are right, Albric, the game has changed, and some men will be weighing their loyalties once more. Be ready for more surprises in that regard.'

We retired early that night, into my privy quarters on the top floor of Laxton donjon where Orva snuggled up lying on the covers next to me. My mind was spinning and neither of us were ready for sleep, there was much to think about so we chattered for the rest of the night until there was a commotion in the bailey.

'Listen, Orva, there are riders coming in.'

'It's dark, it must be near midnight,' she said from an uncovered window slot. 'It's Ælfgar, he's back.'

It only took an eye-blink to pull on my breeches but by the time I reached the door Orva was enveloped around her man and they were already joined at hip and tongue by the look of it in the flickering brazier light.

'You're sooner than expected, Ælfgar,' I said by way of parting them.

'Aye, my lady,' he replied, talking to me but looking at Orva, 'Cuckney surrendered and I sent the garrison Serjeant and his men on their way without swords or horses, they are walking back to Nottingham.'

'Oh, then they might not have reached the sheriff yet.'

'If they ever do. There are terrible outlaws in the woods, and they don't like the sheriff's men, I'm told.'

'Have you heard the news about King John?'

'Our guard Serjeant told us as we passed his brazier. I told him to see to the horses and I will inspect them at dawn, I suspect that we are going to be busy for a while now.'

'Aye,' added Captain of Archers, Brant, 'and we'll sharpen our other weapons too.'

'Oh dear, this is not good,' mumbled a sleepy Albric, 'I must pray.'

'Aye, sharpen your prayers, we'll need them, Father Albric,' added Brant, but I could not tell if he were jesting or not.

'Never mind all that, we should be about our business,' I cut them off. 'Nicholaa wants me back in Lincoln, to sort matters out. I need to know about the succession, will young Henry be allowed to succeed his father? Will a different king stop this war? Will the French accept Henry or will Louis continue in his efforts to seize the crown of England? Ælfgar, will you see to the defence of Laxton until I return? Orva, you will come with me back to Lincoln. And you can come along too, Father Albric,' I ordered.

The remainder of the night proved to be mostly sleepless, until I was awoken by Orva's voice in my ear, I must have dropped off.

'My lady, my lady. The sky has light in it.'

Orva was dressed and armed, and I scattered about to get myself ready.

'Let's get going, is Father Albric awake?'

'He is, my lady, he's chasing his pony around the bailey.'

We went down and were helped to mount by the stable hands.

'Look at him, Orva,' I giggled rudely, as we sat safely on our horses watching Father Albric's attempts to get a leg over his new pony.

'He might pray for a miracle, my lady,' responded the wicked girl.

'Up you go, Father Albric,' said the wrangler encouragingly.

'No mercy for my aching backside, little sleep, and little to eat; this warfare business is becoming one long pain,' was the priest's response. 'Thank you, I hope to stay up here until we reach Lincoln.'

'You will. Hold the reins tight, Father, and pray a lot, you'll be fine,' added the wrangler with much more confidence than I felt, watching.

It was a lengthy journey and there was much time for contemplation along the way, for there was little to admire in the nearly bare trees and the soggy ground beneath our feet. My thoughts were broken into as we neared the town, the cathedral and castle looming large on the horizon as a call rang out, 'There's a patrol ahead.'

The call came from one of Ælfgar's archers, sent ahead as protection, as he came galloping towards us from the track ahead.

'That's good,' I said, 'if there's any trouble in the town the extra protection will be welcome.'

The patrol was following him at the gallop. They had obviously been chasing our archer, probably mistaking him for one of Louis' men on the prowl. They pulled up to block the track, with seeming hostile intent. The Serjeant in the lead peered closely at me and held up an arm to restrain his men, five in total.

'I knows you, don't I? You is that lady from Laxton. Hain't you just gorn back there?'

'Yes, Serjeant, and now we are returning, news of the king's death has reached us, you see. And you may escort us, if you please.'

That was more of an order than an invitation and the good fellow took it as such.

'Ahem, of course. Lady Matilda, isn't it? I remembers now. Follow me, if'n you pleases, my lady. We'll soon have you safely inside, these townsfolk are spoiling for a fight now that King John is gorn and passed over. There's many a contender a-wantin' his crown, I'll be bound, hincludin' the Frenchie prince. Not that I fancies it, oh no, 'tis too risky a job for me, I means —'

'Yes, yes, very good, do you think that we can get on with it?'

I had heard enough of that prattle and we soon continued our progress turning along Earninga Straete, through the Roman arch, between the houses, to turn right into the barbican, and through the east gate of the castle — still glowering at the cathedral behind us across the close.

Riding on to the bottom of Nicholaa's steps I slid off the damn thing, happy to ease my aching muscles. *How can sitting on the back of a horse cause so much pain?*

I could see as I looked up those steps, Nicholaa was there, seeming small at the top.

'Sorry to drag you back, Maud,' she said with a kiss, 'but we need to agree some precautions. Now that King John has left us, all sorts of mischief might happen.'

The guard chamber was packed but Lady Nicholaa wafted her way through the throng, and we stuck close to her until she reached the great table at the far end and sat us down. Captain Oswald and Geoffrey of Serland were already there and greeted us cheerfully enough. Father Albric found Father Bernard and joined him behind the great table — we seemed complete.

Rattling an empty pot on the table top Nicholaa called for order and the hubbub fell into silence.

'Well!' she said, 'now that everyone is here, I shall tell you of all that I know ... and all that I think might happen ere long. Two days ago a new king was crowned at Gloucester by the Bishop of Winchester, Peter des Roches. It was King John's dying wish to confirm his son Henry as his successor, and so, my friends, we have a new king, Henry, the third of that name — and nine years old he is.'

There was a silence before the chatter began, then was stilled again, this time by Oswald who held up a hand and glared at the gathering.

'Hear Lady Nicholaa out. There is more, I'm certain.' Then he faced his castellan and asked a question which was probably in everyone's mind. 'My lady, the kingdom is in turmoil, we are almost under siege, how can a nine-year-old boy control this mess?'

'His father also appointed William the Marshal, our greatest soldier, as regent, so the kingdom is as safe as it was. Whatever comes next we are in the hands of a competent man. Besides, the coronation was proclaimed by the Bishop of Winchester, with the blessing of Cardinal Guala Bicchieri.'

'Who?' asked Oswald.

'Guala is the papal legate, so the succession has the blessing of Pope Honorius.'

'Which is more than John ever received,' chirped Geoffrey, remembering King John's excommunication, and received a withering glance from Nicholaa for his wit.

'Should we still consider a war with the French likely, my lady?' asked Oswald.

'I should think it definite,' blurted out Geoffrey, unbowed by glances from anyone.

'You have the truth of it, Geoffrey. I expect that the prize of England is still in their minds, and we know not the mind of the Scottish king, Alexander. Father Bernard,' she sought out her confessor who was standing close behind, 'what do we know of the mind of the church?'

The chubby face of the pleasant priest frowned a little before responding, 'It seems to have several, my lady. Excommunications and coronations are not comfortable bedfellows, and with Bishop Hugh still absent from Lincoln, Archdeacon Peter has developed sympathy with the townsfolk and King John's taxes have borne heavily upon the church. How it feels today? I know not, my lady.'

Lady Nicholaa stared at him for a while before coming to a decision. 'So, off you go, Bernard, go and find out what *Mother Church* is thinking today. Do we know if any messengers have reached Archdeacon Peter's ears yet, Oswald?'

'The sentries reported no arrivals as yet, my lady. They may well be imminent at the cathedral, although they have not beaten the king's couriers ... or rather William Marshal's men, and William is...?' he asked, looking at our priest.

'*Regent constituit*,' clarified Father Bernard before exchanging glances with Lady Nicholaa, picking up his skirts and trotting off to the door with Albric scuttling after him. The archdeacon was about to receive some news which he might find uncomfortable.

'He is what?' I whispered to Nicholaa.

'*Regent constituit*. He is in charge of the new king, Maud.'

Nicholaa waited until the priests had left the chamber before speaking again to Oswald and Geoffrey.

'Regardless of what news Father Bernard returns with from Archdeacon Peter, are we in all respects prepared for war within our stronghold? There are still rebel forces out there on the loose and we know not what their reaction to the new king will be.'

'Aye, my lady, all that can be done to protect these walls has been done, is being done, or is well advanced,' replied Oswald.

'All that you asked for and more,' added Geoffrey.

'Very well. Then I shall make a tour of inspection, both inside and along the outside of the castle walls. Nothing shall be left to chance, I shall visit the kitchens, storerooms, wells, stables and smithy; everything will come under my scrutiny today. Now get off and make ready, I shall be with you in an hour.'

The guard chamber cleared in an eye-blink as those with responsibilities vied with each other to squeeze through the door, brave the steps, and see to their duties.

'Come on up to my privy chambers, Maud, we need to talk.'

5.

Father Bernard

I was pleased to have Albric by my side, although his short legs slowed progress somewhat; it gets a bit lonely facing Archdeacon Peter on my own.

'This is a messy affair, Bernard. My lady was busy emptying the forest of sheriff's men, now this. I say, could you slow down a little?'

'Sorry, Albric, I am rather looking forward to seeing Archdeacon Peter. I am also hoping, and perhaps praying a little, that news of young Henry's coronation has not yet reached his holy ears. We might have a little fun at his expense if the church couriers have been tardy about their business.'

'Quite. I vaguely remember meeting the man once, but I doubt that he will remember me. I am looking forward, as are you, to causing him some discomfort.'

'Then we are alike as two peas in a pod, Albric.'

The captain of the guard was a little baffled by the appearance of two chuckling priests in front of him and when he learned of our intent he insisted on sending us off with an escort, two Serjeants — which identified us as castle priests, which I did not entirely welcome, nor were we, when we presented ourselves at the small door of the cathedral.

'Oh, it's you,' said the voice of the eye peering at me through the partially opened door. 'Who's that with you?'

'A friend of mine,' I replied.

With no further explanation furnished he relented and with reluctance said, 'You'd better come in.' The door opened and the face attached to the eye revealed itself. It added, looking at the soldiers, 'Those two should remain there.'

I objected. 'If you leave them standing there, there's likely to be a battle erupting outside the door — when the rabble become bold enough to throw stones at them.'

I pointed out the mob which had formed, loitering on the far side of the graveyard.

'Humph, bring them in. I'll conduct them in a few prayers.'

This was not going well; not exactly a warm welcome.

'You know the way,' commanded the voice, now complete with a body, which I could see as we set off for the archdeacon's door.

'You soldiers, let us pray,' he demanded as we went on our holy way.

I knocked a little louder than normal and a familiar voice called out. 'Enter! Ah, Father Bernard, come on in.' This was delivered in Archdeacon Peter's usual sonorous tones so I detected no change there. 'Do I recognise your companion?'

'Good morrow, Archdeacon,' I offered hopefully. 'This is Father Albric of Laxton. Are you well?'

'Oh, you know, the autumn damp chills one's bones. You seem warm enough. Good morrow, Albric, live in the trees, eh?'

'In the greenwood, Archdeacon. It suits me fine — God's cathedral, you see?'

'Not really, too damp in there. Did the pair of you dash here, you seem a little flustered.'

'A little, the folk outside today are about as warming as the clime, and that's freezing.'

'Ah, yes. I need to tell you something unpleasing, I fear.'

'Oh. Is it about the weekly mass? Lady Nicholaa would like to know —'

He stopped me in mid flow. 'Lady Nicholaa will not need to know anything, because Lady Nicholaa will not be welcome. The celebrations are for the people.'

I stood silently digesting this not wholly unexpected news. Still, he could have been less brutal.

'I see. That is final, is it, no possibility of an appeal to better judgement?'

He looked up sharply, annoyed, I could see.

'The judgement, as you call it, is mine … and yes, it is final. Now you may convey that news to her ladyship, with my blessing.'

I stood still for a moment, wondering about how to begin my counter-attack, until Albric coughed, as a hint to make myself heard.

'Erm,' I began, as a way of letting Peter know that I was not ready to be dismissed, 'You've had no news from the south?'

'We've had no news from anywhere except that they've separated King John's remains, the innards to Croxton Abbey and the carcass to Winchester. God knows why, he will be in hell from wherever they despatch him and in however many parts.'

'Mmm. That's as maybe, but the *new* king is in one part, and one place, as we have heard in the last hour or so.'

That silenced him. Perhaps he had been awaiting the announcement of Prince Louis as the new King of England. That hope lay in pieces, much like the last king. He stood up from behind his desk, his knuckles white on the writing surface, his miserable face seeming even longer than normal.

'Is this true?' he uttered in barely a whisper.

'Surely. King Henry, the third of that name, has been crowned and anointed at Gloucester by Bishop Peter des Roches, attended by the papal legate, Cardinal Guala Bicchieri.

Young Henry hath the blessing of Pope Honorius. Good news, eh?'

He sat down again.

I felt a tad sorry for him then. *Perhaps siding with the people against the castle, the visible sign of regal power, might have been done with more discretion.*

'Think you that this … dispute nonsense might be brought to an end? How can young Henry govern? What is he, eight, nine?'

'Nine, but he has William Marshal and the Earl of Chester by his side, and a council of twelve, chosen by John on his deathbed in full support. What's the worry?'

Peter was twisting a quill in his hands and some ink scattered about the desk; the top of his head was shiny with sweat and glistening in the candlelight.

'What if the French king will not accept it? What if he sends more men from France?'

'What if's, Archdeacon, what if's; what if Lady Nicholaa wanted to attend weekly mass as usual? What if.'

'Don't be trite, Bernard. Sit a while and we'll work something out. I'm sure that we can return to normal, if it is required. Please sit.'

'Thank you, Archdeacon, but if things are returned to normal then there will be little to discuss, which I'm sure that one of the new king's judges, your bishop, Hugh of Wells, will be pleased about whenever he returns.'

For that remark I received a startled stare of recognition as the sudden alteration of circumstances hit home.

'I see,' said Peter. 'Then we shouldn't disappoint him, should we, Bernard?'

'Best not to, Archdeacon.'

I saw no point in prolonging the debate, such as it was, and gathered my skirts around me to leave.

'Come, Albric, let us leave the archdeacon, he hath much to ponder and plenty to do, I am sure. God bless you, Archdeacon Peter, I had hoped to reach a satisfactory conclusion rather than be forced to choose a side in this matter, and I will pray for a peaceful outcome.'

'Indeed, as will I. God bless you, Bernard.'

So with that we went to find our escort. We were left to open the cathedral door for ourselves, prayers for soldiers evidently at an end, whereupon the senior Serjeant took it upon himself to stick his nose out to spy any danger lurking before he almost ran us across the cobbles of Castle Hill and into the sanctuary of Lincoln castle's enveloping walls once more.

'Quite a good day,' I gasped to the guard captain when he asked after my mission, 'it could not have gone better.'

He told me that Lady Nicholaa was in the Lucy Tower: *those steps*. I was still puffing from the dash across from the cathedral, so when I stood before her, I was, to say the least, dishevelled — such a contrast from the lady's own sweet face, lined it may be, but the skin visible under her coif was flawless and radiant. Albric was some way behind me.

'Fetch Father Bernard a tankard and a flagon,' she ordered, with a glint in her eye, 'he appears to need some refreshment.' The cellarer dashed off to see to my needs and Lady Nicholaa pointed at the bench opposite her.

'Where is my confessor?' asked Lady Matilda politely.

I pointed over my shoulder towards the stairs. 'Hear that, my lady?'

The noise of someone breathing heavily echoed up the spiral stairway.

'Albric?'

'I pray so,' I replied as the little fellow made an appearance in the doorway.

Lady Nicholaa called for another tankard and gestured for Albric to sit at the end of the table. He said naught but breathed a lot. She returned to her examination of my face, as my breathing returning to normal.

'Is that a happy face? Basilea,' she asked, 'you see our priest? Has he good news?'

'Perhaps, my lady, he seems fit to burst.'

'With joy, I trust. Tell all, Bernard, let us hear our fortunes. Geoffrey,' she called, 'come near and listen to this.'

I was recovering now and decided not to hold back.

'Hostility grows in the people, it is worse every time I venture out. And we were *persona non grata* in the cathedral.'

'Don't pad it out, priest.' Geoffrey could be a bit short on courtesies.

'That doesn't mean me, surely?' retorted Lady Nicholaa.

Geoffrey, gazing at my forlorn face, grimaced. 'He does. Methinks that he does.'

There was another long silence before Lady Nicholaa found words to speak.

'I trust that your archdeacon has not made any wrong decisions, Bernard. Now that William Marshal is keeping the young King Henry's backside firmly on the throne, we can expect some support from him, and some changes in appointments ... especially in archdeacons, I wager.'

'Err,' I mumbled, 'the archdeacon.' Spinning it out, teasing, and looking at Lady Nicholaa.

'There's more?'

'He was inclined to chuck me out.'

Geoffrey threw back his head and let out a loud guffaw. 'I've never heard the like! A priest chucked out of church, now there's a turn up.'

'Oh, Geoffrey, behave. This is uncalled for. What was the outcome, Bernard?'

'I left him pondering, but you might prepare yourself to continue to attend the weekly mass.'

'Oh, you old fox, Bernard, had they not received word about the coronation before you arrived on their doorstep?'

'No, my lady, I had the privilege of relaying that good news.'

'It made a remarkable difference to the air, my lady,' Albric was talking again, 'but there is no guarantee that the church will choose its course wisely. The archdeacon was heading off in his chosen direction.'

'I would have loved to have witnessed that,' chortled Lady Nicholaa, 'what say you, Geoffrey?'

'I say be wary, the archdeacon may shift his feet but the town won't sway so easily. We stay prepared for war. That's what I say.'

'I agree,' said Oswald. 'If 'tis true that Prince Louis has returned to France to bring back an army, then what care will he have for a new English king? Especially a boy, he will see that as an opportunity. And who knows which of the rebellious lords will accept young Henry?'

'What think you, Maud?' asked Lady Nicholaa, her face growing more distressed by the moment.

'I feel troubled, Nicholaa. I would like to think that a settlement with Mother Church would bring this evil which lies upon our fair land to an end, but something tells me that the matter has not yet run its course. I agree, war is lurking, we prepare for war, and I will away back to Laxton. We must keep in touch and stay together in this: if Laxton falls then the wolves will be quickly at your gate, Nicholaa. And who's to say that they won't visit you first? This stronghold here in Lincoln is the most superior prize in all of England.' The lady stood and transfixed the hall with a steady gaze, catching everybody's eye before her strong voice commanded silence. 'We are the embodiment of the monarch's power in middle England. If Lincoln falls, England falls to the French … is that what you want?'

'NAY, NEVER.' A tumultuous shout went up and rattled the plates on the table.

She raised her voice to ask again, 'Will we defend our realm against the poxy invading Frenchie?'

'WE WILL.'

'Then see to your duties, there is much to be done. God bless King Henry.'

'GOD BLESS HENRY.'

'God bless you all.'

'GOD BLESS NICHOLAA.'

If the shout had not reached across the close to the cathedral then word of it soon would, and no one will be in any doubt that Lincoln Castle will be the toughest nut in England for any French prince to crack.

The next day I bade farewell to my good friend Albric. I had come to like the man and we agreed to try and visit more often when this nonsense was brought to an end.

There were tears when Nicholaa and Matilda tried to drag themselves apart and it was not much different between Basilea and Orva; the area of the western barbican began to look as if it had rained for a week before they went through the gate and on their way. Jesu! Women and tears, never far removed.

I managed to write down the doings of the day after Sext prayers. Things generally calmed after the Laxton convoy left and the following days seemed to drift towards Christmas with not much happening except endless discussions.

At the evening table the smallest scrap of news was picked over, chewed, spat out, and re-chewed countless times, mostly by Geoffrey and Oswald, although it has to be said that Oswald was easily distracted when Basilea entered the hall. Whispers began, as whispers do, but no impropriety was observed.

'As I see it,' Geoffrey began, as he usually did, ignoring that Oswald's gaze was elsewhere, 'the fact that William Marshal and twelve good nobles now have a firm grasp upon the reins of power, and are keeping young Henry secure, must be sinking into the consciousness of the church.'

'Why?' responded Oswald. 'Just because we continue to be welcome at the cathedral?'

'Sort of, but he can change his mind again, welcome or tolerated, it swirls around like a trout in Braden pool,' said Geoffrey.

It was a very odd time leading up to Christmas. Strangely quiet hereabouts and our cause had suffered setbacks elsewhere. Then came rumours that young Henry would be taken to Ireland to keep him safe.

The day after the latest conversation, Archdeacon Peter sent for me, or rather wrote to Lady Nicholaa asking if I could attend him, an improvement over a demand, I thought.

He wasted no time in blether, coming straight to the point.

'This is a strange period, Bernard, do you not agree?'

'Indeed, Archdeacon. Most of the south is in the control of Prince Louis. He even occupies Westminster.'

'Unfortunate, but true. However, now that young Henry's council has handed the conduct of the war over to William Marshal, surely we can expect him to begin the task of ridding England of the Frenchies?'

'Things will alter when the spring comes, Archdeacon, but the rumour is that Prince Louis has crossed back over the sea to request more men from King Philip. If he grants his request, then we will have ourselves a war.'

'I cannot see that we will escape it in Lincoln. Feelings are still high against the dead king, and the people are not particularly attracted to the new one… It will not take much encouragement to entice the townsfolk to rebel against the castle, I fear.'

I had the sinking feeling that Archdeacon Peter was right. Lincoln still seethed with discontent. If we could get past Christmas without incident we would be fortunate, I believed.

'We are to go ahead with the Christmas celebrations?' I asked.

'Of course, it will take more than discontented townsfolk to halt those. Besides, it might bring some calm to the town, do you not agree?'

'It might, but it seems that most people are simply waiting to see which way their masters jump before declaring which side they favour.'

Part Two: The Reckoning, Lincolnshire and Nottinghamshire 1217

6.

Lady Matilda

'If you can spare me a moment, Ælfgar, here is the message for Lady Nicholaa.' I handed him a scroll which he shoved inside his gambon.

'Certainly, my lady. Is there anything else?'

'No, if you can drag yourself away from Orva, get along with you, and take your eyes with you, you will need them.'

'Yes, my lady,' he replied as he went off for his daily meeting at the ferry.

When Ælfgar returned, it was with the alarming news that in the woods surrounding us he had spotted throngs of marching troops. Two horsemen had broken from the fray and rode out to join him. The men had wild red hair and a strange manner of speech, and it soon became clear they were Scots. The man told Ælfgar he was from north of the New Castle on the River Tyne. They were returning homeward with the Scottish king.

'What does it mean?' I asked Ælfgar.

'It is good news, my lady,' he replied. 'They are homeward bound. It seems they have deserted the French, and Prince Louis has crossed back over to France. Are you of a mind that this war will peter out, my lady? Given that the French have lost an ally?'

'No, I am not. There is much to play for and too many are willing to change sides if the winds of chance alter. William Marshal has handed over young Henry's guardianship to Peter des Roches in order to concentrate on war, and they have reissued the Magna Carta to try and tempt the remaining rebel barons to return to the royal fold, but the French and their allies still hold Westminster, and many other places besides. I fear that the return of the warm weather will see our foes pulling on their boots once more, especially if Louis's father, King Philip, gives him the resources he has gone off to France to beg. Keep your blades sharp, Ælfgar, and your eyes sharper.'

'I shall. Geoffrey was at the ferry and I gave him your parchment for Lady Nicholaa. He had some food for us and we shared a meal. The castle seems well prepared for a siege, should it come.'

'What was Geoffrey's latest intelligence?'

'There are worrying signs of activity in the forest, we are close to action, I believe. The forest on our side will, I fear, soon be infested by rebels and Frenchies. I want to try and grab one of them, see what we can squeeze out of him.'

'And how are things in Lincoln, ready for a siege?'

'Yes, Geoffrey said the Lady Nicholaa has thought of most things, and what she hasn't someone else has. But she asks could you lend her a few of your archers? The defensive plan depends on keeping the rebels away from certain areas outside of the castle walls.'

'You mean marksmen?'

'I do, to deny access to a gate in the upper town wall. Geoffrey intends to use the west gate of the castle for comings and goings, if possible. And if they are already under attack, our men, skilled in concealment, could go out from the walls and discourage the rebels.'

'Give her as many as we can spare. And what news from the south? From William Marshal and all the other royalists?'

'Geoffrey said Marshal is to take the Frenchies head-on, there is a muster at Newark. If the rebels head for Lincoln,

Marshal shall be not far away. How prepared are we in Laxton, my lady?' he asked.

'Very well. While you are off touring the countryside we are busy strengthening the walls, covering the roofs with turf … all the things that they are doing in Lincoln Castle — although we are slightly different from that mighty citadel. Our outer palisade is too long to defend with what we have at our disposal, the first plan is to retreat into the inner bailey, with its eastern facing gatehouse and with the north gate guarding my motte with its own palisade around the top, we have several lines of defence. Worry not, you keep your eyes outside and we will manage Laxton.'

'Good. I hope that if they go for Lincoln they will bypass us here and not cross the Trent.'

'We can but pray. 'Tis turning dark now. I shall not need you for a while. Orva, attend me later at the evening meal if you please.'

'My lady, thank you.'

The next day Ælfgar came to find me with a messenger, breathless from his ride.

'What's ado, Ælfgar?' I asked.

'This man has news for you, my lady.'

'Where have you ridden from … fellow?'

'Serjeant Will, I am named. From Lincoln, my lady. Things are on the move.'

'Come inside, we will hear you in privy.' I turned and led him into the guard chamber. 'Wine for our visitor! Have you eaten, Serjeant?'

'Not before it turned light, my lady, we received couriers during the night and Lady Nicholaa sent me immediately. Prince Louis has returned and has divided his force. Half are at

Dover, where the constable Hubert de Burgh is defending the castle with great vigour. There has been a success at sea and Louis' reinforcements have been disrupted. However, half of his men are marching north, we know not where, but Lincoln might be in Louis' mind. William the Marshal has control of the army now and is expected to challenge the French at some point.'

'We will need his assistance, of that there is no doubt,' agreed Father Albric.

'Well, Ælfgar, with God's help and your arrows we will be secure,' I declared turning to him. 'What shall we do now?'

'Have all the families gathered into the bailey for a briefing. Everyone has a part to play should we come under attack. You should be the one to tell everybody, my lady, but these are the main points to include. Archers will defend the walls and men-at-arms will carry wattle shields to defend the archers, all men will practise with a weapon each morning and each afternoon. Women will support them and carry spare arrows to the walls as required, it will be dangerous work and they should stay off the battlement. The women will also be responsible for filling as many buckets as we can muster with water to douse fires caused by fire arrows incoming. I will split the garrison into three watches, some guarding, some working and some resting. You, my lady, need a plan for everyone to retreat into the inner ward when pressed and consider your final move if you are forced into the donjon. That, my lady, is well within your capabilities to organise.'

'Very well,' I replied. 'And you, Ælfgar?'

'I will increase our daytime patrolling and institute a night-time patrol.' Ælfgar turned to the now-refreshed messenger. 'Get back to Lincoln, Serjeant Will, and ensure that Oswald or Geoffrey will meet me tomorrow at the Dun Ham ferry. We must coordinate our defensive strategy. I will provide you with a fresh horse.'

Orva asked quietly, 'And me, what shall I do, my lady?'

'I will place you in charge of the females,' I replied, 'and all children of an age to help. 'Tis clear that we must shift for ourselves, Ælfgar will have enough to do outside but we must work out in detail what we require within these walls.'

'And worry not,' Ælfgar interjected, 'if the Frenchie's target is Lincoln, he will have enough to bother about without sending troops across the river to here.'

'And I shall coordinate all,' I added. 'Check that there are turves on all the roofs, timbers around the well, and stockpiled around the compound for reinforcing breaches, sharpening the weapons… Anything else that I have missed, Ælfgar?'

'Have Albric write everything down in a list to ensure that you have not missed anything. And be of good cheer and keep the folk occupied.' Ælfgar turned again to Nicholaa's messenger. 'What of William the Marshal? Has he a plan, Serjeant?'

'Lord Marshal has decided to mirror Prince Louis' movements. He is at Oxford now but has sent word to all loyal men available to gather at Newark, and there he will reveal his response.'

'Well,' I declared, 'along with everything else, I intend to get on with planting the crops. If we survive this spring then we need to survive next winter. So, Ælfgar, we'll need a guard to ensure the safety of our crop sowers, for if you are to turn all the farmers in our domain into soldiers the women will have to do the sowing.' I looked to my priest. 'See, Father Albric, never a dull moment here in Laxton.'

'Indeed, my lady, and is there aught else that I can do?'

'Yes, go and see the chirurgien, tell him that he might have more than sick horses to deal with, and you can help him to prepare for the wounded, God forfend that there are any.'

7.

Father Bernard

As a priest, one did not expect to be so near to a war, at least here in the centre of England, as it seemed likely that I would be soon, but the Lord has his own paths to test men with, I supposed — although not for the first time.

My reverie was broken into by Lady Nicholaa.

'What's that fuss, Bernard, over by the west gate?'

I was with her on one of her endless tours of the defences and we were standing by one of the wells. It was covered with great beams and turves to protect it from harm.

'It's Lord Geoffrey, I can hear him clearly. Should we go across?'

'We should, come along, Bernard, listen to the man.'

'We should not get too close, my lady, hear his language.'

'Dover?' Lord Geoffrey was outraged, and loud. 'Dover soddin castle, that which watches over the whole of the sea betwixt England and France? Besieged, you say?'

'Aye my lord, and worse.'

'Worse! Worse, you say? What can be worse?'

Geoffrey greeted Lady Nicholaa as we moved closer to hear more.

'D'ye hear that, my lady?' he demanded of Nicholaa.

'Yes, Geoffrey,' she responded.

'This fellow has ridden with haste from the camp of William Marshal near Oxford, and he has more to say. Good morrow, Father Bernard,' he turned his attention to me. 'The game's afoot, I fear.'

'Good morrow, Geoffrey. Is this the news we have been fearing?'

Lady Nicholaa gave me a sharp glance and retorted, 'Yes, yes, never mind all this greeting and such.' Then she demanded of the messenger knight, 'What more news have you that can be worse than the siege of Dover Castle?'

The fellow bowed, recognising the famous Nicholaa, and straightening up told her, 'Prince Louis still has a force blockading Dover, but…'

'But?' Lady Nicholaa and Geoffrey chorused.

'Lincoln… My lady, he also intends to take Lincoln.'

'My God,' said Lady Nicholaa, a rare blasphemy indeed. 'What help can we expect? What has William Marshal planned?' She glared at the fellow as if he had an army camped outside the castle gates.

'I know not, my lady, except that we are losing strongholds everywhere, saving west of a line twixt Bamburgh and Bristol. Everywhere else, including the Tower of London, is lost, threatened, or under siege. My lord William begs that you hold firm in Lincoln else our cause is lost.'

Lady Nicholaa drew herself up to her full height. Her face tightened and a fire entered her eyes. 'Get the principal men into the guard hall, Geoffrey, I will talk to them.'

Then with a swish of her kirtle she marched off towards the Lucy Tower. I sensed a strengthening speech was in the offing and followed along behind the purposeful lady.

The guard hall soon became crowded, and having spoken with Oswald and Geoffrey while many of the garrison gathered around, she was now ready to act. Standing next to a small table she picked up a flagon and used it to draw attention by striking it on the table top, with more enthusiasm than I expected, and some drinking vessels toppled over. It had the desired effect and she launched straight into a tirade.

'In the name of God, and in the name of young King Henry, no French prince will command this castle, this garrison, or this town as long as I draw breath. By the grace of God, Prince Louis, and the odious collection of ragged-arse English barons who have sided with him, will find their cause dashed on the rocks of Lincoln ere there will be any surrender of this place.'

A silence greeted this oratory, which had been delivered with surprising volume. Then a great cheer rang out, and soon I was deafened by the cacophony which must have been heard across the close at the cathedral door: Lincoln was going to war.

The separation of town and castle was now complete. Archdeacon Peter sent me a note telling me to stay away and I was now the sole representative of Mother Church within the castle walls. A giddy prospect, but my tumbling thoughts were interrupted by a shout from the guard door, it was the guard Serjeant of the day.

'The messenger has returned from Laxton, my lady.'

'Thank you. Oswald. Geoffrey, pay attention, everyone draw near.'

The three most powerful and skilful now sat down to confer. I took a seat just behind Lady Nicholaa, next to the beautiful Basilea; always a trial of the flesh, was that girl.

'Father Bernard, this is exciting,' she murmured in those compelling tones of hers, enough to set a spark in the mind of any man of any maturity. The aroma of her body was also compelling, but it served my soul well to resist her charms and put sinful thoughts away.

'Indeed it is, Basilea, but it augers darkness. It will not be long ere bad deeds follow bad news, methinks.'

She swallowed, coughed, and shuffled before responding.

'Will it be so bad, Father? That God cannot resolve the matter?'

'God watches the result of giving men free will, he will note what they do with it, be assured. Now listen, Lady Nicholaa is about to speak.'

She had a plan of the town, castle, and cathedral spread out on the table. As well as Geoffrey and Oswald, her chamberlain, steward and larderer, and some of the leading artisans were present.

'So it is confirmed, we are now the target,' stated Lady Nicholaa, as if we had not noticed the occasional missile flying over the castle walls already. 'Remind us of our plans, Oswald.'

Oswald, with the thick, horny fingers of a battle-hardened soldier began to prod the plan. Conceived and agreed some three months ago, now it must be made to work.

'As you know,' he reminded us, 'we are relatively protected to the south of the castle. There is the castle curtain wall, then the ground falls steeply downhill and the lower town lies well beneath us: we can watch that side with a sentry or two.

'Next, our eastern curtain wall and gate must be fully manned because the ground between it and the cathedral is level, and vulnerable from the north along Earninga Straete. The western wall likewise; it must be fully manned at all times as it represents our safest route in and out of the castle.

'Now for the dangerous side. The northern castle wall looks down into the upper town which itself is enclosed by the town wall. Access into this area is through the Roman gate, the New Port, already held and guarded by the town rebels. It is from along here, and from behind the houses along Earninga Straete, already missiles are flying in from the ballistae hidden among the houses.'

'It will be worse if the French bring up heavy ballistae, as is rumoured,' added Geoffrey.

'Indeed,' said, Lady Nicholaa, 'God preserve us from that. Finish your briefing, Oswald, if you please.'

'Indeed, my lady. There is an opportunity here.' He pointed to the plan. Only one hundred paces north of the west gate of the castle wall was a postern gate set in the town wall. 'Lady Nicholaa, in her foresight, has had this gate reinforced. It can only be opened outwards, and as expected the rebels have blocked it with rubble on the inside, this means that it could be opened and cleared from the outside, which we could do if we wanted to send an attack force into the upper town. Are we all clear?'

The chamberlain had an observation. 'How do we prevent them from clearing the rubble and breaking down the gate from the inside?'

Lady Nicholaa answered, 'There are be crossbowmen posted at the north-west corner of the castle wall at all times. Anyone attempting to open that gate will be discouraged.'

'An arrow or a crossbow bolt will suffice to keep them away,' added Oswald.

'How many arrows and bolts have we stocked now, smithy?'

The smith, a great thick-armed fellow, yet with a pleasant demeanour, answered with a smile. 'Twelve thousand bolts, my lady. The attiliators have been busy making more. But not so many arrows, we have only two fletchers and it takes longer to make arrows than simple bolts; three thousand of those.'

'Is that a problem, Oswald?'

'We have but a few archers, unless you can persuade Lady Matilda to lend us some more.'

She looked at Geoffrey. 'You are meeting with Ælfgar on the morrow?'

'Indeed. I have noted that, I can but ask,' he said without much hope.

'Well, do your best, I have a task in mind for some skilled archers. Oswald, how far has the treeline been moved back on the west side?'

'About one hundred and fifty paces, my lady.'

'Right, gather all the able-bodied men you can and clear it back to two hundred. We will effectively close the east gate to traffic and use the west gate. If we clear the remaining trees we will create a better killing ground. Make certain to gather all the tree trunks to bring within the castle, they can be used for defensive purposes. Agreed?'

'Agreed. I'll arrange for a woodcutters' fair, they can chop while my sentries watch, it should be fun.'

'Oswald! Keeping up the spirits with jest? You do right, there'll be plenty needed ere this game hath run its course. Now, any questions? We needs move quickly, I cannot tell how much time we will have, and Geoffrey, ensure that the patrolling areas twixt ourselves and Laxton are clear. We do not want any gaps, either of understanding or location to let the enemy enter without our knowledge.'

'No, my lady, all will be clear from tomorrow.'

'And I will begin the tree-clearing right now, my lady,' confirmed Oswald.

'See, Basilea,' I said with confidence, 'all is well. Your lady has prepared with much thought. This place will be at the centre of the young king's realm, its very beating heart. Fear not, we shall triumph.'

'Oh,' replied that sweet mouth beneath those engaging eyes.

'I must go now,' I said, 'and see what the chirurgien hath need of.' *And stop gazing at her face.*

On my way back from my cell at the back of the garrison church where I finished off my latest scribbling, as I reached the bottom of the gatehouse steps I found Oswald standing.

'Father Bernard, how fares your archdeacon today?'

'Have you not heard, I've been declared *persona non grata*, and he thinks that we are all doomed.'

'Then he is correct in that regard, we will none of us live forever.'

'Yes, but he thinks that our end will visit us earlier rather than later.'

'I shall resist that thought.'

'Are you expecting visitors?' I asked. He pointed towards the west gate, which was hidden behind some huts from where we were standing.

'Ælfgar's archers are here, Father. Lady Matilda has lent us some of her silent assassins.'

'Oh, and who are they going to assassinate, if I may ask?'

'You may ask, but the fewer who know of their purpose the better. Here they are.'

Three very dark and drab men were leading ponies across the bailey. They were certainly not destrier nor even sumpter horses, but creatures not much bigger than Irish wolfhounds.

Oswald stepped forth to greet them.

'You are from Laxton?'

'Aye, lord, Ælfgar's finest.'

'You have names?'

'Aye,' said the one in the lead.

'Which are?'

'Garr,' came the reply.

'Pardon!'

'Garr. 'E's Hengist, and 'e's Peter of Mansfield.' Garr waved his hand at the man loitering at the rear.

'Why is he from Mansfield?' Oswald asked hopefully.

'Because 'e's not from Laxton.'

'Is that important?'

By now this conversation had all the merits of the deaf shouting at the dumb, so fractured was it in understanding. Nevertheless, Oswald persevered. He gazed at me as if seeking divine help. I shook my head and clasped my hands in prayer, so he took the hint and tried a little more.

'So, Garr, what is your understanding of your presence here in Lincoln?'

'What?'

'Why are you here? You have been sent to help us, have you not?'

'We have.'

'What are you going to do, Garr?'

'Find rebels in the dark, kill them, and return, my lord.'

'I see, and that is what you like to do?'

'Born to it … my lord.'

After a little consideration, I could see Oswald's mind racing as I considered these men of dreadful aspect. They were immense in the shoulder and narrow in the hip, the result of archery training from the age of ten. Their clothing resembled dark rags, green and brown in hue, and although they did not smell badly nothing about them shone. They carried short swords at the hip but they were secured to the thigh so that they did not swing, then a quiver of arrows tied to the other thigh with the missiles secured so as not to jiggle about. Finally they all held long bows, clutching them as if they were a part of the hand which grasped them.

I was curious. 'You do not have the bows strung, Garr?'

He fixed me with a terrible stare, as if I were a target. 'No, priest.' He removed his leather cap and from the top of his head produced some strings for my inspection. 'Keeps 'em dry, priest, can string it in a flash.' His hands moved with the speed of a lightning flash and the bow was upright and drawn before I knew it. 'Keeping it stringed weakens it. Can do this in the dark, we can ... want to see me do it with my eyes closed?'

'God's miracles, not now!' exploded Oswald. 'Can we just get on with it? Garr, come with me and meet Lady Nicholaa. Father Bernard, escort Hengist and Peter of Mansfield to the stables, then see about their quarters, if you please.'

I did not want to miss this interview so I almost ran across to the stables. There I passed on my instructions to a stable lad, and picking up my skirts trotted back and up the steps into Nicholaa's tower.

Lady Nicholaa was in her place at the far end of the guard hall. Standing respectfully at a distance awaiting a summons was Oswald and the oddly dressed Garr. He was gazing up at the walls, which were richly festooned with tapestries of the finest quality and most interesting prospects. Beasts, hunting scenes and depictions of the life of Christ abounded, and some long ago battle scenes completed the circumference, for this chamber is circular, most unusual for a donjon.

Puffing I went to stand alongside Oswald, trying to smile, although my lungs would have had a grimace on my face if they'd had their way.

Looking down on me, he remarked, 'That was quick, are they settled?'

'Indeed, your stables are very accommodating,' and I was about to say that it was not my position to organise archers, but at that moment Lady Nicholaa looked up from some parchments she had been occupied with and beckoned Oswald forward. I shuffled along with our new ragamuffin man, Garr.

Inspecting Garr up and down Lady Nicholaa smiled at him — she knew his purpose of course, before greeting him.

'Is this a tree you bring before me, Captain Oswald?'

'More of a bush, my lady, a very spiky bush.'

That raised a laugh and even Garr smiled, before managing a quick bow of the head.

'You've come to inflict some damage on our enemies? You have a name?'

'Garr ... my lady.'

'Welcome, Garr. Are you alone?'

'No, lady, us'n three.'

'The others are at the stables,' I interjected.

'Thank you, Father Bernard. Now, Garr, how do you intend to operate?'

'If it please your ladyship, Lord Ælfgar has instructed us. We exits the castle after dark and looks fer trouble, we expects to return afore light. All else is between us and them rebels, I wus told to say, if you please.'

Glances were exchanged between Oswald and Nicholaa before she made her mind up.

'Captain Oswald, find these, err, bushes, somewhere quiet to sleep during the day. Garr, when you come back tell the guard captain what you have done, and then you can eat and sleep till the next time you go out.'

'Thank 'ee, your ladyship. Owt else?'

'Oswald, take him on to the walls and show him the dangerous areas. I wish you well, Garr; may God be with you.'

Oswald and the spiky bush left before Lady Nicholaa remarked, 'These are strange times, Bernard. I had not thought to rely upon ragamuffins to help defend this place.'

'Yes, my lady, strange times and stranger methods; but if God wills we should employ all our talents, do you not agree?'

'Indeed, Bernard, indeed.'

Next day we were at breakfast, after I had conducted Prime, when Oswald came into the donjon to report on last night's activities.

Geoffrey nudged me. 'Bernard,' he said, nodding in the direction of the approaching captain.

'Are they returned safely, Oswald?' asked lady Nicholaa.

'Yes, my lady. Garr heard French voices on patrol last night, they are setting up heavy machines, hidden behind the houses along the Earninga Straete. He heard the English with them talk of the main French army due here very soon.'

'I see. And you say that they did not suspect that our ragamuffin men were among them in the dark?'

'No,' replied Oswald, 'they come, they go, and before they arrive you do not suspect that they are there, and when they leave there is no trace of them … they are as spirits. Garr has asked when you will require him to begin killing.'

'They must remain silent, I will deploy them to keep us informed. I do not want them to become trapped inside the upper town walls, they are no use to us strung up. Make certain that he understands this, Oswald, they are our secret weapon and we must ensure that they are not lost in some madcap adventure.'

'Aye, my lady.'

'What of other things? Do we know how many men the rebels have at their disposal?'

'We think about six hundred. The upper town wall is too long for them to defend in all places so they are concentrated around the old Roman gate, they have withdrawn on the west side so that they are out of range, they do not go too near the cathedral and they are not in the lower town in any numbers…'

'And that is where we expect the French to come from, through the wet lands and across the river?'

'Yes, the access via lower Earninga Straete is narrow, constrained by the wetlands on either side, and easily defended. If we want reinforcements then they must approach from the north, and attack the Roman gate.'

Lady Nicholaa gazed at her loyal captain and smiled. I knew then that she had a plan, and somehow I suspected that the little postern gate used by Garr had a place in it. Sweet plotter: what a devious mind hath the female of the species. It was not unnoticed.

'What're you grinning at, Father Bernard?'

'Gates, my lady, the gates of heaven.'

'Then we are like of mind, but do not discuss the gates of heaven save with God, and ensure that he understands our needs.'

'I will pray, my lady. I think that should go and try with the archdeacon one last time, see if he will alter his stance, the church should be neutral in matters of Christian souls. I should go across to the cathedral and pray while there is a chance, and see if the archdeacon will assist us in prayer.'

'Very well, go carefully. Oswald see that Father Bernard is safely escorted there and back. Now, chamberlain, a report from you if you please.'

We left her presence and made our way down those steps, turned smooth and tricky, even beneath the newly constructed gallery, by myriad muddy footfalls, then past the smithy, where the farriers had joined the blacksmiths and atilliators in forging arrow heads and crossbow bolts, along the side of an open shed wherein dwelt the fletchers, busy with their goose feathers, making arrows straight and true, past the shambles where the meat of the day was being carved up and so on, the air heavy with kitchen smells and smoke as we approached the eastern gate.

Coming near I could see that Geoffrey was already at the gate.

'What's the kerfuffle?' mused Oswald out loud, 'and why's Geoffrey there?'

'Ah, there you are, Oswald. We have a problem. The French are in the lower town now and there are many loyal townsfolk waiting outside begging shelter.'

'Then we'll accommodate them. Lady Nicholaa has given instructions to harbour as many as we can inside, God knows what will happen to them if they are left out there.'

'Are you still going out, Father Bernard?' asked Oswald.

I answered 'yes' but was beginning to feel as if 'no' should be the answer — too late.

'Guard Serjeant!' he called out.

'Captain,' replied the alert soldier.

'An escort for Father Bernard across the close to the great door of the cathedral, if you please.'

Soon I was dwarfed by three burly fellows, who grinned at me, no doubt hoping for a confrontation.

'Open the gate,' commanded Captain Oswald, and as the great gate began to swing open the crowd began to press forward.

'Wait, slow down. Line up by the wall, women and children on the left and men on the right,' he commanded, then to Geoffrey he explained, 'e will question them all and ask those whom we know to vouch for their fellow citizens, those we don't know will be turned away.'

Oswald gestured to my escort and we began to make our way out of the gate but we heard a whistling noise as a small rock flew over the gatehouse battlement to land with a crash inside the bailey behind us. At the same time a dozen bolts peppered the gate and we all fell to the ground.

'Get back inside!' came the shout and we variously crawled or ran back inside, half crouching.

The gate was hurriedly closed and all was still, until I heard someone moaning nearby and a shout went up.

'They've got one, see to him. Guard Serjeant, all your men to the battlement and call out the reserve, I want all of the battlement fully manned. Send word across to the west gate and post sentries on the southern wall. I want reports from there, as to what activity there is in the lower town. Father Bernard, you might want to postpone your visit, hurry along and attend Lady Nicholaa, the siege is begun. Tell her that they are using small machines to hurl rocks at us and it is not safe in the open anymore.'

The war was here. I began to run back to Lady Nicholaa's steps. Steps to heaven, heavenly gates, the fate of all within the castle was now in the hands of our God in heaven. Who would He favour? A question that time would answer in due course.

When I entered the guard floor I asked a soldier for the whereabouts of Lady Nicholaa and was directed to the upper chambers.

'I think that she has received some bad news, Father, a messenger came in through the west gate and then she went up to her privy chambers.'

I found her, together with Basilea, in the chapel. She was in distress and I did not want to deepen it, but asked, 'Have you heard, my lady?'

'About my son Richard? Sad news indeed, Father Bernard, sad indeed. He has died in bad circumstances.'

This flummoxed me and I hesitated. She saw that, and wiping away a tear, asked, 'More? You bring more?'

'O-only the missiles landing in the bailey, my lady. But your news, how terrible. Shall we pray?'

'Oh dear God, later. This is a day to forget already.' She fixed me with a teary look and said, 'Explain, Basilea, I need a few moments.'

The girl pinned me with her enchanting eyes and commenced the explanation.

'Lady Nicholaa's son, Richard, did pass away in Northampton. He was not well when he returned from Ireland with King John, but he lost his love for the king and insisted on joining with the rebel barons against our cause.'

Nicholaa completed the explanation. 'He turned against me, but he was still my son and I must forgive him.'

'Oh, I am indeed sorry, my lady, we shall pray for him,' I said.

Basilea held her lady and embraced her kindly, and Nicholaa said to me over the girl's shoulder, 'Indeed, but there is his wife, my daughter-in-law, the lady Eustacia, and my granddaughter, Idonea, they are on their way here. They must be prevented … and missiles landing, you say?'

'One chased me up here, my lady. Should I go and arrange a rider to be sent to find Lady Eustacia, turn her back?'

'Please do. She must not come here, I have suffered enough bereavement, only five years since my husband Gerard died … I will not risk another death in the family.'

'Gladly. And Geoffrey has allowed more loyal townsfolk access to the castle, the French are taking the town, I fear.'

'That was expected, 'tis well that we are prepared. You are keeping a diary, Bernard, if I do not survive this…'

'Your story will be told, my lady, and I have no doubt that you will have the telling of it, as God wills.'

I went to find Geoffrey to arrange a messenger to find and conduct Lady Eustacia to a safe place, and my heart was heavy. Poor Lady Nicholaa, eyes so sad and yet determined. I knew that she would hold this place, there was none better, but in the face of so many blows she would be forgiven for turning to despair. I thought that I heard a sob from Basilea as I went through the door.

Today is the tenth day of May, in the year of our Lord, Twelve Seventeen.

I sat back to admire my script. It had been quite a while since I was bent over a desk learning the craft of calligraphy, hard taskmasters in the abbey had ensured that I learnt well, right through the chilly days of winter and the heat of summer, and it had stayed with me for all these years.

'Father Bernard!'

The call echoed up the steps from the guard floor into the chapel in Lady Nicholaa's privy chambers, a quiet place to write, but no escape from the rigours of these days under siege.

'Yes!' I called back through the open door.

'The chirurgien requires some assistance, there are more casualties,' came the urgent demand.

'I'm on my way.'

Setting aside my wet quill I rushed down to the guard, but before I stepped out a Serjeant thrust a wattle shield into my hand.

''Ere, Father, you needs one o' these pavises, there's too much objects flying around out there for comfort.'

'Is it that bad?'

'Something strikes every now and agin, so you take no chances, and listen for the whistling sounds, that means a ball to take yer 'ed off is a-comin' over the wall.'

'God preserve us.'

He looked at me before replying. 'Yerrs, but while you is waiting for God, keep one of these over yer 'ed, if you please.'

As I was bidden I flew down the steps, unhindered by my priestly skirts, for I had discarded them in favour of breeches, being much more practical to wear for war, and with my new pavise over my head — Jesu! We are as rats scuttling in a trap.

I was shocked when I reached the shelter of the chirurgien's hut, for there were at least four people lying on the floor moaning, and blood everywhere. Two bodies lay outside, lifeless.

'Father!' exclaimed Chirurgien Godwine, arms all bloodied. 'See what you can do for those two over there.' He pointed at a man and a woman sitting against the wall looking quite dazed. 'I'm treating these two, they have taken a bolt each, one in the leg, but this one…' He indicated a man with a bolt near buried in his back and shook his head. I assumed that the man was close to death and went to attend to my wounded.

'God bless you,' I said to the woman. She looked at me dumbly.

The man sitting next to her said, 'You're on her wrong side, Father, her ear's been taken off on that side.'

It was true. I prised her hand off the side of her head and blood spouted over me; she had lost that ear.

'One o' they bolts took it off, Father. And another cracked me on the leg, look.'

'There's some strips of cloth in that bag, Father, use them to stop the blood flow, if you will.' Godwine was issuing instructions as he attended to the man with the leg wound.

I did what I was asked and soon the woman's bleeding was stemmed, although it did not prevent her from moaning.

When I had done as much as I could I took a look outside. It was very busy near the sheltering cover of the west and north walls but there were not many folk moving about in the open, except soldiers with shields, running and watching the skies for flying objects.

'Don't feel too sorry for these silly sods, Father, they was warned about wandering about, serves them right.'

Harsh words, but he was right; in these circumstances everyone had a duty to take care of themselves, else we would soon be reduced to too few to defend the castle.

Leaving Godwine to tidy up I ran across to the east gate, as the missiles were now coming at us from the close in front of the cathedral. It was sheltered here and I could see Oswald was in attendance.

'Captain Oswald; bless you.'

'And good morrow to you, Father Bernard. What are you doing here?'

'It's as safe as anywhere. I've been attending the wounded with Chirurgien Godwine, there are bodies to bury.'

'Aye, and there'll be more if these folk don't do what they're told, damn their eyes.'

'They are not trained soldiers, Oswald. You need to be firmer with them.'

'I'll find you a place away from the wells. Could you dig the bodies up later, when all this nonsense is done with?'

'I'll need an indulgence from the archdeacon.'

'Whatever you need. When to do it? That is the puzzle. At night we're sending people around the castle bailey to pick up all the crossbow bolts and those stones which they're hurling at us. I intend to send them back with venom when the time is right, we're making our own rock catapults. I'll get some graves dug over by the west gate, if that will suit you.'

'It will. Why are you waiting to respond to this assault?'

'Because we have limited supplies and no certain means of gaining more. These missiles are but pinpricks. If the Frenchie does his job properly he'll be bringing up some real ballistae, big ones capable of throwing rocks at us. Mark my words, these pebbles are but a beginning.'

'Quite. And we'll need a hospice too; the chirurgien's hut is not the place for the dying … or those likely to live.'

'What's a hospice?'

'Somewhere to die or live. A hut will do. Have one cleared and put beds in it, and ensure that it is properly protected with a turved roof and timbers around the walls. We will need scullions to keep the place provided with hot water, and the chirurgien's hut too.'

'God's bollocks, man, d'ye not think that I've enough to do?'

'I'm sure that you have, Captain Oswald, but this is, as you say, going to get worse before there is any relief.'

Oswald eyed me up and down, but I was firm on this one, it had to be done. At last he brought one of his attending Serjeants forward.

'Work with this priest and ensure that you carry out his instructions well.'

'Captain.'

I made to thank Oswald but he was already trotting across the bailey towards the western gate so I repeated my request to his Serjeant and received a swift and positive response.

'Leave it to me, Father, it'll be done by the evening … if these damned missiles miss us, that is.'

He grinned at me, and I suspected that he was rather enjoying the chaos. Soldiers! Never happier than when surrounded by mayhem.

On the way back to Nicholaa's tower I experimented with my pavise. With arms above my head I carried it on my shoulders with the handle, thus protected from unseen rocks coming at me from behind. My arms were tired by the time I reached the galleried steps, and I got shouted at from the top for lowering the damned thing too early.

Geoffrey was at the top, laughing at my misfortune.

'That got your speed up, Bernard. And look at all that activity, it has taken a few casualties to drive home the message, don't you see?'

I did see. Watching from the narrow slits at the top of the steps I could see a new intensity within the castle bailey. People had taken action to add to their protections, and the trees and wattle which Lady Nicholaa had ordered to be brought within had been utilised by those sheltering here. Some had found a place in the existing huts, protected by the turf-covered roofs and walls reinforced by new timber, and for others timber shelters were being constructed right against the castle walls, and some were digging trenches to shelter within, it was very busy, and very noisy. And still the occasional crossbow bolt or fist-sized rock whistled in from outside. It might have been comical under different circumstances, but every time those toiling heard a shout or a whistle, they disappeared from view and the bailey appeared deserted.

'Amusing, eh?' asked Geoffrey.

'Only if one retains one's head,' I retorted. 'I must report to Lady Nicholaa, are you coming?'

'Right,' he said, 'there are things to discuss. See that over there?'

He pointed to some goings-on within the walls of the west gate barbican, a long tunnel which covered the gate entrance and extended some way within the castle. It was a killing ground. If an enemy could cross the ditch, smash down the portcullis, and then break through the metalled gate, they would find themselves assaulted from above while trapped within its confines.

Today it was a busy site and I could see a large throwing device and some smaller ballistae under construction.

'Is that what Oswald is collecting rocks for?'

'Aye, we will return them from whence they came. But first that ragamuffin man, Garr, is going out to locate their throwing machines tonight. If he can destroy them or kill the machine crews it will give us some respite.'

'This is an evil business, Geoffrey, would that it could be averted.'

'It'll be over when we receive reinforcements. Generally in wars, the side with the most men wins, and we have barely enough to man the walls, certainly not all around the perimeter.'

'No, it is quite a distance around. We must keep Lady Nicholaa in good spirits, don't you think, Geoffrey?'

'Indeed, indeed, come along, keep up, Bernard,' shouted the soldier, running up the stairs and leaving me puffing in his wake.

Nicholaa greeted us when we arrived at her privy chamber.

'Ah, Geoffrey, how goes it below?'

'Patchy, my lady. There are more casualties, but Oswald intends to do something to relieve matters tonight.'

'I see. I presume there is to be some kind of foray?'

'Indeed, we intend to discomfort the bombarding troops.'

'Are our machines ready? The artisans seem much occupied within the confines of the barbican.'

'Another two days, my lady.'

'Good. And is everyone safe within the bailey, all those who have escaped from the town? Upon my soul, Bernard, you are all of a dither, sit down and take a breath.'

'Thank you, my lady, you are too kind,' I gasped, still struggling from the climb.

'I can report on conditions for the townsfolk within the bailey, my lady,' said Turstan.

'Good. Bernard, you sit and listen, see if Turstan misses anything.'

'The dangers are coming from the north and east, from within the upper town buildings, as expected, and your orders have been carried out. Trenches have been dug and covered with logs as shelters next to the south walls for the women and children. The men are accommodated at the bottom of the north wall. That way all the missiles hurtling into the bailey are falling short of those sheltering on the south side and the men are available for defensive duties to assist the soldiers. All the existing buildings and the wells are protected, but, in discussion with Captain Oswald, and Lord Geoffrey, we feel that it will be better to take food to the people, rather than have them all cross open ground back and forth to gather at the kitchens.'

'And those carrying food and water will be protected?'

'Indeed, my lady.'

'Bernard, you've something to say?'

'Yes, my lady, I have asked for a burial ground. Captain Oswald has promised me an area, I will bless it and move the bodies when this matter is done with.'

'There were casualties today?'

'Indeed, two more deaths, and several injuries.'

'You hear that, Geoffrey? Two deaths too many. Make sure that there are no unnecessary movements, and we'll take your advice on feeding, no one is to be in the open unless it is essential and unless they are protected.'

'They have had such instructions, my la—'

'Then tell them again.' Lady Nicholaa was sharp, cutting in and discomforting Geoffrey. 'Punish those who disobey, we must have discipline. Do you understand, all of you? Discipline will get us through this. I will go on a tour of inspection as soon as you are ready. Geoffrey, make arrangements. I want to see the people and they will see and hear from me. We are all in this together and we will die or survive together; be sure of it. *Together.*' She fixed us all with a stern glare before turning to me. 'We will pray, Father Bernard.'

'I will prepare your chapel, my lady.'

'No, not there, here. Lead us now, all here can join in. Basilea, your arm, help me kneel, if you please.'

My homily must have been too lengthy, because it wasn't long before the Lady Nicholaa sighed impatiently.

'We must go now, Bernard. Where is Geoffrey?'

'He has gone down to arrange you an escort, my lady,' replied Turstan. 'I fear that he would prevent you leaving your tower if he could not keep you safe.'

'Oh, well, let him do his duty. Come now, attend me, I will be seen around and about, we must let everyone know that we care for them, and they are not alone. Bernard, we will visit the wounded first.'

'Yes, my lady.'

I was reluctant, but I could not stop the lady from getting into the thick of things if that was her wish.

'Oh! My Lord!' she gasped as we emerged from the tower.

Looking to one side of the gallery and then the other the wreckage was visible in the bailey; it was as if a powerful wind had scattered the place with rubble. At the bottom of the steps soldiers waited, all carrying pavises to protect her and her entourage.

'Geoffrey, Oswald,' she demanded, 'is this really necessary?'

Just then a very large rock came over the northern wall, bounced its way across the earth, up the Lucy Tower embankment and smashed into the bottom of the tower wall. It hit no one along its way, thank God, but put the frights on all who witnessed it.

Geoffrey shouted to Oswald, 'Get rid of these willows, they will not protect the lady; get some proper shields to form a *testudo* over her head before we go further.'

'Very well, Geoffrey. Rush her over to the shelter of the north wall until I get them sorted.'

Geoffrey escorted our little party across to the shelter of the north wall, arriving at the same time as a half-dozen soldiers with metal shields. He quickly reorganised his pavise carriers into a *testudo*, a sort of moving tunnel, using the more substantial Norman kite shields. Only when beneath its protection did Geoffrey allow Lady Nicholaa's tour of inspection to begin and we shuffled speedily about the bailey, praying hopefully to remain untouched by rocks, balls, boulders, or bolts launched from their infernal machines.

'This is awful, Oswald. What if they move their machines round to the front of the cathedral? We will be certain to be hit standing here, and all these folks sheltering.'

'You are correct, my lady, however our defensive plan is to deny them the ground to set up their machines on the cathedral close. It is reachable by bolt and arrow from the top of the eastern gate, and they will not enter the open ground there without peril.'

'But those raggedy men of Matilda's will be out there lurking somewhere,' added Geoffrey.

'Are they? What will they do out there? Surely they would be better placed, as you say, Oswald, on top of the gate with their bows?'

'Quite, my lady, but their mission is to affright the enemy, they move and kill at night and lie silent during the day. They left last night in the dark, but I expect them back tonight. The French machine crews are in danger all the time when Garr and his friends are out in amongst them.'

'Dear Lord, has it come to it that we send men out to kill in the dark?'

There was a series of whistling noises as half a dozen balls hurtled over our heads and struck various huts, ripping the roof off one.

The astonished occupants, a knight and his family, were left staring into the sky as they sat at their midday table — they were fortunate, the heavy turves and logs piled around the house had saved them, and many ran to drag them, mud-bespattered, from out of the wreckage. But attention quickly turned skywards again as the sound of a heavy rock split the air as it passed overhead to land on top of a store hut, sending the contents scattering across the bailey.

The larderer appeared from in front of the kitchens, soon to be joined by Turstan the chamberlain, to survey the damage. The dutiful man called out for assistance from his scullions and ran to take stock of his provisions. The chamberlain ordered them back into cover and Lady Nicholaa added to that demand by directing Captain Oswald to 'See that the larderer gets some protection, we *cannot* have anyone out in the open.'

Geoffrey was somewhat agitated now. He had thought things through, he believed, but now we were coming under increased bombardment from a certain direction he made a suggestion. 'Your tower, my lady. The Lucy Tower is on the safest wall and is the furthest away from the ballistae; let us concentrate on reinforcing that area. We have enough timber to build a wall around the base and get more people and supplies behind it. The missiles will have lost a lot of their velocity by the time they reach there and it seems to be the safest spot.'

'What about the wells, Geoffrey?'

'We can extend the steps gallery and build wooden tunnels from the tower to reach them under cover.'

'Good, let's do it. I pray that William Marshal will arrive before too long, we cannot withstand this constant barrage forever.'

'Indeed, my lady. Should I send word to Laxton, they can reach the royal army easier than can we?'

'Do it.' We ducked a little as another shower of balls passed overhead. The soldiers who were covering the activities of the larderer and his helpers with their shields were bowled over, but after a few moments they all staggered back on to their feet, no harm done, except that the larderer redoubled his efforts to retrieve his scattered supplies, and the shields were somewhat dented.

'Get a move on, you scurvy sod, we cannot wait all day.'

We all heard the shouted order of the Serjeant in charge, but I doubted if the fellow could go any faster. I'm sure he was running about as fast as his legs could take him.

'Our preparations are inadequate, Geoffrey, we must do more.' Lady Nicholaa was becoming annoyed.

'Aye, my lady. They,' he said, pointing at the sheltering townsfolk, 'are in peril, they have naught but the back of this wall to keep them safe.'

'Oswald, you should be at the eastern gate. Go now, I'll manage.'

The captain ran off carrying his shield aloft towards the gate to command his troops, as Nicholaa faced Geoffrey.

'Geoffrey, gather our miners, and the masons, and see about digging some more trenches over in that south-west corner, 'tis safest there. Get these people to help and get them out of harm's way as quick as you can.'

'Aye, my lady.'

'Father Bernard.' She turned to me. 'Come with me, we will visit the chirurgien … which is where you should be anyway … indeed, why are you following me around like a lost lamb?'

'I'm not at all sure, my lady, this is all quite beyond me.'

The noise was tremendous, the voices of people both within and outside the walls, Serjeants calling orders, the desperate whinnying from the stables, flying objects filling the skies, the crack of struck timbers and the wounded crying out; it was a chorus from hell.

I followed the dauntless lady across to the hospice. If a woman of years past sixty could brave this mayhem, then so should I.

Near midnight, after hours of bombardment, Lord Geoffrey and I were summoned by Captain Oswald. They had received reports on the rebels' activities and now knew who the leaders were. The banners of Prince Louis of France were prominent, together with those of the Count of Perche, and Gilbert of Gant; he who had made an attempt to dispossess Matilda in earlier times. There was also the English rebel baron, Robert

Fitzwalter — formidable opposition, I was thinking, all lined up to feast on the carcass of Lincoln castle.

Oswald was with the raggedyman Garr and his two men. Garr dragged a scruffy parchment out of his gilet and handed it to Oswald to spread out. It was a rough map of the area with scribbles all over it.

'How do you do it, Garr? Where have you been all day?' Oswald asked.

'We only moves at night, so us'll need to find a place to lie still during the day, if'n us can't get back to here, that is. Mostly we lies still in muck heaps, us aster stay away from animals and the like; dogs are a right pain in the arse. Sometimes us'll be in plain sight, if the dozy turds would just look proper like, that's when us can't move when it gets light and just lies still.'

'Is this where their machines are placed?' Oswald asked, prodding the plan.

'Aye, here be Onagers, catapult-like machines that hurls the small balls, and here they has the large crossbows, strapped to a wagon to hurl over-size arrows … they've not brung 'em inter use yet. And here is their trebuchet. And here and here, they are building two more.'

'God's bollocks! We can't withstand much of that, those rocks are deadly.'

'You won't like the extra-long arrers either, when they get going.'

'How long are they?'

'Twice as long and twice as heavy as yer normal arrer. A bit like your lance.'

I sat quiet for a while. This was the third assault which Lady Nicholaa had resisted on her castle, but this one was serious, with the French and openly rebellious English barons involved.

There would be no way out of this save for a victory, and that would only come with a relieving force.

'What thinks ye, Cap'n?'

The question startled Oswald out of his thoughts.

'I'm thinking that 'tis time we struck back, Garr, give them some shite.'

'Good. This time we will choose our targets and kill, as ye've said we can. Us'll do owt fer't lady.'

'We all feel like that,' I agreed.

'Let's sit under the gate, Garr has a tale to tell, Father Bernard, for your diary, if you please.'

'Of course. Let's hear your tale, Garr.'

He was obviously enjoying this, very proud of their craft were Garr and his men. We sat captivated as he related the events of his outing.

'Captain Oswald and the rest of 'is guard watched as us'n got ready to exit the castle through the west barbican gate. We carried only short hunting bows, wi' a short sword strapped to a thigh and a seax across the belt — last night was a lookabout, us wanted no noise and no fuss. Others had come to the west gate to see us off as us slipped out of the small postern set in the great gate, then slithered down into the ditch which ran across the front of the western wall. The postern creaked shut and apart from the voices way above us heads on top of the castle battlement it was silent. The sentries above had been instructed to behave normal so as not to cause suspicion in the upper town.'

Garr paused in his narration and looked at Oswald.

'Very important to us, Cap'n, everthin' must be as normal, thank you for that. We laid still for a while to set us eyes to the dark and when I was sure that there was nobody stirring, us crept along the ditch until we come to the postern in the upper

134

town wall. I 'ad a length of rope with a grappling iron on the end and hurled it ower, tugging at it gently until it snagged in the rubble on the other side. Nuthin' stirred so I pulled mesen up and waited for the others — we could jump down from there on to the rubble piled high behind the door. With the grappling iron secured us dropped the rope back ower the outside of the wall, an escape route if things went wrong.

'It stayed all quiet in the upper town and so us could move around easy. Creeping along in the shadow of the walls us heard the rebel troops clumping about, then, entering the shelter of the various buildings — those that wus still standing, us soon got near the old Roman gate in the north wall. Taking shelter in a handy bush us settled down to watch the town guard and their habits.

'They wus careless, sitting around a fire which destroys night vision. We coulda been upon them and separated heads from shoulders wi'out a fuss. I picked up some conversations, foreign it were, and saw how often they patrols went out, then after about three hours us made our way back to the rubble-backed postern, over it and into the ditch. A whistle to the sentry above the castle gate soon had it opened and we were inside in an eye-blink to be greeted by your'sen, Captain Oswald.'

'I was watching from the top of the battlement, Garr. I neither saw nor heard anything, you are very skilful. Did you kill anyone?'

'Naw, Cap'n. I've told 'e what's what, and your lady can decide if'n she wants anybody killed, now we 'as a good idea of what them rebels is like. Can us tek a drink, 'tis powerful dry out there.'

'Certainly, Garr, you've earned it. Get off for some sleep and we'll plan something for later.'

'Thank e' Cap'n.'

And they were gone as silently as they came.

'Glad they're on our side,' said Geoffrey, the spell of Garr broken, 'shouldn't like to bump into them in the dark.'

'They are seemingly deadly shadows, Oswald,' I added, 'I'm not certain that they are altogether Christian in their doings.'

'We'll send them out again tonight, Geoffrey, we won't survive many more of these continuous daytime bombardments.'

'I agree, Oswald, they're turning the bailey into a shambles,' said Geoffrey.

Oswald responded, 'Garr will go out again tonight into the upper town. They will strike at the ballistae crews as they sleep and try to do some damage to the machines. I will have rope ladders over the castle wall in the north-west corner and hope they could climb swiftly up if they got into trouble — scrambling over the town wall near the postern gate would be another option, but I want them to have the very best chances, and will have as many archers and crossbowmen as possible lined up on the castle battlement to give them cover if they are pursued. Agreed?'

'Agreed.'

'And you, Father Bernard, ensure that this is all recorded in Lady Nicholaa's diary, the efforts of these men should not be unrecorded.'

'As you say, Captain, as you say. Should I tell lady Nicholaa of this tonight?'

'No, let her rest tonight. If Garr fails we may expect an intensified bombardment in the morning, the Frenchies outside will not take kindly to our efforts to sabotage their siege. Just write it down.' He turned to Geoffrey. 'We need to craft a strategy to contact this army of William Marshal's, if it exists.'

'Indeed, how are we going to do it?'

'We can't lose you to go looking for it, let's see if Ælfgar can go.'

'Shouldn't be difficult, finding an army.'

'Yes, but Ælfgar can do it without being seen, he moves fast enough to escape if he is spotted. Will you ask him when next you meet?'

'Consider it done. Are we finished for the night?'

'Aye, go and get some rest, we'll be up all night tonight again.'

I went to my lady's chapel and tried to sleep but was too restless and set to work on my diary. It was full of detail, too much I fear for I nodded off at one time and awoke with my head on the table, thankfully no ink was split but my quill had dried and was useless. It being late afternoon I had something to eat out of the garrison pottage, not a particularly pleasant experience but that was what was available to all now. Then I went back to the western gatehouse to keep vigil for the night while Garr and his men left to do their damage.

'Father Bernard!' It was Oswald.

I had asked to be in the western gatehouse; with so much going on I wanted to witness it for myself. Besides, if the soldiers were to be up all night why should their priest not join them?

Oswald had tried to discourage me. I'm sure that he expected me to be a nuisance but I made myself small and stayed in a corner — which is where I was when I nodded off, to be wakened suddenly.

'Is it day break, Oswald?'

'Nearly, but there has been some action, a man has been killed.'

'Oh, dear God. Who is it?'

'Peter, Garr's man.'

'How?'

Oswald related the events of the night, how I slept through them with all the noise he described, I know not, perhaps the endless living under threat of danger was taking its toll.

When he had finished Oswald appeared.

'Lady Nicholaa wants to speak with Garr. Bernard, will you take him up?'

The bailey was quiet as we crossed to Nicholaa's tower refuge.

'It seems that you have silenced the Frenchies, Garr.'

'At a price, Father, at a price,' he responded glumly.

Pausing at the chamber door I asked Garr to wait and entered. Lady Nicholaa was busy scribbling at the table but stood when she saw me.

'Bernard, you have brought him?'

'Garr is here to see you, my lady. He awaits your pleasure outside.'

'Thank you, Bernard, will you stay and help me? I'm not looking forward to this, and you, Geoffrey, if you will.'

'Certainly, my lady, we must show our gratitude. Last night was a spectacular success, save for the death of Garr's man, Peter.'

'Indeed, they have much to answer for, those who begun this war among our fellow English.'

'And invited a foreign prince to lead them,' added Geoffrey.

Just then there was a fuss at the door and Oswald came in hurriedly, Garr being kept outside.

'My lady.' He went close to her and as he whispered in her ear her face took on an ashen appearance and she looked to me.

Geoffrey asked, 'What is it, Oswald?'

'Tell him, Oswald,' said Lady Nicholaa with tight lips.

'It's Peter. We have recovered the body. A patrol went out and under the protection of archers on the battlement brought Peter's remains back.'

I crossed myself. 'May God have mercy.'

'Well, I will not,' was the predictable response from the man of Serland.

'Calmly now, Geoffrey, be still. Does Garr know?'

'I think not, my lady. I passed him outside the chamber, he is leaning against the wall and looks tired from last night, and not much interested in anything at the moment,' replied Oswald.

'Bring in Garr, and then go, and prepare a burial,' commanded Lady Nicholaa.

Oswald and Geoffrey left the chamber grim-faced, saying naught, so I popped my head out of the doorway and smiled at Garr to beckon him in. He entered, a shadow as ever, and seemingly a trifle awed in the presence of Lady Nicholaa. He need not have worried. Lady Nicholaa went across to greet him, and grasping him by the shoulders she planted a kiss on both cheeks and held him while she offered her words of comfort.

'I am deeply saddened by your loss, and it is also our loss, Garr. That was a brave action last night, but at too high a price, I fear. Has the man Peter any family?'

'No, my lady, he was a loner, a man who lived for dying. He is … was, brave, of that I'm certain, but he will be happy in heaven. I cannot have him left there, what can be done?' He turned to me when he said that, as if to have it confirmed that

Peter died in a righteous cause. I looked at lady Nicholaa and she responded immediately.

'Worry not, Garr, we have him back inside, and he will be given a Christian burial.'

Garr cheered up a little before replying, 'Thank'ee my lady, 'tis only right.'

Lady Nicholaa released Garr and took a step back before addressing a remark at me. 'Then he will be content that he died protecting the rights of our realm and our God-anointed king.'

'I shall lead us in prayer, my lady. Shall we do it here, with all your lords present?'

'Indeed, Father Bernard, let all know how brave are our saviours, here on earth as in heaven.'

Then Chamberlain Turstan bustled his way into the chamber closely followed by Geoffrey, who nodded at Lady Nicholaa. She nodded back in understanding, and then addressed Garr.

'Be assured, Garr, that Peter will be buried with the best of dignity and the prayers will be led by Father Bernard himself.'

She looked at me and I nodded in eager assent. It would be a privilege to conduct a service for such a brave man.

'I'll come to see you later, Garr. Leave the arrangements to me,' I confirmed.

He nodded his understanding and Lady Nicholaa looked at Turstan next.

'What now, Turstan?' she demanded. 'More bad news?'

'Nay, my lady, quite the reverse, there have been no more flying objects, the skies have fallen silent.'

'Hah!' declared Geoffrey, 'that's buggered them up. Garr, your man did not die in vain.'

'Geoffrey, have a care. The man is yet still warm.'

Lady Nicholaa's sensitivities had been offended and Geoffrey looked suitably admonished. Garr ventured a few words.

'Peter will be happy, my lady, do not fret on his behalf, 'e will be enjoying this day in a better place than here.'

'So be it. On with the day. Garr, how much damage did you inflict? Geoffrey, how long have we got before the bombardment recommences?'

'It depends on whether they have brought enough rope to make the machines good again. Did you damage the timbers, Garr?'

'No, lord, there was not time.'

'Then perhaps two days to re-rope the trebuchet, one day to bring the Onagers back into operation ... if they are left unhindered.'

'And what can we do to hinder them?' asked Nicholaa.

'Let Oswald return their rocks and balls, make their lives difficult. It would have been better if you had damaged the wheels.'

Geoffrey looked at Garr, as if the wish could be the fact.

Garr shook his head. 'Us took them pins from the wheels, but they can be replaced.' Then he put the question back to Geoffrey. 'Have ye got Greek fire, lord? A goodly dose o' that will slow 'em.'

'It would, but we do not have any, although there might be a way. Chamberlain, in your kitchen supplies how much fat can you gather?'

Turstan's eyes lit up. 'Quite a lot, and we have tar and lots of sawdust and splinters and the like. We could make our own Greek fire. Leave it with me.'

Turstan looked to Nicholaa for permission and received it with an unhappy nod.

She noticed my look of horror. 'Needs must, Father Bernard?'

I could only nod in agreement, but to hurl the fires of hell at Christian enemies, this war was indeed an unhappy event.

Then Lady Nicholaa straightened her back and standing erect pronounced a decision.

'Turstan, gather as many as you can around the great hall, what's left of it. I will see them and speak with them while this interlude lasts. They should know that the Lord is with them and that we are determined in our course. Garr, we are deeply saddened by your loss and your part in the defence of this place shall not be forgotten, but we need more from you. Please go back to Lady Matilda to carry your sad news, then ask that she sends out patrols to the south to see if they can contact William Marshal and his army. They must tell him how we are bottled up and that some early help is vital if we are to maintain the king's presence in Lincolnshire and its forests. Tell her to do all that is possible to impress upon him the urgency. Can you do this?'

'Gladly, my lady. 'Tis a strange circumstance when a man needs to serve two women, I had not thought it possible to be so steadfast in my loyalties. But you are a pair better than any men that I have seen. God bless you, my lady.'

Geoffrey spoke up. 'We are due a meeting tomorrow with Matilda's man, Ælfgar. We can go down to the river together, eh, Garr?'

Garr nodded and Geoffrey took him by the shoulder.

'Shall we leave now, my lady, to make arrangements?'

'Indeed. Now I will speak with my people. Let us go, Turstan, we'll gather them in as we progress.'

Lady Nicholaa led off down the steps, across the guard floor and down *those* steps into the bailey.

It was very busy within the castle with everyone taking advantage of the lull in the French bombardment to repair and strengthen the defences. I wondered how long it would last but Nicholaa had seemingly no such thoughts as she made her way swiftly over to the rubble of the former great hall, calling as she went, 'Keep up, Bernard, we might not have much time before they begin their bombardment again.' And to all who could hear her she urged, 'Follow me, put down your tools, I want to speak to you all.'

She was silenced as a tremendous bang and a whoosh went off to our left as a ball of fire left the castle to speed across the sky and land behind the houses in the upper town.

Oswald was sending back the fires of hell. The racket was echoed as another salvo of iron balls, fired from our Onagers, followed the fireball.

'Jesu!' I cried. 'This is Hades in Lincoln.'

But the folk did as they were bid and despite the clamour Nicholaa was soon standing in front of the hall, crowded all around with her hard-pressed people.

She was dressed immaculately, splendidly attired with a cotehardie made of camocas gold and silver stripes, and topped by a bejewelled hennin cone on her head — the very picture of a lady.

Standing quietly for a moment as if to gather her thoughts, she held up a hand and the crowd stilled.

'My friends, you have chosen the protection of the king in the form of my poor self in this matter, and I will not forsake you. It has been hard, so far, and I cannot promise that it will become any easier. Some of us will die, that is certain, but if you stay here, all of us will be blessed, that is also certain —'

She was interrupted by a burst of cheering. I was not sure whether they were looking forward to being blessed or dying, or both.

'That is certain because our cause is right: the king is our proper anointed king and the foreign prince, Louis, is not, and his proper place is in France with his father, King Philip.'

That raised a greater cheer; the French and their prince, and in particular the English who had sided with him, or more accurately, summoned him over the water, were held in contempt by a lot of the townsfolk — and that was why they were inside this beleaguered castle.

The lady surveyed her audience, and judging it proper, continued, 'If any here wish to retire, especially those with families embattled within my walls, they will be conducted away safely under a flag of truce, and we will hear no more of it.'

She waited for a response, until a solitary shout was heard, then enjoined, then the cry was lifted to the heavens.

'We stay! *We stay*! WE STAY!'

Then a great tumult went up, accompanied by yet another flaming ball sent over into the town without response, and I prayed that they could hear our voices on the other side of the walls.

Such cheering drowned all and Lady Nicholaa was forced to give up her speechifying and set off to return to her tower.

She was praised and blessed by all as she made her way through the pressing crowd and in the end Oswald surrounded her with soldiers to make her passage possible — it took me ages to push through the herd and the lady had gone into her tower long before I made it to the bottom of the steps. When I eventually reached the top and gazed down at the town and the lands surrounding it, I was hoping to see a glimpse of shining

144

armour in the distance, or a messenger at the gate, or another sign of a relieving force — but it was to no avail. All I heard were the sounds of industry coming from within the houses surrounding the walls on the northern side. The sound of hammers, the shouts of men, and the creak of rope, as those infernal machines of war were prepared in readiness to be set off again. Our present safety, I feared, could not last, and I wondered if we would have one night of peace before we were damned again.

8.

Ælfgar

The river was wide and deep, still swollen from the winter rains and I could hardly hear Garr's shouted response, but I recognised the knightly figure of Geoffrey from afar.

'Odd,' I said.

'What's odd, Ælfgar?' asked Brant.

'Where's Peter?'

We stared at the approaching craft. It had been slowed in midstream to avoid a pair of barges toiling their way up towards Nottingham. Heavily laden as the ferry was, the wind aided their sails, but the stream was against them, and progress was sweaty and slow as the four oarsmen put their backs into the oars. Then the ferry grounded in the shallows and stuck in the burgeoning springtime reeds. The ferrymen dropped the ramp to allow Garr and Hengist off, their ponies splashing through the mud then stopping to face me.

'He won't be joining us, Lord Ælfgar,' stated Garr. He knew the question in my mind.

'What happened?'

'Us had a successful mission ... until the end. 'E's staying within them castle walls ... forever.'

'Oh, I am sorry, Garr, he was a good man. I'll hear the full story later. How is it within the castle?'

'Bad. They needs relief, now.'

'I see. We know that William Marshal is at Newark, I should go there now.'

'You do right. Tell him to approach Lincoln from hereabouts. Us'll sketch it out on the ground. There is a way to confound the French, get around their forces and reach the castle.'

'Have you anything for Lady Matilda?'

'Aye, from Lady Nicholaa, tucked within me gambon, and a map for thee, lord, of the Frenchies' positions.'

'Show me the defences and then you go back to Laxton and report to Lady Matilda. We'll go across the river and seek out our commander-in-chief at Newark.'

'Aye, tha does right.'

'Dismount and gather in,' I called in my men. Looking across the water I could see Geoffrey disappearing into the far trees — we were on our own now, all decisions were mine.

'Brant, tell the ferryman to wait, we are crossing over soon. Now listen to Garr, he has a map to report on.'

It was near dark by the time we had been briefed by Garr and crossed the swirling waters. His map was now tucked inside my gambon.

'Stay by here, lord, my wife has a goodly pottage on the go.'

That was the ferryman's kind offer and although his hovel by the water had more than its share of aromas, mostly to do with the three pigs wallowing nearby, we sheltered in its lee for the night, ready to move at first light.

I gave him two pennies for his troubles, one for the crossing, and one for the horrible mess which he and his wife gobbled down greedily, and tempted my empty stomach to overcome the appearance of, and do likewise.

'Are we ready, Brant?'

'Aye, let's go, Ælfgar. Sixteen miles?'

147

'Sixteen. The track runs a little away from the river. It goes in the right direction but it should be dry.'

We reached the track half a mile from the riverbank and as we turned southwards Brant asked, 'When we reach a hostelry can we stop? I need to wash out the taste of that … stuff.'

So we headed south with our tongues hanging out until we reached Spalford and crowded into the local hostelry.

'Stopping to eat, my lords?' asked the host.

I looked at Brant for agreement, and he nodded faintly.

The host seemed to be clean enough and his fare might not be as greasy as last night's so I asked, 'What are you offering, fellow?' while looking at his ample girth.

He rubbed his stomach and chuckled. 'This hamlet is named Spalford Warren, my lord, on account of the excellent rabbits which is bred hereabouts. As you see I'm not averse to a bit o' rabbit pie mesen.'

I looked around me at Brant, Dunstan, and Raulf, all with their tongues hanging out.

'That'll be beer and rabbit pie for four, fellow. And we have not much time.'

''Tis on its way, my lord, fear not.'

The host was as good as his word and soon we were on our way, one groat short, but with full bellies and bearing down on Newark.

Soon reaching Langford, and as we passed the church, a priest, leaning over the wall, coughed politely and asked, 'Who be thee, strangers?'

Brant responded somewhat rudely, 'Matilda of Laxton's men; who be thee?'

'Easy, Brant,' I said, 'he means no harm.'

'True,' the priest agreed, 'I am the priest of Saint Bartholomew's and bid thee good morrow. However those fellows over there,' he said, indicating the trees nearby, 'might not have your best interests at heart.' So saying he waved at the trees and they came alive with half a dozen archers stepping out.

'Stay still, Matilda of Laxton's men, the men of William Marshal want to speak to thee.'

'Ahh!' I breathed a sigh of relief, *we had made contact — but such carelessness. It would not do, we could have been cut down for our neglect.*

A mounted knight emerged from the trees and headed towards me.

'Stay still,' I commanded my men, 'lest any move be misunderstood.'

'Good morrow,' he said, 'what business do you have here?'

'The king's business,' I stated bluntly.

'From whence?'

'Lincoln Castle.'

He paused, fiddling with the reins. 'You are?'

'Ælfgar, Lady Matilda of Laxton's man.'

'We still hold Laxton?'

'Aye, and Lincoln, if the commander-in-chief is so minded.'

'What can you tell us about Lincoln?'

'I can tell William Marshal a lot.'

I could see him thinking *are you dangerous, or useful?*

'Very well, I'll take you to my captain. Will ye unstring your bows?'

'We can. You are?'

'Serjeant Gerard of Winchester.'

'Pleased to meet you, Gerard of Winchester. Lead on,' I said, stuffing my bowstring into my gambon.

The presence of a large army became apparent even before the gatehouse of Newark Castle loomed high before us. Large detachments of troops were encamped in the fields all around and I suspected that they formed a metal ring with the castle at the centre. Passwords were demanded and responded to by our escort as we rode through the town, the thoroughfares increasingly busy as we neared the location of the commander-in-chief, William Marshal.

'Wait here,' commanded Serjeant Gerard. 'Dismount and I'll be back.'

I slid off my steed and stood still, like a cow outside an abattoir, watched by many eyes from all sides, and from above atop the monstrous gatehouse, with much metal clanking around our ears.

'I've never seen so many soldiers in the one place,' said a nervous Brant.

Our mumbled conversation was curtailed by the reappearance of Gerard.

'The commander is interested in seeing you. Come along, Ælfgar, your men can stay here in the guard chamber. If you would hand over your short sword, please.'

'Thank you, Serjeant Gerard. He is in that marquee?' I asked with some surprise, having expected to find him in the castle's great hall.

'Aye, he likes not the steps these days, and prefers to remain near the ground.' Gerard looked at me and with his admiration clear informed me, 'He is past seventy, but is as bright as the sun. Be careful what you say, he will test you on everything that you tell him.'

'Seventy, Jesu! Still, if he is that sharp you should prepare yourselves to move from here, for what I have to tell might well cause him to act.'

I was stopped at the entrance to the marquee where two enormous fellows took time to search me for concealed weapons. One of whom, it seemed to me, was a bit too interested in examining my crotch, but I underwent the humiliation in my duty to the king with forbearance.

The marquee was curtained inside, and I was stopped at the next drape by some imperious knight. Finely clad he was with a penetrating eye, and I confess to shuffling a bit as I met his gaze.

'You are Ælfgar of Laxton?'

'I am.' I left the response hanging, I would not be subdued.

'I am Peter des Roches, aide to the commander.'

'I have news for him.'

'For him alone?'

'It would save time in the telling.'

'Of Lincoln?'

'Of Lincoln.'

'How fares it?'

'Dangerously close to surrender.'

A somewhat curt conversation, but I would not bend to this Norman; I knew little about him.

'Wait a moment … if you please, Ælfgar of Laxton.'

He disappeared inside the drape but reappeared shortly and beckoned me to come forward.

Inside was quiet, with only three or four people present. Behind a table was the one I could see was William Marshal. He fixed me with a no-nonsense stare.

'What's this, fellow? What's to tell, Ælfgar of Laxton?'

He was curt, direct, and short of words. So I responded in a like manner.

'I met with Geoffrey of Serland last evening; he came directly from Lady Nicholaa. She is concerned about the lack of assistance for Lincoln, my lord, and they are hard pressed.'

'Hard pressed? Then they are in good company, the governance of England is a pressing matter.'

'You said that Geoffrey came from the castle. Who conducts its defence?' asked des Roches.

'Have I not made that clear, my lord? 'Tis Lady Nicholaa.'

He was unimpressed, and made *that* clear.

'That *woman*. Have the men lost something necessary for leadership?'

'I think not, and Lady Nicholaa manages very well without them.'

'Hah, a nice response for you, Peter. This Nicholaa sounds interesting,' said William Marshal. He waved a hand in the direction of a churchman sitting near the end of the table. 'This is Cardinal Guala Bicchieri, the papal legate in England. You've met Peter des Roches. You may speak freely, Ælfgar. Tell me how you come to be involved in this matter.' He paused, and, as if reading my thoughts, added, 'The king is safely out of this, I left him at Northampton.'

The king! Young Henry. The lad was but ten years old and I knew that the de facto king was staring at me now, and seventy years, if he was a day.

'Well?'

The command broke me from my reverie and my purpose here took over.

'I have … I had a map, it was taken from me at the door.'

Peter produced it. 'This one?' and stretched it out on the table for me to begin my briefing.

It was a full hour before I was done, or rather done with. At one point my briefing turned into a conversation, in which I played a diminishing part. It was fascinating to watch these three men, the most powerful in England, explaining, exploring, and deciding. At last William looked up and engaged with me.

'You have heard all this, Ælfgar, do you agree with the plan?'

'I?'

'Yes, you.' His eyes creased in the first semblance of a smile.

'Only the one thing extra, my lord. The crossing at Dun Ham, it should be guarded, it is Laxton's protection from the French on our side of the river. We have not enough men to hold it but if you could spare a few to help out?' I looked at him hopefully.

He waved an arm at Peter. 'Peter?'

'They can have a troop of six.'

'Archers, my lord?' I ventured.

'Crossbowmen,' was the response, 'we can't afford to give you archers.'

'I am grateful, my lord.'

'Give my greetings to Lady Matilda of Laxton,' added William Marshal, 'the women hereabouts seem to be a peculiar breed. We shall look forward to meeting her one day, when this matter is settled.'

'My lord.'

Time to go. I looked at Peter des Roches, bowed to the papal legate and was glad to return to earth with a sense of relief.

'Thank you, Ælfgar.' Peter had come out of the marquee behind me. 'We really appreciate this, and we shall meet again, I am certain.' He took my hand and smiled. 'God be with you.'

'And you, my lord.'

I went to winkle out my men, and wait for a troop of crossbowmen to take back to Dun Ham.

9.

Lady Matilda

'Orva?' My companion was braiding my hair in my bedchamber ready for the day.

'Yes, my lady?'

'Is your seax sharpened?'

'Always, my lady. Who do you have in mind?'

'Philip Marc.'

'Good target. What're you going to do?'

'*We* are going south. I don't see why we should sit here while Ælfgar is off, leaving us to fend for ourselves. Let's enjoy his absence and go and give the sheriff a poke in the ribs.'

'But who's going to look after Laxton?'

'There's lots who know better than me how to construct defences, and there's at least fifty men in the garrison who can wield a weapon. I'll place the captain of cavalry, Gavin, in charge. He and the Serjeant of the guard can keep the place secure, they have ten men-at-arms, and we, dear girl, will take Cenna and Godric to guard our tails.'

'If you're sure, my lady.'

'Don't look so alarmed, we shall be quite safe. Now, put my hair up and drag out my breeches, we are going for a ride.'

It took the rest of the morning to prepare but before midday we were ready. Father Albric stood gazing up at me when I was safely in the saddle and I knew that he was going to make one more plea.

'Is this wise, my lady? At least let me come with you.'

'You're needed here, Father Albric, to see to the welfare of the people, most especially of the wives and children. And if you will I would like you to organise a hospital for the treatment of the wounded, if there are to be any. It will be good for the garrison to have somebody to care for the sick. What say you?'

'I have not thought about it.'

I looked down upon his pate, shining in the midday sun; neither had I until that moment. I glanced across at Orva, also in the saddle, who smiled and nodded her approval.

Albric looked back up at me, a broad grin across his face.

'Do you know, that is a very good idea, my lady. Now, where should this hospital be, and how are we going to pay for it?'

'Within the inner bailey, it will be safest there. Talk with the carpenters, they can build you a hut. As for money, perhaps we could divert some of the coin which seems to be disappearing into Nottingham Castle. If I need to, I'll empty Sherwood of sheriff's men to do it, that's how.'

'Taxes are the king's to dispose of, my lady, but I'll make a start. I'll set about building you a hospital right now.'

'Good. If the king wants his taxes then I'll ensure that they are sent in the right direction, and make a claim to defend the collecting of them by having the stronghold of Laxton properly prepared to keep them safe. Worry not, I'll think on't. We're off. We'll return by tomorrow night.'

Leading the way to the main gate I halted before it and Cenna and Godric pulled in alongside.

'Where to, my lady?' asked Godric, looking at me boldly.

I was put off for a moment. Something familiar in his eyes, a man's gaze, nudged a vague notion in my head, something hinted at but not recognised.

'Rufford Abbey, and keep a sharp pair of eyes.'

'Two pair, my lady, two pair.'

Looking behind I saw that the sumpter horse was ready, with our food for two days safely in its panniers and some rolled up blankets over its back. The horse was led by wrangler Osbert on his palfrey, and behind that two of Gavin's cavalrymen, Ralph and Stephen bringing up the rear. Enough to keep us safe. But I wondered if I would feel brave enough to use the short sword at my side — I knew that Orva would not hesitate to use her seax... Oh well, the die is cast, Rufford Abbey next and a journey through the spring forest to contemplate.

The seven miles went by without incident although I knew we had been observed. Not surprising, as we deliberately rode through the centre of the hamlets along the way.

Orva had asked why.

'To allow messages to be passed to Nottingham, as they surely will be about my presence in Sherwood,' was the answer she got.

I intended to stay overnight in the environs of the abbey. As we approached, Orva asked another question.

'How far are we going?'

'As far as my southern border near Newstead. If Philip Marc has not reacted by then, we'll come back and assume that he does not want to face me.'

'Do you think that he will?'

'I'm not sure. These are uncertain times, he should have left Nottingham when he was ordered out by the great charter, but he hangs on still.'

'If he holds Nottingham safe for the new king he may have bought himself a reprieve.'

'True, and that's the uncertainty. Here comes one of our scouts.'

It was Godric. He seemed content as he approached, smiling his irritatingly attractive smile.

'My lady, the way is clear. Cenna has obtained permission for you to stay in the abbey in the nuns' travellers' quarters, and me and the lads can sleep against the wall. We'll be fine.'

Fine he might have been, but that was not what I wanted.

'No, we'll stay together, Godric, I want to be seen. I'll go and pay my respects to the abbess, but make certain there is a place at the fire for Orva and I.'

He looked at me oddly before nodding assent. He'll not make arrangements without consulting me again, I was thinking as we passed by where Cenna had stopped to make camp outside the wall.

We continued a few more paces before Orva dismounted and knocked on the great door.

A tiny hatch in the door slid open and a pair of eyes looked at me, but before I could speak the hatch slammed shut, then there was the sound of bolts sliding back and the great wooden door slowly creaked open.

'Lady Matilda, how nice to see you. Please enter.'

A nun, middle-aged and very small welcomed me. I glanced at Orva as the nun closely examined our clothing — and especially the weapons we were carrying — with disapproval, I could see.

'Thank you but no. I called to offer thanks for allowing us to make camp outside your wall, the shelter it provides will be all the welcome we need, I'm sure.'

'The abbess wondered if you might want to stay the night? You'll be most welcome, if you leave those things outside of course.'

Her eyes were flickering between the seax at Orva's waist and the short sword in my belt.

'We do not want to disturb you and we will be off at first light. Perhaps I could visit sometime later in the year, things are a little unsettled at present and there are matters that I must attend to in the forest.'

'I see,' she replied, although I doubted that she did. 'I'll relay your intentions, Lady Matilda. God bless you.' And the door closed.

'What was that?' asked Orva.

'A Cistercian nun,' I replied. 'There's not many around, they're mostly French.'

'D'you think they are on the side of Prince Louis?'

'I doubt it. They are on the side of God, they might not know about Prince Louis, or about men generally.'

'Oh. Don't they really?'

'Come on, Cenna will be setting up. I'm pleased that we brought blankets, it might get cold later.'

'Mm, we can snuggle up if it does.'

'Yes,' I replied, although I wondered if I could provide her with the warmth that Ælfgar would usually. 'Ah, they have a fire going already.'

The men had formed a circle around the fire and with the horses hobbled further out we seemed quite safe. Godric came over to speak as I was tucking my sword by my side under the blanket.

Kneeling down beside me he spoke in a gentle voice.

'All is prepared, my lady.' He was speaking to my eyes because that was all that was showing above the blanket.

'For what?' I mumbled through the cloth.

'A safe night, my lady. Someone will be on watch all night, they will change at intervals, but...'

'But?'

'If you should require someone to be nearer to you...'

'You would be willing. Thank you, Godric that will be all. Goodnight.'

'Goodnight, my lady.'

Orva shuffled in closer and I felt her warmth, I went off with her last whispered words in my ear. 'D'ye think that they *really* do without men?'

'Shh, put that out of your mind, girl.'

It was cold that night, and although we curled up in the glow of the fire reflected back off the wall, at some point in the night I felt Orva wrap herself around my back. Thank you, I thought as I drifted off into deep sleep once more, you're a good friend.

Although Orva made it possible for me to catch a little sleep, she was also the one who woke me up before daybreak.

Startled by the sound of someone retching I sat up to see Godric bent over Orva, who seemed to be in distress. I leapt up, scrabbling for the sword digging into my ribs and ran over to them. He turned, saying, 'She is not well, I'm trying to help.'

'Leave me now, Godric. See if you can find me a flagon of water. Oh, Orva, what ails thee, girl?'

'I don't know, I woke up feeling sick.'

She coughed and spat out, her eyes were red but she gathered her spirits and was soon laughing at herself.

'Phew, what was that? We ate the same last night. Are you well, my lady?'

I was, but I had an idea.

'Has that ever happened before?'

'No, never. I'll think I'll leave food for now. Thank you, Godric.'

Godric was back with the water skin and everyone else was now up and about, the men heading over to water the bushes.

In less than an hour we had cleared up and set off down the well-worn track to Newstead Priory. I was making a point of marking my progress with religious houses, to warn anyone of ill intent that these sacred sites were within my domain.

Around midday we stopped outside the priory buildings for something to eat. I did not bother the Augustine brothers, many of whom were out in the fields toiling, as is their wont — but I had made my point, my forest and I'll patrol it.

We received many a cheery wave as we went by and were soon back on the narrow trail through the forest on our way home to Laxton.

'Very disappointing, that sheriff,' voiced Orva when we stopped in an open pasture for a rest. She might have regretted that remark because there came a shout from up ahead and Godric came at full gallop out of the trees.

'Sheriff's men, I think, coming along behind me.'

'How far?' I asked. But he ignored me and shouted something to our men.

Before I could react Osbert had pulled his horse and the sumpter horse in front of myself and Orva, while Ralph and Stephen stationed themselves on either side of the line of horses. Cenna and Godric went some way off in the pasture with their bows at the ready.

'Ooh, an instant castle, they are good.' Orva had it right; we had been ring-fenced with horseflesh and metal.

I saw the flash of sunlight off a helm before they came out into the open: three horsemen, all fully attired in military garb and one carrying the banner of Nottingham. The leader slowed a little when he saw us lined up across the track. I watched as he noted the archers off to the sides but he continued until he was only ten paces away.

'Good morrow, ladies,' were his opening words, eyes searching the woods.

'Good morrow, knight,' I responded.

'Who are you? Know you not that this is the sheriff's forest?'

'I am Keeper of the King's Forest, which the sheriff is not.'

That was greeted with silence. One of his comrades coughed and one of their horses whinnied which broke the tension.

'*You* are Matilda?'

'*Lady* Matilda to you, knight. Have a care with your manners.' Orva put the fellow to rights and received a filthy glance for her trouble.

'I won't ask who you are, wench. Speak when I question you.'

As we were partially hidden by the horses, he did not see Orva's hand settle on the handle of her seax. I hoped that he would not push his fate much further.

'I'll decide when and who she should answer,' I said. 'What are you doing in my forest?'

'There's a report of strangers, we've been sent to clear them out.'

'I haven't seen any. You can report that to your lord.'

He edged his horse a little nearer, and our archers tightened their grip and raised their bows … visibly.

Then he realised something.

'Why're you dressed like men?'

'Because we're strange. Haven't you heard about us, odd women?' answered Orva and I was hard put to keep the serious expression on my face as she moved closer to me.

A sneer came across his face, such of it as could be seen under his helm.

'I've heard of that affliction. Nothing a man couldn't cure, I suspect.' Undressing us with his gaze. He pulled on his reins

161

and made to pass us by, but not without another barb, aimed at the wrong target. 'I should be careful, you two, there's wild men in these woods, and whether you like it or not you have enough of the appearance of women, if you know what I mean.'

'We'll be careful, thank you for your concern. God bless you.'

Riding by to follow their lord the two horsemen gave us a searching look. One blew a kiss to Orva, to which she responded with one of her most radiant smiles and eased out her seax before smacking it back into the scabbard.

They were out of sight before I gave vent to some quite nervous laughter.

'Where did you dream that up from? My reputation!'

Cenna sniffed and Godric smiled, having returned from their trip across the mead.

'How did you get rid of them, my lady? They seemed unhappy.'

'We prayed,' said Orva.

'Let's get on,' I instructed, 'we've a few miles to cover yet and I think that we might have sent the sheriff the intended message. It's a narrow path ahead, they came along it in single file. One of you go up ahead, and one of you stay in the rear in case the sheriff's men decide to catch us up.'

'My lady,' replied Cenna. 'You take the rear, Godric,' and he rode off into the trees. Ralph entered the trees next and I followed with Orva behind me.

It was rather pleasant in the greenwood, with the new growth showing all around. The birds had finished their morning song but the place had the smell of spring about it.

We had been moving for a while when Ralph pulled up suddenly and I almost ran into the back of his steed.

'What?' I hissed.

He beckoned me forward and I drew alongside him, filling the track.

'What bothers thee, Ralph?'

'I'm not certain. Something, listen.'

I fell silent and did as he had ordered. There was nothing to be heard.

'I can hear naught, Ralph … not a—'

'That's it, nothing, no birds, not a sound,' he said with urgency. 'We might have heard from Cenna, at least a horse whinny. We've not seen him for ages.'

I was flummoxed, what to do?

'We should find him. Could he have taken a different trail, perhaps?'

'We haven't crossed another since the last hamlet and he waved at us from ahead when we passed through there.'

I suddenly felt cold. Orva coughed behind me and I could feel some edginess from Ralph.

'What should we do, Ralph?'

'Carry on, my lady,' Godric's voice came from behind me, firm and confident. I turned in the saddle to find him alongside Orva, smiling that damned smile and daring me to contradict him. 'Weapons unsheathed, arrows nocked, eyes alert, but carry on,' he continued. 'We are here to take control of the forest, are we not, my lady?'

I nodded. 'Of course. We keep going, we'll find Cenna up front somewhere, I'm certain.' Although I did not feel it. 'Move on, Ralph, we can't sit here all day.'

From there on, anything and everything seemed to betoken danger; a twig dropped from a tree, a dog barked in the distance, something scuffled in the undergrowth — all highly dangerous and all about to kill me.

I kept glancing into the trees on each side as we rode along returning my eyes to find Ralph's comforting back after every inspection of the woods — and then he stopped.

'What now, Ral…?'

'Jesu! What the…' He had not time to finish his words when a rock came hurtling out of the trees and struck him on the helm. He fell sideways off his horse, dropping his sword as a rough-dressed man leapt out of the bushes and grabbed hold of his reins.

Ralph staggered to his feet and was searching for his weapon when I felt a tug at my leg: someone was trying to pull me off.

Clamping my knees I resisted as long as I could, holding on to the reins with one hand whilst unsheathing my sword, but I couldn't stop him and he dragged me off the saddle. I might have considered that the mossy ground would be soft but when I fell onto my back all the breath was knocked out of me and it was easy for him to leap on top.

Laughing at me with breath so foul I almost choked, he began to fumble with my waist belt — *oh no, not that*. I struggled, then realising that I had managed to cling on to my sword I raised my arm, but he cackled his stink at me and seized my wrist, almost breaking the joint. I was forced to drop the sword and he returned to undoing my belt.

I kicked and twisted to no avail, trying to get my other hand free from his grip. My wrist hurt so much… He had horrible teeth, and I could see all of them, so wide was the grimace on his face.

Letting go with one hand he struck my face so hard that my eyes lost focus and then he was loosening my waist belt again.

A shadow came over us, this much I could see, and as my eyes cleared his expression changed to one of surprise and he let go of my hand and belt to grip the blade of the seax which had penetrated his throat — all the way through from one side to the other.

Orva pulled it out so violently that his head fell over to one side and I was showered in blood and began to gag, but when he fell off me I sprang up and looked around for my sword, found it and tried to take stock of the scene — Orva had disappeared.

Running further along the track I found Osbert trying to pull a lance out of the chest of someone lying on the ground and looking back I could see Godric, who was trying to reach me by forcing his way past Stephen, himself hanging trapped by a foot from his left stirrup.

His horse had barged sideways into the bushes and so was prevented from moving and injuring further poor Stephen, who was shouting to be let free.

There was a scream from further along the track, and I turned to see Orva wildly stabbing at a man's chest until the fellow fell down leaving Orva straddling Ralph, as if to save him from all evil.

Then it went quiet again, and I could see that the sun was still shining, and the leaves were still green. My shoulders slumped and I started to walk towards Orva.

She threw up on the path and started to tremble. I took her in my arms and tried to calm her.

'Hush, my Orva, hush, 'tis all over now.'

She gasped a few sobs and then bracing her shoulders said urgently, 'Come on, my lady, we cannot remain here.'

'You're right, who's left alive?'

'Osbert, Godric, Ralph lying there, and where's Cenna?'

Ralph moaned and sitting up said, 'What happened? My eyes have gone all funny. Jesu, something's thumping in there.' He took off his helm but I could see no blood.

'You'll be fine, we must move away from here, see if you can find Cenna.'

'Cenna? That's why I stopped. He's staked out on the track, his wrists have knives sticking through them and they've severed his feet. Don't go there, my lady.'

He knew that I would, he knew that I needed to see for myself — even so the blunt horror of the sight was enough to turn my stomach. I said something so banal that I did not know it.

'Dear God, what happened to the nice ride through the trees?'

Orva had calmed now and we stood together, and then I was assailed by a fit of trembling. I had heard men talk of this after a battle, it passes, but she also wanted to leave this place.

'Is he dead?' I asked. I felt a comforting arm come around my shoulders and looked up to see Godric's unsmiling face.

'Of blood loss, my lady, no one could survive that without urgent attention. Come, turn away, I'll prepare his body to take back. But we must be gone, we're in no condition to resist a further such attack.'

'Stephen's got a stab wound in his leg,' shouted Osbert, 'I've cut him free but he can't walk.'

'Get him back on his horse,' I replied, 'then lead him.'

'I'll get Ralph mounted again then we can get off back to Laxton,' added Orva.

'How far are we away from Laxton?' I asked Godric.

'About eight miles, my lady. We can get there before dark, but we'll have to leave these bodies behind.' He glanced at the would-be robbers. 'I'll load Cenna's body on to his horse and we'll make good time.'

It was a horrible eight miles. When I stopped trembling and asked Orva a thousand times if she was well, my body feeling

166

as heavy as a horse-weight, I started to worry about the next thing I, we, would need to face — Ælfgar.

It was a sorry cavalcade that passed through the main gate into the outer bailey at Laxton. Two bloodied women, one knight with his thigh strapped, hanging on to his reins, another with a raging headache, and one footless cadaver draped across his horse.

There was silence at first before the community burst into life, and by the time we entered the inner bailey we were surrounded by the concerned, the helpers, and the curious. Two or three goodwives, partners to knights of my household, more or less dragged me off my steed. There was not much resistance, I felt dead in the head.

'Hold a moment.' I managed to find some strength. 'Some of you see to Orva, she saved my life.' Then she was taken away to her hut as I was dragged and half carried into my own.

'Worry not, my lady,' gasped Ealdgyd as she began to strip me of the stinking shirt, 'we'll have you out of those clothes before you know it. Water!' she cried. 'Elfreda, fill my lady's tub, then get across to Orva and make sure that she is attended to properly.'

Without a word more I was stripped naked and sat down on a chair wrapped in a blanket. I watched dumbly as they filled me a tub of steaming water.

''Ow you feeling now, my lady?' asked goodwife Ealdgyd as she helped me to step into the water.

'Oh, I'll live, no punctures,' I said as I looked down to inspect my body.

'Good, we don't know what we would do without you to guide us,' she said as she rubbed me down with a cloth. 'I've sent that clothing off to be burnt. D'ye think you could refrain from men's clothing now, and be happy in a kirtle?'

'Possibly, probably. Let's up now, I think that I'll take a nap.'

Upright, towelled down and clad in a fresh gown, I climbed the steps to my privy chamber and lay thinking on the bed. I must have nodded off but a knocking on the stairs woke me. The chamber was deserted, water tub all gone and the place tidied up — thank you, Ealdgyd, I thought.

It was not long before Orva poked her head into my chamber.

'My lady?'

'Hallo,' I said, 'come and sit with me. What did he say?'

'I've not approached him, I wanted to speak with you first. I've got a secret to calm him.'

I looked at her stomach. 'Are you?'

'I am.'

'You're going to distract him.'

'I am.'

'You're in no danger?'

'Apart from squeezing his son out of my body, no. He thinks too much of me to hurt me.'

'You are brave, you might save my life again.'

'We get by, my lady, can't be doin' with a dull life.'

'Survivors, that's what we are, life's survivors.'

I pondered on how to deal with Ælfgar, and his pregnant Orva. When I mustered the courage I found him at the doorway of his little hut.

'Good morrow, Ælfgar,' I opened tentatively, 'are you refreshed?'

'That was not wise, my lady,' he began, quietly, so that only we could hear, 'such foolishness can cost us everything.'

'You are the only man that I will take such a comment from, Ælfgar. I apologise, it will not happen again.'

'Then let it be done with.'

'Thank you, Ælfgar. There's more I should say.' I put a hand on his shoulder and drew near before speaking to him quietly. 'That's twice we have fallen out and this time was due to my foolish ambition. I apologise for placing Orva at risk. Will you forgive me, for I love her as much as you do.'

'If you will leave the killing to me, my lady, I will leave the loving to you.'

'But you must involve me, Ælfgar, it is my responsibility, do you not see?'

'As you wish, my lady.'

I released his shoulder as Orva emerged and placed an arm around his waist.

'What're you two plotting?' Orva asked.

'We're talking about you,' Ælfgar said, 'how much we love you, and how I need to take better care of you. Forest patrols are not going out with you in them again, no matter who leads them.'

'Oh, am I reduced to the place of a goodwife now?'

'I doubt that will suit you,' I said, 'I'll find a position for you, as befits your ways.'

'As you say, my lady,' Ælfgar agreed. 'But let's address the business of the day. We'll leave someone at the river to keep us informed, and to show our commitment. This William Marshal is best kept sweet. I should think we will need his good offices in the future.'

'Indeed, Ælfgar, when the armed struggle is done with there'll be a courtly battle to engage in, I'm certain of that. There are some who have eyes on this place … and Nicholaa might find unwelcome visitors at her gate.'

'And the forests?'

'Especially the forests. Now take care of Orva, you need to learn some baby talk, my proud warrior.'

10.

Lord Geoffrey

Another crash resounded across the bailey as I went to find the Lady Nicholaa at the top of her tower. It was daylight again and the French had resumed their onslaught.

'You should come down, my lady,' I implored. 'And you, Basilea, we cannot do without our bravest souls.'

'Oh, Geoffrey, are you certain that Matilda's Saxon will find William Marshal?'

'As certain as I can be of anything, my lady. He and his dark archers will find their way through the fires of hell if they need to. Besides, he loves you greatly, he admires you with undisguised expression.'

'Never mind me,' Lady Nicholaa said, 'I'm well past my allotted time. Every day is a bonus and I intend to make the most of it. Father Bernard, Chamberlain Turstan, attend me closely. Basilea, you go down now, my child, we have no need of you for a few moments, and I'll be down shortly.'

But the girl merely shuffled her feet and shifted towards the steps a little. Another bang took our attention.

'See, Geoffrey,' the lady continued, 'the houses along Earninga Straete and those next to the upper town wall are gradually being demolished by Captain Oswald's counter bombardment, but we are perilously close to having no roofs left within the castle bailey. The people are sheltering in rubble now. Is there nothing else that we can do, nowhere else they can take shelter?'

'Very little, my lady, but we can make better use of the rubble. They'll need to help themselves more.'

'I'll help, my lady,' said Basilea.

'And I,' added Father Bernard, 'I'm sure that I can handle a shovel.'

'I cannot sit comfortably in your tower, my lady, while this…' Basilea waved her hand across the latest vision of hell which the castle bailey had been reduced to… 'worsens by the hour.'

The outlook was starting to seem somewhat helpless. For the first time I could envisage the end, a long lingering reduction of all the buildings inside the castle curtilage and a gradual disappearance of all living bodies within it — pounded into rubble or splattered into the resemblance of a butcher's yard. Who, if any, would survive?

'How are the stocks of food, chamberlain?' Lady Nicholaa asked.

'The water wells, as you know, remain high, but the food is fast disappearing. We had not counted on so much being lost to the bombardment, or so many in here seeking shelter. We have had no new supplies for several weeks now and I reckon that we have two weeks … perhaps three, at the most, before we start cooking our horses.'

'Can we not do more to prevent those damned trebuchets launching?' beseeched Chamberlain Turstan.

'Very little,' said Lady Nicholaa, 'we only had the one chance to dismantle them. They will not be so careless again as to let our men wander around at night. We can only work within the walls to keep our people safe and pray that Ælfgar has found William Marshal.'

'Shall I go out to search, my lady?' I asked.

'Not yet, not until we see the sun glinting on their helms, Geoffrey. I will not lose you on some fantasy journey. We will wait it out. Bernard, have the days of your visiting the archdeacon gone by?'

'Probably. There are not many English outside the east gate, they are all foreign by the appearance of them and I would not expect a safe passage. What did you want?'

'Apart from prayers?' the Lady replied. 'Cannot we get some of these refugees into the cathedral?'

'You can't risk Father Bernard, my lady,' I objected, 'have you seen the ragged-arse collection of scoundrels who wander past the end of the steep hill? I would not trust them by a hand's width not to harm anyone from the castle. When I go out to greet William Marshal, I will be fully prepared, depend on it.'

'Very well, Geoffrey, you are annoyingly correct. Chamberlain, come with me and we will go among my people and try to help them a little more. To begin I will visit Captain Oswald at the east gate, I will see these foreign beggars at first hand.'

When we reached the bottom of the tower steps Turstan went off to organise the terrified people while I set off towards the east gate with Lady Nicholaa and Bernard, where Bernard was stopped by Chirurgien Godwine as we came to the improvised hospice.

'Are not you supposed to be here giving aid, Father Bernard?' he asked.

'Wherever I am best placed, Godwine. Lady Nicholaa, you asked for me to attend you in the tower in case you required prayers.'

'Of course, prayers, but please let him help here, my lady,' entreated the blood-spattered Godwine. 'You will be more use

172

attending the wounded and the dying than on your knees, or perhaps you could do both.'

'Stay with him, Bernard,' Lady Nicholaa agreed. 'You can pray while you work.'

'Yes, my lady.' So saying he rolled up his sleeves and followed Godwine into the shambolic hospice.

We edged into the wrecked building. It was protected by earthworks of rubble facing the northern wall and supported by a palisade of tree trunks, hurriedly sunk into the ground to try and give the place cover. It was a distressing scene, with so much noise from the wounded, and children crying or sniffling with fear. We came across one mother huddled in a corner. She had a baby at one breast and a child of about three or four at the other.

'My dear,' Lady Nicholaa bent over her and tried to tug her shawl around her, 'is that necessary?'

'She has milk, my lady, which is more than most other mothers have, and there is little left for children.' Chirurgien Godwine had come to stand alongside us and spoke with pain in his voice. 'Everything we have is being turned into a pottage which all must survive on, I'm afraid, but some of the younger ones cannot digest it properly, hence that mother for has been driven to desperate measures.'

'Geoffrey.' She grasped me by the arm. 'Has my larderer nothing better for the children off the breast?'

'I shall find out, my lady, there are two cows in the stables with the horses, they have been supplying yourself and the garrison soldiers.'

'Oh, for God's sake, Geoffrey, redirect all the milk into here, Godwine can distribute it as he sees fit.'

'I'll make the arrangements, my lady.'

'Good.'

I watched and wondered, then passing among those lying still and those dying I began to wonder if this was a price worth paying. So much suffering for a king's person. Was this what is required by a kingdom, or by someone's desire for power?

'I'm going on to the gate now,' Lady Nicholaa said to Godwine, 'God bless you in your endeavours. Father Bernard is here to help you, and if there is anything else that I can do…?'

'More cloths for dressing wounds, and more water carriers, another to keep boiling water.'

'I'll see to it.'

We were outside now and I had half turned towards the gate when one of those Onager balls came over the wall whistling towards us. Lady Nicholaa was dragged to the ground by a Serjeant and it missed me but there was a sickening crack from behind and when I looked round Godwine's body was standing upright with no head, his lifeblood pumping skywards, and as I watched his body collapsed backwards to land in a heap in front of me.

'My lady! Are you injured?' Father Bernard was at Lady Nicholaa's side quickly. 'Come, turn your head, my lady, such a sight.'

'A sight, Bernard? A reality more like. Help me up, I think that my limbs are sound. Is anyone else hurt?'

'There may well be, but you are the most important person in this shambles. Can you stand?'

'Get me to the gate,' she commanded. 'I must see our enemy for myself.'

'Thank the Lord. You are unhurt, my lady?' I asked.

'My pride is hurt, my heart is hurt, and my chirurgien has lost his head. Father Bernard, you are now in charge of the hospital. Now get me to the gate.'

We made as much haste as Lady Nicholaa could manage and soon we were in the shelter of the eastern barbican. Captain Oswald had been summoned and soon came clattering down the gatehouse steps, his face a picture of anxiety.

He began to ask me a question, 'What are you doing here ...?' but Lady Nicholaa held up a hand.

'Stay, Oswald, it was my idea. Now, I will go to the gatehouse battlement. Take me up those steps, I'll see these scoundrels for myself.'

Oswald hesitated before replying grumpily, 'If you wish, my lady. May I take your arm?'

Oswald and I competed to help her but Oswald was the nearer and won the task of getting her up on to the battlement.

'Easy, Geoffrey. You can bring me down, if I am still in one piece, that is.'

We brought her up, where she was surrounded by knights and struggled to see through the crenels and a host of shields.

'Good knights, allow me some space to see,' she implored them.

'Please stay behind the merlons to shelter, my lady,' I said.

'Where are these unkempt beasts who surround us and rain rocks upon our heads?'

'Just watch the area between the top of the steep hill,' said Oswald, pointing, 'and the first house on the opposite corner. They scuttle across like the rats that they are, bringing up supplies from the lower town for the war machine crews.'

'Can't you pin them with your crossbows?' I asked him.

'Surely, that's why they are in such a hurry to get across, but there is not much time and we don't hit many.'

'Oh. A practice gallery.'

'Quite. Ah! There's some now,' cried Oswald, as the twang of several crossbows rent the air and we watched at least six bolts as they chased the ill-dressed ruffians across the muddy space. The last one fell with a bolt in his side and sure enough, as rumour had it, he was bare-arsed. The pannier he had been carrying fell and its contents scattered in the mud.

'No more rations from him,' I scoffed.

'What does this tell us, Oswald? Geoffrey?' Lady Nicholaa asked.

Oswald answered first. 'It confirms to me what other things have indicated, my lady. That Prince Louis has brought with him the dregs of the French countryside: his father, King Philip, has sent him numbers, not soldiers. The only competent men he has with him are the machine operators and his fellow leaders' own personal troops, the rest are there to make up the numbers.'

She thought for a moment. 'You are making much of one varlet with a bolt in his ribs.'

I spoke up in support of Oswald. 'Garr's night attack and some more night-time scouting have revealed a lot, my lady. The trebuchet and the other war machines are tended by men of a better class than the others, while such leaders as we have identified are suitably attended with well-mounted and shod knights, but the rest of them ... tch, tch! Rabble! They will not stand and fight against a disciplined army. We can and must hold this place, my lady, if you will allow me to say so.'

'Say it, Geoffrey, say it, we cannot be doing with platitudes in our position.'

It was true, we could hold this place. The French had not even attempted to assault the walls, they had not the quality of men necessary, and if their only strategy was to reduce the place by hurling rocks at us — we could wait them out.

'Oswald, how much do we have in the way of rocks?' Lady Nicholaa asked.

'Near as many as they throw at us, my lady.'

'Is our second trebuchet near completion?'

'Another two days, but we do not have enough timber to construct a third, unless you take away the protective walls that many folk are sheltering behind.'

'Don't do that, but train more crews and keep the counter bombardment going throughout the night. Destroy all the buildings in front of the town north wall and force the French back until they are out of range, then do not waste our bolts and arrows. We will not sit here and be reduced to rubble and torn flesh, do you understand, Oswald?'

'I do, my lady, I do. And tell that to the people on your way back to the tower, for you are now in my way. Geoffrey, escort Lady Nicholaa off the battlement, if you please.'

'Captain Oswald,' she declared, 'you are a rogue, and I love you dearly. Come Geoffrey, let us be off, there is visiting to do.'

Later, when we were eating in Nicholaa's quarters, Oswald came to find us again.

'Is William Marshal in sight?' Lady Nicholaa asked.

'You guessed correctly, you saw the flash of helms in the direction of the river.'

'No, the sentries above our heads told of a kerfuffle at the gate, and we surmised,' I said. 'Time for me to go, my lady.'

'Indeed, Geoffrey, take care. Oswald, see Geoffrey safely out of the west gate, he is going to guide the army here.'

'Yes, my lady, the time is here, time for retribution I believe.'

'No, Oswald, not retribution. Take prisoners when you can, and killing is to be the last resort, if you please. There are enough corpses within the castle walls without adding more Christian souls to the tally. Bernard, write this down in our diary. On the nineteenth of May, William Marshal's army was seen. Off you go, Geoffrey, and may God's grace attend you and keep you safe. Captain Oswald, see him out, our relief is nigh.'

'Indeed, my lady. Come, Geoffrey, how quick are you at descending the steps?'

'Why are we running?' I demanded of Oswald.

'You said that you wanted to leave, Geoffrey,' he replied.

'Jesu, Oswald, throw me out the gate, won't you.'

He laughed but pressed on.

As I puffed my way across the rubble-strewn greensward to the western gate I could see the wranglers preparing my steed. It was only a palfrey, I liked not those destriers, they had an evil eye and besides I was not expecting to fight, merely to gallop off down to Dun Ham ferry and meet William Marshal's army coming northwards.

'Mount up, Geoffrey, your moment of glory approacheth.'

Oswald, the sod, was laughing as he pushed me into the saddle.

'Laugh when I return, cheerful dog-turd, and make sure that the gate is open when I approach, it might get difficult if those Frenchies figure out what's ado.'

'Pull back the drawbridge,' he commanded.

'Done, Cap'n,' cried the Serjeant.

'Open the gates,' shouted Oswald.

I watched as the portal to the next phase of my life, or death, opened before my eyes. My muscles tightened on the saddle as that bugger Oswald gave his final instruction.

'Off you go!' he cried as he slapped my horse's withers. 'Your men are with you.'

I had forgotten about them. Hurriedly checking behind I saw my squire, Elric, and a patrol of six all ready and waiting for me to go. So running out of reasons to stay I kicked the animal in its ribs and clung on as it sped off down the slope, across the bridge and headed for the cover of the woods fully two hundred paces away — and hoped that they would follow me closely.

There were shouts from my right as we made for the cover of the trees. We had been spotted and a few bolts went whizzing past. They had not enough time to load and take aim properly — it would be different when we returned, they would be watching for us then.

Slowing down on the level ground I set a pace that would take us to the river without fatiguing the horses and in due course we broke clear of the trees and entered the boggy lands leading towards the ferry, where we were naturally confined to the track by the wet ground on either side. I called a halt.

'What is it, Lord Geoffrey?' asked my Serjeant, leading his steed alongside mine.

'Ahead, see.'

Heading north, parallel with the river, was a seemingly endless line of men, banners waving, helms glinting. The noise of their chatter reached us from fully a mile away.

'Look, the head of the convoy has stopped,' observed Serjeant Bertin.

'They must have reached the ferry. Ælfgar's men will have stopped them. Come on, we will approach cautiously, lest they misread our intent.'

'Aye, lord,' responded Bertin of Rouen, a man not easily caught out through mistakes, he had lived too long in the shadows of war.

Once we left the shelter of the trees, the track leading to the ferry crossing was nothing more than a long island, surrounded as it was on both sides by the remains of the winter floods. There was no way to leave it save by turning back.

As we approached, the became clearer.

'That's the banner of the Bishop of Winchester!' I declared.

'Good,' responded Bertin, 'I was beginning to worry. There's a patrol coming towards us now, lord.'

'Wave my banner vigorously,' I called to Elric, 'lest you want to be perforated.'

Half a dozen horsemen came bearing down on us at breakneck speed, two abreast and lances lowered. As they closed in I held up a hand and they reined in to halt twenty paces before me.

'Who are you?' the leader demanded ungently.

'Geoffrey of Serland. Here to greet you on behalf of my mistress, Lady Nicholaa of Lincoln.'

'We know of her; follow me.'

Without waiting for an answer he waved a hand in a circle about his head and his patrol began the difficult task of turning around on the narrow track ready to retrace their steps. When they were ready we followed them meekly towards the king's army.

We stopped at the junction of the tracks — or rather our guide did, I ran my horse into the rear of one of theirs and halted suddenly.

'Wait here,' the patrol leader shouted back. I was becoming a bit irritated by the fellow's behaviour. I was, after all, a man of some distinction — not to be treated with disdain by anyone who chose to do so.

The man galloped off to where the banners were flying and soon returned only to shout at me again.

'Geoffrey of Serland, come forth, if you please.'

At least that was polite, obviously someone in the royal party knew of me. I made my way towards him between the lines of his cavalrymen. One of them slipped sideways and he and his horse ended up standing in the soggy ditch. I held back a snigger and smiled at the patrol leader innocently.

His composure broken he said with some irritation, 'Bishop Peter would like to speak to you. Please ride alongside me, my lord.'

'Lead on,' I replied — bursting to laugh.

As we closed on the banners the patrol leader spoke, although I knew not his name, nor did I care, rude sod.

'That's John Marshal with the bishop, William Marshal's nephew. You'd best go forward now, Geoffrey of Serland.'

I left his side and walked my horse towards the pendant gonfalons, and banners, all aflutter in a strengthening wind, a right royal sight they were — but not as impressive as the seeming endless lines of troops waiting behind them.

Jesu! Wait till the Frenchies see this lot.

The Bishop of Winchester, Peter des Roches, the same person being also the Sheriff of Hampshire, sat comfortably on a great white destrier. He wore fine raiments encrusted with various symbols and other statements of power, both spiritual and temporal, with the slightest glimpses of chain armour beneath, and smiled casually at me as I approached.

'Geoffrey, dear fellow, we've not yet met, I believe?'

'Not to my knowledge, your grace.'

'Shall we dismount, Geoffrey? This creature is giving me an unholy ache.'

'Certainly, Bishop Peter.'

Standing to one side of the track, Peter offered the back of his hand, upon which I saw his ring — and taking the hint gave it a little peck as a signal of respect — *something new every day.*

Bishop Peter, looking to his side at a younger man, said to me, 'This is Fawkes of Bréauté, one who witnessed the Magna Carta two years ago. Ah! And here is Ranulf, Earl of Chester: we are conducting the next phase of this war together. Come, tell us all that we should know about Lincoln Castle … and this remarkable constable you have, Lady Nicholaa.'

Before very long a tent had been set up by the trackside on the only small piece of dry ground for miles around, and we were soon sitting around a table, complete with maps and charts, and a pair of scribes writing down our every word — organisation the like of which I'd rarely beheld. I closely watched the two newcomers. Fawkes I was wary of, a mean face and sharp eyes which darted about the place, I thought him not interested in me. The Earl of Chester was an older man, quite short in stature, but holding himself upright in a manner which bespoke his confidence. I thought that I could trust him.

After only an hour or thereabouts the group had the grasp of the problem, including Fawkes, who was deceptively inattentive but showed an understanding of things through his questioning of me; sharp he was.

Then Peter called for refreshments. It was in between snatches of venison and a few draughts of wine that a plan did emerge and was duly written down, with everyone's part in it described in detail. Then I had the pleasure of watching Peter,

Fawkes, and Chester bring forth their captains to explain and allocate tasks to each and all and send them on their way to brief their men in turn.

Three hours only, I thought to myself as I returned to my men waiting patiently at the junction, three hours to plan the relief of a castle under siege — remarkable. I could hardly wait to return to Lincoln and give Nicholaa the good news. Tomorrow the siege would be lifted.

Finding that my patrol had been fed by the royalists in my absence, and were in good cheer, I pulled them to one side to watch as the bulk of the army set off northwards. Led by the Earl of Chester, and the ranks of crossbowmen by Fawkes, they would bypass Lincoln and head for Stowe, some eight miles north of the town. From there they would turn east to join the main north-south route of old Earninga Straete, which passes through the very heart of my town, then treading its path, assault Lincoln from the north.

Bishop Peter remained with us. He kept with him twenty of his arbalesters, and twenty knights of his mesnie, all mounted. He was waiting for William Marshal to catch up. We would set off to the castle before dawn the next day with me in the lead.

I felt great elation. Here was I, Nicholaa's senior knight in Lincoln, now the guiding light for the redoubtable Peter des Roches — fame at last. I prayed that I would not be the moth to someone else's flame on the morrow; a dangerous position, being at the front.

We were a bit exposed here on the flatlands and I worried that I would not get the good night's sleep that my body required and mentioned it to Bishop Peter.

'Do you think, Bishop Peter, that we could move away from the river's meanders and mists and find better shelter in yonder trees?' I pointed to the woods at the end of the track from whence we came, a full mile away.

'Oh, a good idea,' he replied, 'but wait until William Marshal passes by, I'll introduce you and we will tell him of our plans.'

'Introduce me to William Marshal?' I blurted out.

'Indeed, Geoffrey. What you see passing before you now is but a fraction, and glory will be along the banks of the Trent ere long, when our commander-in-chief reaches us. Be patient yet a while and I shall introduce you.'

Jesu! My day kept improving. To meet William Marshal!

The bishop's tent disappeared, loaded into one of his wagons to go onward; all he had left was a pair of sumpter horses with interesting-looking panniers.

'Comestibles, for the morn,' he confided to me, and apart from that we were left with our horses and what we stood up in, hardly an impressive show of force.

'Here he is!' cried Elric, now very excited.

'Calm, lad,' soothed Bishop Peter, 'the commander appreciates those around him who are of a tranquil aspect. It aids thinking, you see.'

Elric nodded enthusiastically, his head bobbing, bending at the waist, and then a half genuflection. To be spoken to kindly by Bishop Peter had the lad all of a dither. I was also impressed with the kindness thus shown.

There were no trumpets sounding but banners aplenty as the very heart of the king's army made its purposeful way towards us. It made no attempt to hide its strength, but instead took every effort to mark its progress and impress whosoever was watching.

The commander-in-chief was in the middle of a ring of metal; large men, iron-clad, and of frightening aspect. Then as

William neared I could see that he was indeed a man of many years gone by, and quite unfrightening.

Bishop Peter hailed him and the convoy came to a halt.

'William, good morrow, well met.'

'Peter. Well met indeed. Who's that you have by your side?'

'This is Geoffrey of Serland. He is the lady Nicholaa's best knight, and hath brought us intelligences from Lincoln Castle.'

'I must hear this, is this why my army has disappeared into the distance? Can't fight a battle without my army at my side, you know. Help me down, I will hear this, er, Geoffrey, at first hand.'

The man was no taller than me, although twenty years my senior and had the gift of seeing past my eyes into my soul, it seemed, as he stared at me: *trying to determine my worth.*

'Well then, Geoffrey of Serland, what advices have you given my commanders that has sent them scurrying onwards? I expected to turn up towards the castle at this point.'

'Good advice, William,' spoke Peter. 'It is in some way a ruse, to fool the French into believing that we are on our way northwards.'

'They are watching, eh, Geoffrey?'

'Aye, Lord William, yonder ridge, upon the end of which sits the castle, provides many a viewpoint. I'd be mistaken if I thought that we were not under observation as we speak.'

I was surprised that I had spoken thus, so openly, my worries about meeting the man dismissed. He was after all a man; flesh and blood as was I.

'So what now, Peter?'

He was blunt. I supposed that he had too much to think about to waste time on pleasantries, but Peter took no heed.

'Chester and Fawkes are taking the army a few miles further. There they will organise it into its attack formations, and then join me up there.'

He pointed out an area at the northern end of the ridge.

'Geoffrey will escort me, and he is to show me a means whereby we can enter the town without needing to assault the north wall and gate.'

William looked at me without an eye-blink, he was churning this plan over in his mind. Then, to my surprise, he stepped closer to me and placed a hand on my shoulder.

''Tis a good plan. I like it. Let's do it, Peter. Geoffrey, we could do with a few sound thinkers in my mesnie. If you want to leave Lincoln, I'll give you employ.'

That stunned me. Leave Lincoln, and leave Lady Nicholaa, but to work close to the king... I had not time to give it more thought because William Marshal was being shoved back atop of his horse and was ready for the off, a fast mover for one so advanced in years.

'See you inside Lincoln Castle on the morrow, Peter. Move!'

And off he went. The silence of his departure left a hole in the very air.

'Doesn't take him long to make up his mind,' I said idly.

'No,' quipped Bishop Peter, 'let's hope that we have it right, else he'll soon change it … about me, and thee.'

Jesu! Fame or infamy, I was in that stew now, right in it.

I watched the disappearing William too long and was brought back to the present by Bishop Peter.

'Are we moving into the trees, Geoffrey? Can't sit here all night.'

'Yes, Bishop. Mount up, men, let's find shelter, we'll need some sleep before we see the sun again.'

I was looking across the turgid waters of the Trent. On the far side the sun was touching the horizon, casting a blood red shadow across the landscape, a portent perhaps for the chaos we intended to wreak when it appeared on a different horizon on the morrow.

I had not spent a night in a forest with a bishop before but it was an unexciting experience. Once we had settled into a grove and posted sentries, he ordered the contents of those panniers being carried on his sumpter horses to be brought out and shared — which was as well, for *we* had naught with us, apart from the usual water skin slung on the side of our steeds.

I settled down with my men, and Peter with his, exchanging pleasantries and sometimes asking questions, but truth to tell we had ordered all the details of the impending action long ago. 'Tis odd that when men settle in among the trees the animals that live there come out only when dark descends. Sitting with my back to a tree, and with increasingly cold and achy bones, I slept but fitfully. As the dark claimed the skies the wild ones came out from the places they had occupied during the day and claimed sovereignty with their voices. Some snuffling gave notice of hedgehogs nearby, a nightjar called, a fox barked in the distance and I was woken from slumber by one of those screeching owls, protesting at my presence from above my head. That startled me so much that sleep fled for the rest of the night.

Thoughts of death flitted through my head and the lightening sky in the east was a welcome sight; actions would now replace my distressing thoughts. I was not alone. Quiet coughing and the increasing sound of wakening men watering the bushes took over the dark spaces of my mind — time to go.

'We're ready, Bishop Peter,' I called gently across the glade.

'As are we,' he replied. 'Lead on, Geoffrey, and God be with you.'

'And with you. Mount up, men, let's be about the business of the day, there's a siege to lift and a town to rescue.'

Sending two scouts ahead did not ease the flutterings in my stomach. I did not expect to gain entry to the castle as easily as we had escaped from it; the French must know that there were comings and goings and although we had got out we had been spotted. So it was with trepidation that I caught up with the scouts at the edge of the treeline on the north-west corner of the city's north wall.

'How goes it?' I whispered.

'It seems quiet, lord, but there were some scufflings in the trees along to our right, and there is an idle fellow lurking by the ruins of that first building over by the corner of the city wall.'

'I see.' I looked behind along the track. Bishop Peter had halted his men and was waiting for a decision from me. I held up a hand to stay him and spoke to one of my men sitting patiently behind me.

'Ask the bishop to wait. I will go out first and trot over to the castle gate. I'll ensure that there are archers on the battlement and give him cover while he rides in behind us. Is that clear? He is to wait until I am inside.'

'I understand, lord.' And off he went, to return in a moment. 'He agrees, lord.'

I gave the signal for my six to close up and whispered, 'Keep close together in two lines, and stop for nothing — we are going directly for the gate. Ready?'

With archers now scattered among the trees and free to shoot or make a dash for the gate, my six horsemen were taking a firm grip on their lances, loosening their swords in their scabbards, and tightening their grip on the reins.

Two hundred paces to go, and I could breathe the tension. It was too quiet by far.

Poking my steed's nose out of the trees, and sensing rather than seeing, I decided to put some urgency to the matter, giving the horse a kick in the ribs. He had hardly put a spring in his step when the fellow by the building gave out a whistle and some men broke cover from the trees to our right ... and—

'Watch out, lord,' called Elric, 'to your left.'

The idle fellow by the city wall had been joined by a half-dozen companions and was bearing down on us as fast as his legs could carry him. I lowered my lance to charge at him but felt it grabbed. One of those coming from the right had closed upon us too quickly by far and was trying to pull me off my horse.

Releasing the lance caused him to fall to the ground, giving me time to unsheathe my long sword and, kicking at the flanks of my palfrey, spring towards him — I merely pointed my sword at his face as he stood up intending to spit me with my own lance, when the tip went into his eye and came out of the back of his skull.

Twisting the blade levered the top off his head and that was him done for — praise to the sword-maker's skill in producing this fine Damascene blade.

Then there was a thud on my left side as a bolt hit my shield, penetrating and lodging in my saddle. This was too dangerous, crossbowmen are the curse of the cavalry knight.

'The gate is opening, lord,' cried Elric, 'let's get through it.'

I looked back. One of my Serjeants was slumped over his saddle, and we would not last much longer out here.

I heard arrows whizz by in the air, our archers were busy.

'Grab his reins, Elric,' I shouted, 'lead him in.'

'Have a care,' he called back, and I looked to my right where another Frenchie was charging towards me. I spent too much precious time keeping my palfrey under control as I turned it towards the running man. The horse was now frightened, it not being a destrier, and unused to war, but it headed for my attacker and we galloped towards him.

The man stopped when we were barely six paces off and hesitated; that was his doom sealed. Kicking into my steed's flanks to quicken it yet more we crashed into him. He went under and I clearly heard the cracking of bones before a scream drowned out the noise.

'Onward, Lord Geoffrey, go for the gate, we are behind you.'

Elric again, faithful, calm young man that he was.

Not hesitating this time I made for the gate. The drawbridge was in sight, the gap over the ditch closed and I crossed it to a great cheer from above — the walls were fully manned by archers and crossbowmen, and the Frenchies were being forced away under a hail of missiles.

Oswald leapt at me to bring my steed to a halt.

'There are more horsemen behind, let them in,' I shouted, fearful for the Bishop of Winchester's life.

'Serjeant!' Oswald shouted up at the battlement. 'More horsemen coming, they are with us,' he yelled.

'Captain!' came a disembodied reply from above and as I slid off my horse Peter des Roches came galloping apace through the gates, and I watched as my men made it through, all safely in.

'Jesu!' exclaimed Oswald, staring at the bishop's colourful tabard. 'Who's this popinjay?'

By now I was sitting on the ground staring at the blood oozing from my left leg; the bolt in the saddle had slashed me.

'That, old friend, is the Bishop of Winchester. Have we a chirurgien nearby? We have some casualties for his attention — and he is also the Sheriff of Hampshire.' And I fell back, exhausted.

'What, in one person?'

'Indeed,' I replied gazing at the sky, 'the very same. Take him up to Lady Nicholaa, I'm knackered.'

'Quite, old friend, but the chirurgien hath lost his head. Father Bernard has recruited some of the town's goodwives to assist in patching up the wounded. You just lie in the middle of the road and I'll take our be-titled person up to the tower.'

'God help us,' I responded weakly.

'He will, but he has the appearance of Father Bernard.'

'By God's miracles, is there any beer to be had around here?' I asked of no one in particular. And no one replied so I sat up and watched as Captain Oswald escorted both the Bishop of Winchester and the Sheriff of Hampshire across the wrecked castle bailey. *Jesu, there's bugger all left standing*, I observed.

11.

Lady Nicholaa

'The Bishop of Winchester, and Sheriff of Hampshire, my lady,' Captain Oswald hollered as he entered my chamber.

'Thank you, Captain Oswald. Please stay and help us to brief our rescuer.'

'Lady Nicholaa,' wheezed the bishop. 'You are well protected up here, it is a shambles below.'

'Bishop Peter, how nice of you to call, you have been expected for some time. Are you the sheriff too?'

'Indeed. Lady Nicholaa, we have…'

'Do call me Nicholaa, your grace, no need for all these titles. We have little time to be doing with formalities around here.'

'I'll manage with Peter, 'tis an honoured name, after all.' He grinned. 'It has been very difficult to bring all the elements of an army together in such a short time, Nicholaa. We have only recently mustered at Newark, you might know.'

'I do. Well, you are here now: what next?'

'Ah! Your fellow, Geoffrey, he wants me to inspect an entrance into the town, it is in the west wall, and I caught a glimpse as we galloped in.'

'Mm, you enjoyed the ride?'

'Not much. You are too much beset with enemies in here.'

'We are, and we wish not to be. Where is William Marshal, Peter?'

'He is approaching from the north as we speak, I am to provide a diversionary assault through the town wall postern while he attacks the north wall portal.'

192

'The New Port Arch, it is a Roman relic. I had that postern gate you seek blocked up, but it is accessible from the outside, the rubble can easily be removed. How much time do you have?'

'None, Nicholaa, I should be on the battlement to inspect the postern from above as we speak.' He turned to Oswald. 'How long has this attack been going on?'

'Several weeks, your grace.'

'We are late bringing help. Sorry for the delay, Nicholaa.'

Oswald asked Peter to follow him outside to form a plan. I insisted on accompanying them onto the battlement, despite their protestations.

'See where the town wall abuts the castle wall directly beneath us, and then runs northwards?' said Oswald, as we hid behind the merlons of the wall. 'Halfway along you can see the postern gate which Lady Nicholaa referred to. It opens outwards so that the rubble blocking the inside can be scooped out and an entry effected. Then the town wall runs along eastwards until it reaches the New Port Arch.'

'The Roman gate?'

'Indeed. Note that the top can be seen from here. We have reduced the town houses which were set against the outside of the wall to rubble, and they have had to move their small catapults and rock throwers back out of range because we can reach them with our trebuchet. They were hidden behind the houses when they first attacked but now we have the advantage.'

'Well done, Captain Oswald. Where is Geoffrey?'

'He has been injured but is being attended to.'

'Good. I'll prepare my men in the barbican,' said the bishop, 'we must be ready when the commander-in-chief arrives, for he will be expecting the fullest support.'

'What plan do you envisage, Bishop Peter, if I might be so bold as to ask?' asked Oswald.

'One in which you will play a full part, Captain Oswald.'

I was also a bit puzzled by the bishop's intentions, and questioned him as we descended the steps down into the bailey behind the western gates.

'You intend to lead this attack yourself, Peter?'

'Indeed, Nicholaa, carrying the holy sword of justice.' After he had explained Oswald's role in support of his coming action we went back up to the battlement so he could begin to execute it.

Oswald shouted out orders to the men: 'Watch for the bishop's men coming out of the gate; they are to open the postern gate and attack the rebels defending the New Port Arch from the rear. We will provide cover for them. Questions?'

'When?'

'As soon as the main army appears on Earninga Straete. They are heading straight to the Roman arch from the north.'

'That's about now, lord; look yonder.'

One fellow was pointing towards the arch where there was much activity. We could hear the noise — something had disturbed the Frenchies.

'Helms, in the distance.' Another shout from the right of the castle battlement. No doubt about that, William Marshal had arrived.

We moved to the top of the barbican and looked down on to the bishop's head.

'Your helm, Bishop Peter,' called Oswald, 'the time is now. Pull the drawbridge, and open the gate.'

The guard sprang into action: the day was for winning.

Peering over the parapet I watched as Peter burst forth through the gate. He was not a normal sort of bishop, not like the archdeacon they had in the cathedral across the way. He led the charge of his knights as they crossed the drawbridge over the ditch and turned right along the town wall. Stopping, they formed a semi-circle around the postern gate as his now dismounted crossbowmen ran afoot after the horses, and ten of them took up defensive positions among the cavalry. Then the second ten, with crossbows ready, joined with some spade carrying sappers who set about demolishing the rubble blocking the gate.

It did not take long to clear and as they burst through the postern I heard a great shout coming from the direction of the New Port Arch — the army had engaged the French. Now was the hour.

Peter's crossbowmen, including the ones guarding the cavalry, were pouring through the postern. Commanded by Serjeants, they formed into lines and began to advance towards the north town wall — the very rear of the rebel defences. The enemy, lackadaisical, but engaged to their front eventually noticed that they were under attack from behind and raised the alarm — but Peter's frontline crossbowmen were picking their targets and loosing, to be immediately replaced by the second line, allowing the first to reload their weapons. By this means they advanced relentlessly upon the rebel positions. Too few to retaliate, they were quickly cut down and left to squirm and die.

Engrossed by this ordered manoeuvre I missed the fact that Bishop Peter was leading his cavalry off to the north, until someone shouted, 'Those horsemen are leaving.'

The bishop was off to circle round and join the rest of the army coming down Earninga Straete — excellent, the flow of things was now in our favour.

I followed Oswald along the battlement towards the north-east corner where we could see the action around the arch clearer. He waved a command down to the trebuchet crew to cease their action as there was now a danger that they would hit our troops attacking the gate and wall.

The top of the New Port Arch could be clearly seen now that those houses between the castle and the arch had mostly been demolished, together with the desperate efforts of the defenders along the battlement to combat Peter's men. I watched gleefully as bolts from the bishop's advancing crossbowmen struck home, forcing the defenders to turn, shocked, as they became threatened from two directions at once.

Scaling ladders must have been brought into play because heads were popping into sight all along the north wall; too many, I judged, for resistance to last with their attention distracted from both sides, and it was true: soon the climbing warriors gained access. I watched them fight their way along, with Frenchies and English rebels being cut down and falling or being thrust off the battlement as resistance crumbled.

'This is no place for you, my lady, your safety,' Oswald said, turning to me, as Father Bernard scrambled to join us.

'A pig's head for my safety, how are we doing?'

'Excellent, look.'

William Marshal's men were now over the wall and inside the gate, which was being pulled open, and then the cavalry burst through the arch and it had become a rout with the Frenchies fighting a rear-guard action along the straete.

Oswald called down into the bailey for the reserve crossbowmen and archers to follow us up to the top of the gatehouse — he was expecting some action in front of the cathedral soon.

The shouts, screams, whoops and groans meant that we could follow the assault as it progressed along Earninga Straete towards us. The battle was coming close.

Oswald called out to the archers and crossbowmen along the eastern gate and wall. 'Make ready and commence loosing when the Frenchies break cover from what remains of that house on the corner, I want them bottled up in Earninga Straete so that our soldiers can get to grips with them. Crossbowmen, pick your targets; archers, I require a rain of missiles; make them fear the very sky.'

The first of the French, now in full flight, appeared and immediately the sky was filled with death. Each archer having three arrows continuously in the air at once, and then the lower trajectory of the crossbows began to find their targets. I heard the thud as the nasty bolts struck home. At this range they would penetrate the best of armour, which few of the French possessed. Cries in both French and English began to reach the gate. But then French horsemen began to emerge from the top of the steep hill. They were fighting back, they made a difference, and the retreating rebels started to push back against our troops coming along the straete. It was in the balance.

'Pick out the horsemen,' Oswald commanded the bowmen, and I watched as the counter-charge started to falter. Neither the archers nor the crossbowmen needed to be particularly accurate, they only needed to strike the horse or the horseman to render them useless, and soon the French cavalry was in disarray, trying to turn and seek shelter back down the steep hill, the screams of stricken horses and men fouled the morning air.

Our joy increased when we heard the unmistakeable thud of horses in full gallop. Our cavalry was now in pursuit and men desperate to escape were chancing the dash from the sparse cover in the straete at full pelt across the open ground to the top of the steep hill, where the fortunate few disappeared behind the houses and out of sight.

Someone tugged at Oswald's arm. 'Captain, look behind.'

'Jesu! Who's that?'

A cavalry troop were galloping across the middle of the bailey from the direction of the west gate, they must have been given access. They pulled up in an orderly fashion short of the east gate, from which battlement Oswald poked over his head.

'Who are you?' he shouted down.

'Fawkes of Bréauté,' was the reply, 'Can we ride through?' He pointed at the gate beneath our feet.

'Admit him,' I told Oswald, before he turned and relayed the message down to the gate Serjeant.

We made our way back to the town side of the gatehouse as Fawkes's horse galloped through the gate. His men were running down or piercing each and every fleeing rebel they caught, showing no mercy, and galloping onward into the front of the cathedral, trampling all over the graves.

There was the sound of more cavalry coming down Earninga Straete. It was William Marshal, at last. Oswald screamed for the aerial barrage covering the straete to stop and we watched as these new horses were pulled up with some difficulty as they emerged onto the open ground and tried to avoid plunging down the hill.

My attention was drawn to the cathedral close where Fawkes's men were taking retribution on those who had hoped to find sanctuary in the house of God. The graveyard in front of the cathedral was now a battleground, it was disturbing — but the doors remained closed and the rebels trapped there perished before my eyes.

As silence imposed itself upon the dreadful scene of carnage, I heard myself breathing as heavily as if I had just run up the steep hill. Calming myself I took a good look around me when the noise of cheering began and soon I could not hear myself think.

A detachment of cavalry had gathered together at the junction of steep hill and Earninga straete from where their leader brought them towards the gate. He stopped beneath my gaze and sheathing his bloody sword, he looked up.

'I say, d'ye think that we could enter, damn thirsty work this.'

'Oswald, let him in. My God what a sight, 'tis a butcher's yard out there,' I gasped, shocked.

'Yes, Lady Nicholaa, a bad day for Christian souls. And the graveyard, oh dear Lord, what a sad day is this,' Father Bernard added.

I took Father Bernard's hand to descend into the bailey and greet my guests.

Making my weary way down the steps inside the gatehouse gave me time to ponder on the events of the past few weeks. How had it come to pass that English had been driven to fight English, and some had sought the assistance of a foreign prince?

'Is it not strange, Basilea, how men make such a difference of the same idea?'

'What idea is that, my lady?'

Basilea was not puffing as we came down the steps, not like me anyway — *I hope that my life's struggles are over for a while.*

'That all men are equal under a common law.'

'King John did not agree,' was her reply.

'He signed the document, the great charter,' added Bernard.

'Under duress, he claimed,' I pointed out.

'Then there should have been more discussion. Look what dissent it hath wreaked upon our world,' said Bernard as we emerged into the shelter of the barbican.

'I agree,' I conceded, 'but to invite a foreign prince to rule over us is a reaction without merit.'

'I agree, my lady. But what's this?'

As we emerged from the gatehouse a sight to cut off conversation lay before us. A line of cavalry was drawn up in an orderly fashion, with the last horseman sat in front of us and the head of the convoy somewhere along the road leading from the east to the west gates. They were being watched, in awe, by seemingly all the citizens left alive who had sought to shelter within the castle walls. Some chatter had begun between the mounted men and the folk but it was stopped by command of their Serjeants — a disciplined lot, I thought; no wonder they soon despatched the Frenchies and their English rebel allies.

'Jesu! God preserve us,' murmured Basilea, as if she were witnessing the chaos in the bailey for the first time.

'Madam!' A man short in stature but long in authority emerged from between the two lines of horses. He was accompanied, or rather surrounded, by a larger, fiercer escort of dismounted cavalrymen.

'That must be Ranulf de Blondeville, Earl of Chester. I have heard that his chin is a bit near to the ground,' murmured Bernard into my ear.

I held back a titter. He still looked rather dangerous, and his height probably didn't matter when he was on the back of a horse.

'You are Lady Nicholaa.' More of a bark than a question, but I nodded gracefully.

'Allow me to congratulate you, madam, your defence of this place is widely spoken of. I am Ranulf of Chester, and privileged to meet you.'

He bowed and held out a hand, I offered mine and received a kiss upon it.

'I would offer you some welcoming food and drink, Ranulf of Chester, however you have entered my domain at the wrong time as we are without much of either. Thank you for coming... As you see,' I waved an arm around the bailey where the wreckage of a once ordered establishment could be seen, 'there are not many vertical walls left.'

'Indeed, a valiant defence. Let me help.' He called over one of his captains. 'Captain Eduard, see to it that the supply wagons are brought up immediately, no nonsense. I want tents erected, clear the ground over there, and set kitchens over there, my tent over there. I want the good folk of this garrison to be properly fed before dark falls.' He looked at me belatedly. 'With your consent, Lady Nicholaa.'

I was stumped for words. Control had swiftly passed from my grasp, I thought that I might say something about that, but it was true, the priority was to get the folk fed and housed.

Steady, stay calm ... and be gracious.

'You are generous, Ranulf. They say that an army marches on its stomach, but I heard nothing about sharing its fodder.'

'Fodder! Hah, I'll give thee better than fodder, madam. You'll eat from a laden table this night, and I swear it. Come, take me on a tour, I want to see how you have resisted this scurvy set of foreigners and treacherous English. We have twenty-six of their leading scallywags shackled up, and they will rue this day, I'll warrant.'

We had hardly set off when there was another kerfuffle at the east gate.

'The commander! William Marshal is here.'

The cry went up soon followed by the beginnings of cheering as the crowd caught sight of the chief knight of all England.

I was left standing, together with Bernard and Basilea, as Ranulf of Chester ran off to greet his leader.

'Well!' tutted Basilea, 'how rude is he?'

'He appears to think that he has won this place. Better watch him, my lady, an ambitious little twerp, I can see,' added Father Bernard.

We were joined by Oswald, and Geoffrey limped over from the direction of the rubble which was now our infirmary.

'I thought that you were helping out in the infirmary, Bernard,' Geoffrey aimed at my priest. He was obviously not enjoying being lamed.

'Be gentle, Geoffrey, I took him away to help me up on to the wall, there was much ado up there.'

'You should see the graveyard, Geoffrey, 'tis an awesome sight,' chipped in Bernard.

'See the graveyard? No thanks, that'll be too soon whenever it is.'

'Here is the Marshal.'

The Earl Marshal of England, William, was upon us before we knew it, and he had more attendants than a shepherd has sheep in a pasture.

'Lady Nicholaa,' he greeted me without hesitation, well briefed I could see. 'I'm sorry that we are late. Ranulf says that you have been waiting on our arrival for some time. I apologise. 'Tis a complicated thing, assembling an army.'

I had heard this before, still, better be friendly, this man controlled the thoughts of young King Henry.

He too, took my hand to his lips. This was becoming boring, could men not think to do something more useful than this?

'He tells me that he has arranged for some supplies to be brought into the garrison. If you can gather all your men together I will praise them for their fortitude over the last … er … period of the siege.'

'A four-week ordeal, William, and the women helped too.'

That pulled his enthusiasm back a little. Arrogant sod, talking to me like that — kingmaker or not, this is my domain.

'Quite. Ranulf tells me that you are to take him on a tour of this … rubble.'

Then he went off without further ado. Any fondness I had for the great man and his organising our rescue was fast diminishing.

I was now surrounded by metalled men and whisked off to tour my beloved castle grounds. I had felt an oddly renewed energy when the battle had ended, but now? Left in the wake of the searching Ranulf, why did he need to dash about so? I'd experienced enough for the day.

As we neared the steps to my tower I propositioned Basilea.

'Come on, help me up the steps, I've had enough of this circus.'

'Yes, my lady,' agreed the faithful Bernard, 'enough is enough. I need to pray, for this has been a terrible day.'

'*He*, can tour without us, he has enough company. The day is late, my lady. Have a little nap and I expect that you will be ready to join the celebrations this evening,' encouraged Basilea.

'Celebrations? What's to celebrate, I might have gained and lost my castle all in one afternoon the way those rude men are stomping all about it.'

'Have a little sleep, my lady, and you will be better prepared to discuss things with William Marshal.'

'Very well, I'll think on it. Ah, here we are, only another two flights of steps. Give me a push, Basilea.'

Father Bernard followed us up to the next, privy floor and went into the chapel. Basilea gave me help up to my bedchamber, where I flopped on to my bed and tried to forget about the day.

It was dark when I felt Basilea's gentle hand on my shoulder.

'There's more to the day yet, my lady ... if you can manage it.'

With my thoughts returning I moved to raise myself up. Creaking and cracking as I was, I wondered if I should bother.

'More?' I asked. 'More of what?'

'You have slept soundly for a while. There has been plenty of activity within the castle, the army has been put to good use and it is much tidier now. And they have supplied food and drink, and lots of men to run around a-doing for them.'

'Oh, those ones? The loud, metal-cote wearing ones?'

'The same. They have set up tents, kitchens, a new infirmary, all the things we have watched being destroyed these past few weeks.'

'Really? Jesu! I can smell cooking. Help me up, please.'

'They would like you to attend a feast in their marquee.'

'Their marquee! When? I stink like a dead rat, of which there are plenty hereabouts.'

'Now means as soon as you can. I've had your tub filled, it steams outside in your ante-chamber.'

'What would I do without you? What should I wear; something regal, as befits a lady, or something befitting a castellan?'

''Tis laid out on the bottom of your bed. Tonight you will be the vision of female authority, both a lady and the defender of the king's realm at one and the same time.'

I looked at this vision of loveliness. Brains and beauty, a dangerous combination I thought.

'You learn well, Basilea, and you have chosen well, make certain that you choose a man with the same attention to detail.' She laughed. 'And don't giggle, you lose authority, and especially do not expose your thoughts, let them worry about that. Now help me out of these mud-spattered garments.'

Ah, the joy of a hot tub, it eases aches and pains and is all too easy to fall asleep within, but not, alas, with my hovering Basilea.

'If you can, my lady,' she said, as much an instruction as a question.

'Is it time?'

'Yes. Lord Geoffrey and Captain Oswald are hovering down on the guard floor, I think that they are waiting to escort you.'

'Escort me?'

'There,' she said, ignoring my remark and standing back to inspect me. 'Every bit the lady castellan.'

She had me in a dark blue cainsil, gathered at the waist by a woven gold belt. Beneath she had teased me into dark blue hose, tied above my knees. In deference to the warmer weather she placed only a light cyclas with armholes finished in an armigaut over my shoulders. And so light were the eschapins which she was now sliding on to my feet.

'Stay seated, my lady,' she commanded as the last thing to be mounted on my poor old body was one of those damned hennins upon my head.

'Can't I make do with a filet ... or a nebula?'

'No, you are to be head and shoulders above the crowd, let no one in the throng lose sight of you. You are the guest of honour at this feast. I care not who organised it, or paid for it.'

'But this hennin makes it feel as if my head is falling over.'

'It seems quite high, but you will get used to it. Besides, we can leave early if you desire, my lady, no need to witness the long awaited bacchanal.'

'True, they deserve one of those, and I am long past such revels, and Captain Oswald is hovering to escort *me*?'

'What do you mean, my lady?'

'You're not blind, and I've seen how his tongue hangs out when you are near.'

'Tongues seem not to be in short supply when men are near me, my lady.'

I was stumped to think up a quick reply to that. At least the girl had the decency to blush, and that was revenge aplenty for dressing me up like some court doxy — hah!

As I suspected, Captain Oswald did not put up much resistance when I suggested that he took Basilea's arm and let me go with Geoffrey. I could do without the usual manoeuvring tonight.

The bailey was heaving, noisy and drunken, and there was more than one couple at it in the shadows; life among the rocks.

'They might have a thought for tonight's romping in nine months' time,' remarked Geoffrey.

A line of braziers and lit rushes led the way from the bottom of the steps across to where this new marquee had been set up, and a pair of army captains waited to guide us. It was all very well organised, and considering that a battle had raged hereabouts only a few short hours ago, quite a miracle.

Inside the marquee was oddly quiet, the only conversations were being held at a gentle pitch, and they were hushed when I walked in. There was a single aisle in the middle of a line of tables, full of strange captains and Serjeants. None of my men were present and I turned to Oswald to ask why.

'I've arranged something for later, my lady,' he whispered, 'fret not.'

Then I was asked by one of the army captains to proceed to the top table with him.

'Bishop Peter and the Earl of Chester await, Lady Nicholaa. Please come along with me.'

I took my time, and nodded and said hallo to someone at each table as I wandered along in a stately way towards the top table, but I lost Basilea, Geoffrey, Oswald, and Bernard along the way as they were guided one to each table as we processed. Separating me from my closest, I could feel my ire rising as Bishop Peter stood and gave me a warming smile.

'Lady Nicholaa, our honoured guest. Please to come and join us here.'

There was a space between him and Ranulf of Chester so I was conducted around the table and guided to sit there.

'Where is William Marshal?' I asked.

'Gone to Northampton, Lady Nicholaa. He needs to attend the king; the news of this victory will cheer him greatly.'

'Where are my people?' I demanded, looking down the length of the tent.

'Each to a table, Lady Nicholaa. They will be well hosted by my captains, see?'

He was right. They had been sat opposite respectable-seeming soldiers and Basilea was already the centre of their attention, although the shadows on the faces of Geoffrey and Oswald did not augur well for future friendships. Then my attention was taken by my hosts as they began to question me about the defence of Lincoln.

We had not gone far when there was another entrance at the far end.

'Ah!' said Bishop Peter, 'here is the archdeacon, with Fawkes of Bréauté. We have invited him in to try and make amends for the looting.'

What looting? What have I missed by sleeping?

'Archdeacon, please be seated,' commanded Bishop Peter. I wondered who the other two chairs were for. 'And you, Fawkes.' The two new guests sat themselves at opposite ends of the table. I was surrounded by strangers and isolated from my people, it all felt quite deliberate.

'Tell us about this looting,' said Bishop Peter to Archdeacon Peter. I paid full attention.

With his face at its most miserable the archdeacon began to recite a list of complaints.

'It began almost immediately the French ran off down to the river. Those of *your* men who had slaughtered the rebels outside the cathedral door lost no time in coming into the cathedral and laying waste to our treasury. There is nothing of value left. Inside the church lies in tatters.'

There was clear tension in the air, and the bishop took the reference to *his* men badly, even though by the telling of the tale they'd clearly been out of control.

'Yes, Archdeacon, there have been punishments and as much as possible will be returned to you in due course. I will point out that rumours have linked the cathedral to the town and the rebels. If my men have dealt out what they see as punishment to both, then that surely is understandable?'

'It is not as clear-cut as you might think, my lord bishop.'

'Indeed? Then we shall discuss matters of the church outside of this gathering. For now we are here to celebrate the marvellous defence of this castle by our honoured guest, Lady Nicholaa.'

That was the moaning Archdeacon's worries dismissed, so now it was my turn. I sensed that I must be on my guard. *There are currents unseen in this gathering, but what are they?*

'How many men have you here?' This was Ranulf of Chester — obnoxious little turd. Brusque and rude. I glared at him to let him know that his manners had strayed, so the bishop spread some unction on the surface of the conversation.

'Indeed, Lady Nicholaa, however many you had they were deployed famously, none could have bettered this epic attention to duty. The king owes you a debt of gratitude.'

I wondered how much of the bishop's oil was real and how much was an attempt to repair Ranulf's damaging remark.

Then he blurted out another. 'I heard that you offered King John the keys to the castle. Had enough, eh?'

'I never tire of my duty, Chester, be assured.'

Fawkes sniggered and the archdeacon coughed into his goblet.

Bishop Peter launched himself into the turmoil.

'As you can see, Ranulf, there is no lacking of spirit in the lady, I'm sure that her offer to the king was merely a polite gesture, she would not have expected him to remove her from office.'

'Hmph, say what you mean, I say.' This was the hobgoblin's response and he gave up on the conversation and turned away from me to try one with Fawkes.

I looked at Bishop Peter and received a conciliatory response.

'Perhaps we should discuss this matter together, my lady, without a lack of understanding, perhaps?'

'Indeed. Perhaps you would excuse me, Bishop Peter. I did not expect this … interrogation, nor did I expect to be separated from my people, and I think that I should give some attention to the rest of my garrison. I'm certain that there are more urgent things to be dealt with than sitting here jousting with the ill-informed.'

I looked to catch the attention of Captain Oswald but he had disappeared. Then there was a kerfuffle behind me as, through the curtains from whence the serving wenches had passed with the wine and food, came Oswald.

Fully dressed he was, as were the escort which followed him, with tabards of Lincoln worn proudly over their mail cotes and bearing arms. Oswald stopped behind my chair and his escort took up positions behind those others at table who had considered me as their guest. I was quick to see the message in this and seized the moment, gladly.

Standing, I held up an arm for silence. I had something to say.

'My dear guests, famous warriors, lords, bishops and knights, my dear friends of Lincoln, heroes and heroines fit to grace the pages of any saga, of any age. I welcome you all. Those who have stood by me during these turbulent few weeks, I pray for you, and I thank you for your fortitude… *No one* could have done better.'

There was a great cheer and my guests began to shuffle in their chairs.

'And, may I thank our guests on your behalf. They have traversed half the land to bring relief to our castle and viands to our table.' I cast my eyes graciously over the now unhappy great men of England sitting next to me. 'For that I thank them. I can also assure them that this great citadel will always, when in my care, remain the most loyal castle in the whole of England to his grace, the young King Henry — we shall always be the defenders of the king's realm. Long may he live, and long may we continue to be his most loyal servants.'

With that I offered my arm to Oswald, nodded to the archdeacon, the bishop, and Fawkes, ignored Chester, and swept me around the table and down the aisle, pausing only to gather my other people as we left my hosts behind sitting in astonished silence.

'And a pox on *their* celebration, my lady,' whispered Oswald as we left.

'Come with me,' I said when we were outside, 'we'll go and see what the larderer has left in his store and dish it out to all in need. William Marshal and his acolytes can stuff theirs up their —'

'My lady!' Basilea broke in just in time.

Geoffrey was hovering, with something to say, I could feel it. 'What?'

'There's nobody left from the town, they all went back home. With Marshal's army on the rampage they needed to go and defend what's left of their property.'

'Oh, so we're on our own?'

'Not for long, Lady Nicholaa, I fear,' said Oswald.

I looked at him, a smart man, done up for me. I loved him at that moment, but he hesitated.

'Tell me,' I insisted.

'Who is William Longspée?'

That sent a shiver down my back, things *were* simmering beneath the surface, and this was bad news indeed.

'Longspée is one of the old King Henry's offspring, the result of a tryst with some woman named Ida, I believe. He is also Earl of Salisbury, having married well. What have you heard, Oswald?'

'Only some table talk that I picked up in there.' He gestured at the marquee, now very noisy with me out of it, and no doubt the butt of the conversation.

'More,' I demanded.

'Only that he might be on his way here … to assist you in rebuilding the castle buildings, and such.'

It did not take long to think this through.

'Assist? He is coming to take control. He was close to King John, and is reputed to be within the young king's closet circle. We must prepare at once. Bernard! Where is Bernard?'

'Here, my lady.'

The priest appeared out of the gloom, in breeches as had become his new habit in his position as chirurgien.

'That diary I asked you to keep, how goes it?'

'Oh, quite well, 'tis only jottings for the few days, we have been occupied with other things of late.'

'Yes, yes. I don't want excuses, I want you to finish it as a priority. Make it a true account of the past few weeks and leave naught out. Then when I am satisfied with it you are to make some copies. We will make it known throughout the kingdom, what we have done here. If they want me out of here I will fight and fight again. I intend to reach young King Henry, and William Marshal, or if it is his cronies that have started something, then I will finish it. This castle and these forests are mine by rights, and I'll decide who discharges the duties of these appointments. For now, send word to Matilda of Laxton. She and I needst talk; there is plotting to be done, and plotting to prepare against.'

12

Father Bernard

The peace of Lady Nicholaa's privy chapel made a welcome change from the chaos of the castle bailey. I lit some candles and the quiet of the place wrapped itself around me. I used the silence to consider the events of the past few days, or weeks. Confessor to my lady, Nicholaa, diarist and advisor, chirurgien to the garrison, as the proper man had lost his head to a large rock, hurled over the ramparts by the unfriendly French, and finally, witness to the ungrateful William Marshal and his army of rescue.

What meaning had this? To resist and repel the French invaders and hold the castle of Lincoln safe, the last stronghold left to the king in England, and then hear rumours that a new castellan was on his way to assume my lady's appointments — how could they be so dismissive of all that was sacrificed in the defence of young King Henry's realm.

A noise on the steps, a dress brushing against the narrow staircase, a woman.

'Ah, you're here, Bernard.' Lady Nicholaa had made her way into the dusky calm.

'Yesterday, my lady,' I replied. 'A day of rejoicing and regret, it seems.'

'Yes, but it remains to be seen who will do the regretting.'

'You will resist William Marshal's man?'

'No-one takes my castle, nor my forests. But hold your judgement, Marshal, like all leaders, has advisors whispering in his ear, I have my own whisperers, time to deploy them.'

'I'm wondering whether to be cheered or despondent, after the struggles of the past few weeks you might have been expected to take your ease, my lady. If you don't mind my observation, that is.'

'No time for that, Bernard, I'll take some ease upon my knees, join me if you will.'

She went to kneel at her prie dieu I offered a hand, which she took reluctantly.

'Lead us in prayer, Bernard.'

I knelt on the hardwood floor facing the tiny altar and studied the crucifix standing there.

'Punishment and pain, my lady, seem to be the reward for striving to do right.'

She turned sharply towards me. 'You mean if Jesu suffered for righteousness, then we should not complain?'

'It had occurred to me, my lady.'

'But are not the virtuous duty bound to seek righteousness here on earth, here in Lincoln? Else what was the crusade for?'

'You've a crusade in mind?'

'I intend to face those who seek to diminish me, yes, call it a crusade if you will.'

'I'm certain that there are many who will follow you, my lady.'

'I won't need many, a few chosen ones will suffice.'

'Then let us pray for them.'

Spending a few moments more in silent contemplation before I led in a suitable prayer, I had hardly ended it before there were more noises on the stairway. Another lady judging by the swishing sounds made by a gown within the narrow walls.

'My lady.' A questioning voice from the doorway.

'Ah, Basilea, come and join us for a moment.'

The young woman knelt, as had I upon the bare floor alongside her lady and I said a prayer suitable in memory of Mary, our lady of Nazareth, the mother of Jesu, in recognition of my female congregation.

When I finished I listened as Basilea spoke gently into her lady's ear.

'The messenger has gone off to Laxton, we should have Lady Matilda here on the morrow. Such of Marshal's army who have been left behind are exchanging stories with our men in that marquee.'

'Is Geoffrey in there?'

'Yes, he stayed to keep an eye on that person.'

'That person. You mean Ranulf of Chester?'

'Him and his strumping cavalrymen think they own the place, they only turned up at the end —'

'I think that you might mean, strutting, Basilea,' I added, 'but they are an odious lot, that's true.'

'Now then, Bernard,' tutted Nicholaa, 'they did come to our rescue, be charitable.'

'Sorry, my lady.'

'And our people are crowded into the guard hall below, my lady,' concluded Basilea, with a flash of eyes at me, determined to finish her report.

'Good,' responded Nicholaa, 'there is much to plan. Come we will attend the guard hall, I need to be seen in this time of doubt and mourning.'

'Doubt?' queried Basilea.

'Some doubt that I will be in charge around here for much longer, I'm going to divest them of that notion.'

Basilea helped the ageing castellan to her feet but held onto her hand for a moment.

'I have a favour to ask, my lady.'

'Do you indeed, as if I could refuse you anything, my child. What is it?'

'Captain Oswald is in the hall, he will ask it of you, my lady.'

'Oh, hear that, Bernard, our courageous Saxon has sent his amore to ask if he can try and capture her heart.'

'From what I have seen, my lady, he has already achieved that,' I replied.

'How do you know that?' demanded the blushing Basilea.

'The whole garrison knows that, what could ever remain a secret within these constricting walls? Fret not, we could all do with something to look forward to, a spring wedding perhaps?'

'Oh, my lady, we are hardly near that.'

'And you've exchanged nothing more than glances, my child?' I thought to add a little spice to the conversation, wicked, I know.

'Oh, Father Bernard, how could you say such a thing?'

'Yes, Bernard, behave yourself before you find yourself on the wrong side of Oswald's anger.'

'Sorry,' I exclaimed, 'sorry, my lady, sorry, Basilea.' Words chasing after the pair as they swept out of the chapel and headed down the stairs.

I tumbled into the noise of the guard floor after the ladies, quite different from that of two floors above with braziers and sconces well lit, fires burning, scorching the pork and venison that had been gifted by the army cooks to add to our larderer's fast diminishing supplies, and obviously a lot of beer and wine already hitting the bellies of the celebrating garrison — mostly sergeants and their common wives, who had been excellent throughout, together with some of the townsfolk who had remained — most of them having gone to inspect their properties, and a few of the senior soldiers invited in.

Captain Oswald had installed himself in front of one of the fires with some of his most trusted sergeants but seemed to be surprised by the presence of Lady Nicholaa with Basilea in close attendance. Her next move surprised us all, leaving Nicholaa's side she went and kissed Oswald on the lips then turned to stand in front of him — beaming at everyone. Looking back over her shoulder she mouthed, 'now.' That was easy to interpret and I expect that I wasn't the only one to notice.

'What?' he said. Then, when Nicholaa moved in close and stood on front of the pair, I smelt a plot, they had worked something out on the journey downstairs, I was certain.

'You saw the mummery across in the marquee,' she said, 'you heard the mention of a name, you must now know that there is a plot to relieve me of my posts.'

'It must be the suspicion, my lady. What will you do?'

'Resist, repel, and fight against it. No invaders have passed my gates in these past few weeks and none shall now. King's bastard, Longspée, nor anyone else.'

'I agree.' The man spoke truly, if loudly against the background hubbub. 'But as Lady Nicholaa knows all too well, for a warrior there is no rest until all enemies are defeated and put down.'

'Why thank you, Captain Oswald, you class me as a warrior,' chuckled Nicholaa. 'A sixty year old, lady warrior.'

'Quite rare, I'd have thought,' I added.

'Basilea tells me that you have something else to tell me, Captain Oswald?' said Lady Nicholaa with a straight face. 'I came in to make an announcement, what is it that you have to say?'

'My lady,' he responded, moving a protective hand around Basilea's waist, 'I … we, have a request.'

'In all this chaos?' demanded Lady Nicholaa, she still has the wit to jest with the man.

'My lady, 'tis precisely this chaos that brings it about, we have come so close to death that we see that life needs to be grasped whilst it is still there for the taking.'

'I see, very wise, and you and Basilea want to grasp it?'

'Indeed … how did you know?'

'Everyone in Lincoln knows, but I shan't go through that again.'

The tall Saxon had an attack of the blushes as he was faced by a lady who had learned the art of directness over the years. I took a glance around me and noticed that the crowd had fallen silent, they had picked up on the conversation and were expecting an answer. I passed a hand over my mouth to hide my titters as Oswald spluttered out his request in front of an audience.

'May I ask your tending lady, Basilea, to walk out with me, my lady?'

'Of course you can, and may we have a spring wedding to look forward to.'

It was Basilea's turn to blush as the crowded hall erupted into a thunderclap of cheering.

That was it, done as far as Lady Nicholaa was concerned. Oswald and Basilea were now in a state of confusion, as if it were all too easy, getting betrothed. I smiled at them and they relaxed a little as my lady called for my attention.

'Here, Bernard, help me onto that chair at the top table, I'm going to speak to them.'

Nicholaa led off towards the top of the hall to where she would normally sit and we got her onto the chair whilst the crowd calmed itself and turned its gaze away from the canoodling couple.

As Nicholaa rose above their heads an expectant hush descended.

'Thank you, my friends,' began the brave lady, 'for friends you are, no curious bystander would have willingly joined me in this wreck of a castle.'

That raised a laugh and a cheer.

'Thank you. But as much as we won the battle, a new threat faces us.'

The mood in the hall changed.

'It has come to our ears that some lord from young King Henry's court is on his way to cast me aside and assume my duties and appointments.'

A howl of derision erupted, voices were heard above the general tumult.

'Is that Longspée?' cried one, evidently rumours had spread already.

'Long gone, more like,' shouted another.

'Don't let 'im in,' came the shout, soon followed by, 'Out, out, out!' Although the miscreant mentioned had not yet entered.

Nicholaa held up a hand and the throng calmed down.

'If you are agreed then I shall take all steps necessary to remain in my office.'

'Stay, lady, stay,' commanded the crowd.

'Very well,' responded the lady, 'but first there is much to do. Captain Oswald will get you organised on the morrow, there is much damage within the castle, and no doubt some of you will find your houses have been used by the soldiery, you need to go and check on them in the morn. We will need as many tradesmen and labourer's as can be found, all work within the castle I will pay for, and we will form working parties to help you with your premises. But that is for the morrow, tonight is a feast, enjoy it but be sensible and you men care for your wives, I'll brook no nonsense else you'll occupy my stocks for a week.'

And that was it from the lady, still in charge, gratitude, reward, and the prospect of a managed return to normality — what else could they expect?

'Right!' she declared being helped down from her giddy chair, 'that'll do for tonight. Basilea, we are off to bed. Oswald, draw up a plan for the restoration work, but go and see how Geoffrey is getting on in the company of that weasel, Chester.'

'It'll be done, my lady, good night.'

I followed Nicholaa and Basilea up the stairs before snuggling up in her chapel — I doubted if my small chamber behind the great hall in the castle bailey would be as peaceful tonight with all this celebrating going on all around.

I slept but fitfully, too much in my head and the floor was too hard, so I used Lady Nicholaa's prie dieu to say a prayer and then went down, intending to go to my chamber at the back of the great hall and write a few more lines of Lady Nicholaa's diary. Most everybody in the guard hall was asleep, some on the benches where they had suffered from too much beer, a couple of the curtained off cubicles for couples sounded quite lively though, early morning marital duties being performed there it seemed.

I received a surprise when I exited Nicholaa's tower and took in the view of the bailey, it was already buzzing with activity, drink a lot they might, but early to rise and get on with their task was the driver for the soldiers of the garrison, of that there was no doubt.

Ranulf's cavalry had disappeared, chasing after William Marshal I presumed, and what was left were the myriad members of the baggage train, packing away the many parts that made up the marquee we had occupied last evening. At least two hundred men, skivvies, mule handlers, waggoners, cooks, all packing kitchen equipment, and several clerks making lists — all that was necessary to feed and house an army on the march. I wondered when and where they would catch up with their leaders. Still, that was not my problem and I passed them by and made my way through the wreckage of the once great hall, little of the roof left, rubble piled up everywhere. But many of the townsfolk had fashioned shelters for themselves and their women, some were up and some snored on as I stumbled past them saying 'good morrows' here and there on my way to my chamber, fortunately hidden in the lee of the build and mostly untouched, my records intact.

I needed to collect my thoughts before going back up to Nicholaa's floor to lead her in morning prayers and there was light in the eastern sky already.

William Marshal, was by design of fate, a very busy man, but I wondered if he had too few wise advisors around him and too many ambitious men. The fact that Lincoln had held out as the last stronghold in England, and had been led by a women in that success, seems not to have been explained to him in sufficient detail for his complete understanding. But he had departed, rather rudely, and gone south, now Nicholaa needed a strategy to get to him and make him listen. The alternative, as I see it, is that Lincoln retreats back into itself to become neutral in the affairs of State, an unhappy contrivance, but one which might well persuade the royalists to listen more carefully than hitherto.

I will engineer this, but how?

Unsettled and anxious to get on with things I did not tarry long and wandering deep in thought I found myself at the bottom of those numerous steps leading up into the Lucy tower. I paused on the guard floor for a puff before ascending further, most everybody was up now, light outside and curtains drawn with cooking pots steaming on the fires at each end of the hall. Chamberlain Turstan was fussing about organising his skivvies, trying to tidy the place up — a new day had dawned and a very busy one in prospect, I'm certain.

Hearing nothing as I ascended the stairs to Nicholaa's chambers I contented myself with a visit to her chapel where I engaged in prayer for a few moments before I heard the swish of skirts and Basilea entered.

'Father Bernard, have you been here long?'

'No, Basilea, I thought that a longer sleep might be of benefit to Lady Nicholaa.'

'You thought right, yesterday was a busy day. She is up now and will be along in a moment.'

'Have you seen your brave captain this morning?'

'No, I expect that he is busy making out lists of things to do.'

'Yes, it will be a long time before things are back to normal.'

'Normal! Hah, if God will provide some justice we will be, but it seems not to be in the king's plans.'

'Oh, despair not, Basilea, I'm sure that Our Lord is watching, these matters will be resolved ere long.'

'They'd better be…' The strident voice of Nicholaa entered the conversation. 'Else the king's ears will be burnt. Has Matilda arrived yet, Basilea?'

'I know not, my lady, I have not been down yet but it is a bit early to expect her, besides I'm certain that Captain Oswald will inform us immediately she comes in sight.'

'Captain Oswald, very formal for your lover.'

'My lady, he is not that.'

'Oh, tush, I jest, I know that. Come on, Bernard, a short prayer and then on with the day.'

I prayed for those who had died in pursuit of their duties, for those who are suffering their loss, and for the intervention of the Lord in the matter of governance of Lincoln.

'Right, downstairs.' Nicholaa, back to her imperious self. 'We'll grab something to eat and then go on a tour of inspection whilst we wait for Matilda to put in an appearance … unless she has been waylaid in the woods on her way here.'

'Not likely with Ælfgar and Orva by her side,' I quipped.

Basilea brought an end to that speculation. 'Orva might be beyond horse riding, Father Bernard.'

'Oh yes,' responded Nicholaa, 'I'd forgotten about that, I pray that she is making progress in the matter of producing Ælfgar's first born. Come along Bernard, I smell cooking.'

I always struggled to keep up with Nicholaa, even going downstairs.

'Coming, my lady, coming.'

William Marshal's army had cleared up space yesterday, the twentieth day of May, to set out their grand marquee, so the devastation we were faced with in the castle bailey today was all our own.

Basilea had prepared Lady Nicholaa to the best of her ability, and from a glimpse that I had handing her down the steps, managed to get her into doeskin boots, not courtly but essential in the mess we were about to inspect. Geoffrey was waiting at the bottom, limping to make the most of his injury.

'Where to first, my lady?' he asked politely.

'Is that Captain Oswald by the eastern gate?' she asked, squinting her eyes the hundred paces to the barbican.

'Yes my lady,' answered Basilea, much attracted to the vision of her brave soldier.

'Well,' replied Nicholaa, 'send him your squire, Geoffrey, and tell him that we are going for a walk around the wall and will be with him soon.'

There was a sergeant in charge of the gate and he demonstrated his pleasure in seeing Lady Nicholaa with a black-stumped grin, and some kind of curtsy. I had met the man before and he was often minded to clear his throat onto the ground around him. I prayed that he would resist such a clear-out in Nicholaa's presence.

'Good morrow, Sergeant, is all well with you this fine morning?'

''Tis indeed, ladyship, 'tis indeed. We saw off them Frenchies, eh?'

'We certainly did, and are you unharmed?'

'I'm missing some bits, ladyship, but I lost them some time ago. That French rabble got nothing more from me.' He grinned ever wider, a bit like a pet puppy before Nicholaa, they all loved her beyond sense.

'Well, that's good. We are going up onto the battlement now, Sergeant. Well done, very well done, and make certain that you pass on our appreciation to your men. And I will pray for you all, be sure of that.'

'Aye, ladyship. And if a barrel of beer came our way ... as well as some prayers?'

'I'll see to it, rogue.' She laughed and the stumpy gap widened beyond belief in response. 'Geoffrey, take my hand — Basilea, shove from behind, let's survey the world of Lincoln.'

Oh dear, the world of Lincoln was full of steps, or so it seemed as I followed along behind.

We came onto the battlement eventually, and I worried for Nicholaa, stopping once on the way up to gather her breath, but we were rewarded by a fine view across the treetops, over the Vale of the River Trent and towards the distant hills beyond — somewhere in there would be the spiky Lady Matilda and her aggressive companions, they should be here soon. The sun was well up, it was a nice warm end of May day, and turning towards the cathedral gave us a fine view of it.

Inside the perimeter of the castle was not such a fine view though, there were not many roofs left untouched by the bombardment of the French trebuchet, only Nicholaa's Lucy tower being unaffected. The rest of the buildings had fared badly. By now Captain Oswald's work parties were busy trying to repair the damage and the chamberlain could be seen below scuttling about the place trying to get everything done at once.

'Some hope,' said Geoffrey, 'why doesn't he settle down and work out his priorities?'

'Yes,' agreed Nicholaa, 'shout down, tell him to concentrate on getting the kitchen working properly, the weather is fine but everyone must be fed properly.'

'Right!' said he, and set off a coughing bout as he strained to make himself heard by the scurrying figures far below. Eventually he ordered a sentry to leave his post on the battlement and go and instruct Turstan as to Lady Nicholaa's priorities, and we progressed further around the perimeter, myself taking down observation notes.

Basilea cheered up no end when we got to the top of the eastern gatehouse, her amore now visible below.

'My lady,' said the proud captain, 'everyone is hard at work, as you can see.'

'Indeed, Oswald, and have you sent a working party into the town to help out?'

'We have and already lists of materials required are coming in — timber mostly, and nails and pegs and tools.'

225

'Oh, spare me the details. Father Bernard has some more lists, our observations from the battlements.'

'I expected that. I have been for a complete circuit and it is a distressing sight.'

'Ah well, let's take our time and get things done properly. Kitchens first, women and children's accommodation, then start on the barracks.'

'My thoughts exactly, my lady. Listen, there is activity at the western gate, Matilda perhaps?'

Shouts were coming from the far end of the bailey and I could just see daylight appearing at the far end of the barbican as the great gate was opened and the portcullis raised — it must be our other beloved lady, Matilda.

First through were two of Ælfgar's scouts, men dressed in dark clothing, festooned with raggy swatches sewn on to disguise them in the woods, then four horsemen, lance carrying cavalrymen riding two by two, then two females, Orva and her lady Matilda. Immediately at their rear the unmistakeable Ælfgar, no attempt being made to hide this giant, any threat to his charges would be met by this hammer of Thor. Behind Ælfgar, two by two, six of his archers, also raggedy men but carrying their fearsome war bows with a short sword belted to their sides. Thus entered our friends from Laxton to great cheers all around.

'Ah, they've arrived,' said Nicholaa, unnecessarily, but gladly, 'we can begin our plotting.'

It was well beyond two hundred paces from gate to gate and the leading scouts had not yet identified Lady Nicholaa as they turned towards the Lucy tower, where they would expect to find her. They were stopped by one of the working parties who, with much arm waving, turned them towards the eastern gate where we stood.

As they approached the leading scouts and the four cavalrymen turned aside to form an alleyway though which Matilda and Orva made a stately progress.

'Matilda!' called Nicholaa.

'Nicholaa, my dear,' responded her friend. 'Your housekeeping has gone astray, I see,' grinned Matilda, 'has there been a festival?' Her dark, unrestrained hair blew about in the slight breeze.

Matilda and Orva were both quite indistinguishable from their escorts, both wearing dark breeches over doeskin boots, dark green blouses, half unbuttoned, and the coif being thrown back displayed the barely hid fact that they both wore a mail hauberk.

Matilda leapt down from her steed, and soon both leaders were grasping each other tightly.

'You would not believe it, Matilda, the trials we have undergone, rocks, blood, destruction — and to cap it all, treachery.'

Matilda stood back, and grasping Nicholaa by the shoulders looked into her eyes with growing concern.

'I had thought you safe, rescued. Pray tell me.'

'We will go to my tower, and when you are settled we will recount our ordeal in all its inglorious detail. Good morrow, Orva. Ælfgar, I see you have not shrunken much since your last visit.' Lady Nicholaa turned her attention to the Saxon. His palfrey, although quite a large horse, seemed only as a dog between his ample thighs as he sat watching.

'Lady Nicholaa, are you well, in this wreckage?' He waved an arm about him.

'We have survived, and now we will effect a return to normal.'

'You have done well, my lady, we all admire you. As for shrinking, I have not, but growing? I have left that to my brave lady, Orva.' He grinned a shy grin at the woman, also wild of hair, who grinned back and passed a hand upon her stomach.

'Oh, my dear,' said Nicholaa moving to embrace the raven haired beauty, 'how nice,' she said, careful to keep her stomach away from Orva's seax. 'When are you due?'

'Oh, January or February, we … I am not certain, my lady.'

'They are very close, Nicholaa,' added Matilda with a cheeky grin, 'sometimes we do not see them for days at a time.'

Nicholaa turned her attention to Ælfgar. 'Ælfgar, take your men across to the stables, such as they are, your horses will be seen to, there is a pottage available over near the remains of the kitchen for your men. Then please join us in my tower. We will brief you all and I would appreciate your advice. I believe that you have met with William Marshal, I need to know more about the man.'

'As you wish, my lady,' was the response and Nicholaa set off towards her tower, arm in arm with Matilda.

Things were returning to normal within the tower and we moved above the guard floor into Nicholaa's privy chambers so that we might be undisturbed. The house steward quickly provided a table and benches and filled up the space with sparing amounts of bread, cheese, and meats, wine and beer, a lot left over from the previous evening but very presentable nonetheless — and we spread ourselves along the benches ready to listen to Nicholaa's new plan.

I scuffed about setting some papers in order and prepared to take notes. Nicholaa noticed and it reminded her of something.

'Bernard, our copy of the Magna Carta, you have it in a safe place, I understand?'

'Indeed, my lady, a very important document, it reposes beneath the altar cloth in your chapel.'

'Sly fox, but very important it is, it started a civil war, after all.'

'Indeed, my lady, although that might have been brought about by man's treachery to his promises.'

'You mean a king's treachery to his promises, Father Bernard?'

The Saxon captain, Oswald was not one to miss rubbing salt in the wounds of the late King John's failings, so I merely nodded and went off to collect the vellum in question.

Removing the crucifix and other embellishments from the cloth beneath which the document reposed took only a moment and I soon returned with the charter and some more writing materials — this might take some time.

Ælfgar had arrived when I got back and Nicholaa was issuing some new instructions to the steward. 'Get him a bench of his own, he's not sitting on this side he'll have us all on the floor.'

Ælfgar grinned and grabbed a rather large fistful of bread and cheese.

'Sit down, Ælfgar, if you please, we need to get on with it.' Lady Nicholaa now commanded our undivided attention. 'There is a problem in the offing which might more surely see me out of this castle, town, and forest, than the French managed.'

The eyebrows of Matilda and her people shot skywards, the rumours seemingly had not reached the sixteen miles across the treetops.

'Did not my messenger say anything about this, Matilda?' asked Nicholaa.

'No, we thought that we had been invited to a celebration.'

'Aye, Lady Nicholaa, what's to do?' Ælfgar's bass voice rattled the tankards and glasses on the table.

'Yesterday, William Marshal and his army had a large marquee set up in the bailey, and we,' she looked at Oswald and Geoffrey, 'were invited to a feast…'

'Damned nerve,' interrupted Geoffrey, 'invited, in our own castle.'

'Quite!' Nicholaa continued, 'and during this feast I heard certain things which discomforted me, as did Geffrey and Oswald, who were elsewhere in Marshal's tent.'

'What things?' asked Matilda.

'Things, Maud, things like there is a new castellan on his way to shove me out of my holdings.'

'What!' A chorus of astonishment. Matilda sat up, wide eyed, and Ælfgar stood up to darken the chamber, Orva's hand slid down to grasp the handle of her seax.

'Calmly, my friends, calmly, 'tis but a rumour yet, we have time to prepare a response if it becomes needed. Bernard, the charter, if you please.'

'Yes, my lady.' Although the thing had been laid flat beneath the altar cloth, it has a tendency to roll itself a little, so I flattened it out on the table and awaited for instructions, not entirely certain as to why it was needed.

'Is that what started the war?' asked Ælfgar.

'Yes, and it's likely to start another if I do not get my way,' replied Nicholaa. 'This has implications beyond my doors, Maud, and affects you and many beyond yours, so listen to Bernard. Read article seven.'

'"*Vidua post mortem mariti sui statim et sine difficul…*"'

'English, Bernard, English, you have lost Ælfgar already,' corrected my lady.

'Ahem,' I started again, but slower this time. '"At her husband's death, a widow may have her marriage portion and her inheritance at once and without trouble. She shall pay nothing for her dower, marriage portion, or any inheritance that she and her husband held jointly on the day of his death. She may remain in her husband's house for forty days after his death, and within this period her dower shall be assigned to her."'

'And that applies to me?' asked Matilda.

'Indeed, and you can wave it in the faces of any who would have you out too,' replied Nicholaa.

'What's that bit about forty days?' Geoffrey had been listening, despite appearances to the contrary.

'Yes, that might be important,' added Matilda.

'There is a will, I made sure of that long before Gerard died. Our holdings were assigned to me and the forty days does not apply.'

'What about you, my lady?' asked Orva, not to outdone in matters of the law.

Matilda laughed before replying. 'You are aware, I take it, that both Nicholaa and I have Saxon roots, but here we are about to turn Norman law back upon them. I inherited my holdings as the eldest child when both my parents were laid to rest, God bless them…'

I repeated the prayer and all signed the cross.

'…and before I married my first husband we made out a will of assignation to each other, and I did the same when I married Adam, God rest his soul, so in the law of the land, written here before you — I am the Constable of Laxton and the Keeper of the King's Forests in Sherwood and part of Derbyshire. Who will gainsay that?'

'Phillip Marc,' growled Ælfgar.

'Him,' cackled Nicholaa, 'this document relieves him of his appointments. It would appear, Maud that our Norman overlords have sat upon a thorn of their own fashioning.'

'Yes, but he is still there, and still doing some tax collecting of his own — in my forest.'

'Who's in bother now?' asked Geoffrey, eyes glazing over, the past few days and his leg wound evidently catching up on him.

'The Sheriff of Nottingham, Geoffrey, that's who. Tell him Bernard,' commanded Lady Nicholaa.

'That's article fifty, it is written, "*Nos amovebimus penitus de balliis…*" then follows a list of names, including, "Phillip Marc and his brothers, with Geoffrey his nephew, and all their followers".'

'Yes,' responded our tetchy Geoffrey, 'what about them?'

'Oh,' I responded, he had perhaps not understood the first part of the conversation, 'they are to be removed from office.'

'Hah, scoundrels, the lot. So why are they still there?'

Lady Nicholaa glared at him with stern brow and replied, 'Because we have been dealing with a war, Geoffrey, your leg should remind you of that. We are nearly done here, take yourself off and get some rest then we'll continue on the morrow.'

'Ah, good.' And without further ado the tired old fellow hobbled off to find his bed. His squire, Elric, who had been waiting by the door, took an arm to help him down the stairs.

'Right, ladies, and men, we can fashion a plan,' said Nicholaa.

'Who are our friends in this matter, my lady?' asked Oswald.

'Good idea,' replied Matilda, 'let's write them down.'

'You've met William Marshal, he left before we could talk, what about him, Ælfgar?' asked Nicholaa.

'He is one of the regents appointed by the grand council, along with Hubert de Burgh, they are both signatories to the Magna Carta so should be amenable to its contents.'

'Who was that you were next to at the feast, my lady?' asked Oswald. 'That soldier-bishop fellow.'

'That was Peter des Roches, Bishop of Winchester, he seemed sympathetic, although he might have been more interested in your charms, my dear Maud.' Nicholaa grinned at Matilda.

'Yes, he was, I was waiting for his hand to stray, but Oswald marched us all out before that happened.'

'He didn't like Archdeacon Peter,' chipped in Basilea, 'I was watching.'

'No, they did not seem as one on some matters,' agreed Nicholaa. 'What about this great council? Do you know much … anyone?'

Matilda replied, 'Only that they have been appointed to guide in matters of governance, the real power lies with William Marshal, he is the late King John's appointed guardian of young Henry, and des Roches is the chief Justiciar of England, you need those two by your side Nicholaa.'

'Then they are our targets. How do we get to them, Bernard?'

'On a horse, my lady?'

'A jesting priest, spare me, Bernard. Oswald, has my carriage survived the bombardment?'

'No, 'tis kindling now.'

'Oh, then work out a plan as to how I get near the king, I'm not going to sit here worrying.'

Oswald agreed, and the worry passed to him.

The candles burnt late that night and by the time my eyes were heavy I had several lists and a well-worn copy of Magna Carta, together with a promise to copy relevant articles from it for Lady Matilda by the end of the next day. The document had become a weapon for threatened ladies, one which provided a legal basis for the several other actions which they had agreed to enact in defence of their domains.

God blessed us with sunshine in the morning and I felt better than I had done for many a week since war loomed over us. I slept comfortably in my little chamber behind the wrecked great hall and no doubt the comfort of my bed helped me to rest. After a quick wash I went to take breakfast in the guard hall with the household, as was Nicholaa's usual habit, and with everyone refreshed our next actions were discussed.

'Father Bernard, when will the copy of Magna Carta for Lady Matilda be ready?' Nicholaa asked me.

'If you only want the two articles in question, by mid-day, but if you want it all, perhaps three or four days.'

'We've got time to wait,' responded Matilda. 'Ælfgar, would you work with Oswald for a couple of days, perhaps he could use some support during these difficult times of restoration. Oswald?'

'I could, what do you say to that, Ælfgar?'

'What is it you need?'

'Let's take a walk around the place, see what you think.'

'And I'll go and get on with my writing,' I said, excusing myself.

The whole document contained fifty-three articles, including lists of who did what. Truth to tell I became quite absorbed by the thing and often broke off in contemplation, thinking about what it had meant to those involved and those whose lives it would affect — but I made good progress and expected to be finished by the end of the following day, God willing, and I burnt not a few candles as I scribbled away.

The morning passed in comparative peace, accompanied, of course, by the banging and crashing and shouting of the busy repair parties outside. I learned to ignore it in time, but then, in the afternoon, a new commotion.

I put down my quill and sanded my document before venturing out. I was met by the vision of Ælfgar, gazing at the eastern gate. He had across his back what was evidently a whole tree truck, shaped for use as a roof beam.

'Is that not heavy, Ælfgar?' I asked rather unnecessarily.

'What? Oh, this. I'll stand it against this wall, or what's left of it. See the gate, Father? They've opened it, must be an important visitor, and there's cheering in the town.'

I trotted along behind Ælfgar as he made his way towards the gate. Oswald was on the top and as he watched us approach, called down, 'It's William Marshal, Ælf, with an escort of twenty or so. Have you seen Lady Nicholaa?'

'We've sent word, she should be here soon. Are you going to let him in?'

'Yes, just as soon as the guard has assembled, he'll not find us distracted from our duties.'

It did not take long to line them up on both sides of the barbican before Oswald shouted down for the great doors to be opened.

The cavalcade entered with William at their head. Trotting past he spotted Ælfgar.

'Saxon,' he called, 'pleased to see you again. Is the lady here?'

'Aye, Lord, in her tower, like as not,' came the response. 'Will she be pleased to see you, Lord?'

William pulled up his steed and gazed at Ælfgar, twisting the reins in his hand. 'You're a scoundrel, Saxon, but well chosen.

Follow me, if you please.' And he grinned as he moved off again.

Ælfgar set off behind Marshal's horses towards the tower. He walked as fast as a horse could trot and I was left puffing along behind.

By the time I'd reached the bottom of the tower steps, William's cavalrymen were dismounted and using buckets of water brought to them by our stable hands to water the horses. Their leader had disappeared up into the tower. I followed, into the guard floor then up again into Nicholaa's privy chambers. Everyone was sitting down when I puffed into view and Nicholaa motioned me to sit at a small desk nearby. She made a writing motion with her hand and I knew to take notes. The pleasantries were still in progress and I presumed that I had not missed anything of importance.

'I know that it must have seemed a little rude of me when I did not stay for the celebration,' William was offering an explanation for his early exit after the castle's liberation, 'but, my first priority is to the king and his needs, he should be told of the victory here, by me, and before any other tales or rumours reached his ears. I trust that you can understand that, Lady Nicholaa, no offence was intended.'

'Thank you, Lord William, I'm sure that you had your reasons, but rumours have spread here too.'

'What rumours?'

'Rumours that I am to be replaced, my inheritance, my life and achievements set aside for one of the old King Henry's bastards to push me out of my stewardship.'

The old warrior's eyebrows lifted to the heavens and he reddened a little before answering.

'I know nothing of this. Who began this rumour, who was mentioned?'

'That little dog turd Chester.' While Nicholaa was searching for a polite form of words Ælfgar came out with it and it was confirmed by Oswald who had stomped up the stairs in time to hear it.

'It was common talk around the table, my Lord. William Longespée was mentioned.'

'Then it needs investigation. I must tell you, Nicholaa, that bastard or not, Longespée is a good man, notwithstanding some errors of judgement, but sound, and not one to enter gladly into some underhanded type of treachery. After all that you have achieved the idea is preposterous.'

'Then if he is sent, by whom? He will not gain entry if he presents himself outside my gate.'

Nicholaa was bristling and William knew it, but there was still trouble in the kingdom and Prince Louis was still active in the south, he needed the assurance of Lincoln holding firm.

'I see that, Nicholaa, please allow me to explain my position. I am by the last written testament of King John, given me long before he died, to have responsibility, together with Hubert de Burgh, for the safekeeping of the new king's person, and wise council — however, there is the matter of the Council of Lords and Bishops, whose task it is to administer the king's wishes, and sometimes, I suspect, wishes of their own.'

'Is the realm still at risk, Lord William?' asked Ælfgar.

'Indeed it is, as long as the French have a foothold and believe that they can turn the tide, we are still at war. Which is why I have returned.'

'Returned you are, but what is your intention?'

Nicholaa remained suspicious, as did I. It seemed to me that William Marshal was testing the waters, watching to see how he could proceed. On the one hand he needed Lincoln, but on the other he needed to be certain of its security. If the King's

Council were uncertain, probably because of Nicholaa's age, then would they send someone to succeed her in her appointments? We were getting to the point where that unspoken truth needed to be on display, I thought.

William, unsurprisingly, for his age and reputation bespoke of his wisdom, felt confident enough to cut straight to the chase.

'I need to say some things, Nicholaa, which might be better said in privy.' He eyed up Nicholaa's companions and even I felt the weight of his gaze before she answered.

'They have been my prop and defenders throughout the past weeks of turmoil, they remain.'

'Including the ladies?'

'Especially the ladies.'

William turned his gaze in the direction of Basilea and Orva, who gave him a scowl back, and Matilda received a passing glance, but he knew of her importance, although he had not mentioned her … yet.

'Very well, as you wish. There is, Nicholaa, the question of who might succeed you in your appointments, your eldest son, Richard…'

'Has gone and his wife, Eustachia cannot take my appointments.' Nicholaa's suspicion was replaced by her enduring sadness.

'No, Eustachia, as his wife, could only have inherited if Richard had survived you and inherited in the normal way.'

These statements were followed by a silence. I surmised that both parties were exploring their options.

'Lord William, we discussed the Magna Carta yesterday,' Oswald ventured.

Nicholaa affixed him with a questioning eye.

'Indeed?'

'Yes. Is it to remain as our guiding document within the new king's realm and law?'

'Indeed it is. This is the advice that Hubert and myself are keen to make clear to young Henry, that which his Father repudiated is to be extant at the end of this war. When we rid the kingdom of the French and peace is restored, the Magna Carta will remain our chief guide in such matters. That has not changed and I will reissue it, with some amendments.'

'Widow's rights, my rights, and Maud's rights, we have them written down within the Magna Carta.'

Another silence, then a smile spread across the wrinkled face of the chiefest knight in England.

'Ah! That. You've read through it all, well done, so now we can talk. So, Lady Matilda…'

'Maud will do.'

'Indeed, Maud. The question of your succession, we should clear the matter now, if possible. Who is involved to succeed you?'

'Not many. I have a niece, Isabella, she is the next natural choice.'

'Another female Caux? But not your heir.'

'Indeed, and that is the problem, William.'

'It needs discussion. I've heard the name Lexington mentioned.'

Matilda's face assumed an expression of some disregard. 'William, he is the bastard of the family, he has been sniffing around, but I've heard that he fell out of favour with King John.'

'More than once,' replied William.

Maud and Nicholaa looked at each other, then Nicholaa spoke. 'Basilea, send for the steward, this may take some time.'

The atmosphere relaxed a little and Oswald filled it with questions about the wider conflict which William was conducting across the country. It soon became clear that we were not at peace, and William was wise to point out, especially to Matilda and Ælfgar, that they might expect to find bands of disaffected Frenchies, or even deserting English roaming the forests trying to survive in a hostile land, or looking for a chance of profit.

Making a decision Nicholaa asked Matilda if she would go for a walk with her. I rose to accompany them but was motioned off and stayed with the others.

'I must say,' said William when the women had gone, 'that I am filled with admiration for your two ladies, valiant and loyal, they are a credit to England, and you all may take pleasure in how you have given them both your support. I salute you.' He stood and proffered a glass before drinking a toast. 'And you Father Bernard, your prayers have surely helped, God bless you all. Now I must tell you that I shall do all that I can to ensure that your ladies remain in office as long as they want, but that we must also consider the question of succession — it comes to all in high places, or low, as I'm sure you are aware.'

'There is another thing which has not been mentioned, Lord.' Ælfgar was not going to leave it there.

'Tell me.'

'Phillip Marc, he remains in office ... and in our forest.'

'Ah! Of course. Then Maud should discourage him. Try and use persuasion, my Saxon friend.'

The ladies could be heard puffing their way back up the stairs.

'Are you settled in your minds, ladies?' asked William, but gently, when they had made themselves comfortable.

'Some things are clear and others are not,' replied Nicholaa. 'I can't go on living forever … that I'm aware of.'

'And I'm not for leaving either,' added Matilda.

'Well, Maud,' responded Will, a little too cheery, 'your case is the easy one, keep what you have with my blessing.'

'And I, I suppose, I am the awkward case?' grumbled Nicholaa.

'Perhaps, Nicholaa, perhaps. Have you a suggestion?' William asked hopefully.

'Short of a suitable marriage?' replied she.

William Marshal's face lit up. 'Did you have anybody in mind?'

'Not I, however, Idonea, my granddaughter is unspoken for.'

'So there is someone in your line, but needs a suitable marriage? Well, the arranging of marriages is something which I may be able to influence. You know that you, as a widow with holdings, cannot remarry without the king's permission?'

'Yes, as I said, we have studied the Magna Carta,' she replied, a softening of her position, I thought. I wonder what the pair of them had discussed when they were outside the chamber.

'Then let me test it in court, I will try and persuade the King's Council, and then try to persuade the king as to the best interpretation of the law. As you know not all laws cover every eventuality and this will be a test for it. What say you, Nicholaa?'

'You seem quite confident, Will.'

'I would not give you false hope, Nicholaa, but there is always a degree of uncertainty in these things, until they are tested.

'Is the way forward set out then?' asked Nicholaa.

'As far as I am concerned,' responded William Marshal. 'A solution, Nicholaa, it might meet your favour. Meet Longspée, you might like him, see if you can work together, and see if you could share the duties of castle, town, and forest. Also, there is another dice to roll.'

We all held our breath, the old scoundrel had kept something in reserve, and he looked at us one by one and grinned — holding the suspense.

'Longspée has a son, William, he is five years, perhaps, if things go aright, you could engineer for him to become betrothed to your Idonea.'

Nicholaa's eyebrows were raised, her eyes widened, and a half smile played around her mouth. 'You are a devious old goat, William Marshal. Have you been told that before?'

'It's not been said within my hearing, Nicholaa, but no doubt it has occurred to some. To survive the succession of kings and be left standing at the end of wars takes a certain set of skills. Do you see a way, dear lady?'

'Yes.' She laughed. 'I see a way.'

'Then may I suggest it to the king's council?'

'You may.'

'They may wish to see you.'

'Then I'll appear.'

'You can meet the king.'

'An honour, I'd like that.'

'Consider it done.'

A NOTE TO THE READER

Dear Reader,

Thank you for taking the time to read this, the first book of the new series, **'Wars of the Magna Carta.'** And as you may have gathered, the attempts to bring a codified and written set of laws into England met with a mixed reception, and a civil war.

It was a chance visit by my wife, Mandy, and I, to the village of Laxton in Nottinghamshire, which led directly to this exploration of the times. Laxton is the last surviving estate in England still managed as a Saxon strip farm, through a bailiff's court. Quite fascinating in itself – but there is more. From the top of the original motte can be seen the towers of Lincoln cathedral, twelve miles away, which sparked off, in me, a cauldron of curiosity. My research then began to unearth the fascinating story of two women who I, at least, had never before heard of.

The astonishing fact is that these two ladies, Nicholaa of Lincoln, and Matilda of Laxton, controlled the King's Forests from the North Sea to the hills of Derbyshire. The tombstones of both Nicholaa and Matilda can be found in churches within their old family domains. Nicholaa's is in St Michael's church, Swaton, Lincolnshire, while Matilda's is in the church of St Peter and St Paul, in Old Brampton, Chesterfield.

I would like to especially thank Dea Parkin and her team at Fiction Feedback, professional and patient as usual. Without their encouragement many a novel would founder in the stormy seas of writing and publishing, I'm sure.

Please find time to leave a review on Amazon and on my website. Reviews are the author's lifeblood.

More detail can be found on the website:

https://www.history-reimagined.co.uk

Thank you.

Austin Hernon

Sapere Books is an exciting new publisher of brilliant fiction and popular history.

To find out more about our latest releases and our monthly bargain books visit our website: **saperebooks.com**

Printed in Great Britain
by Amazon